OTHER BOOKS
BY AUBREY MACE
Before the Clock Strikes Thirty

Love on a Whim

a novel

AUBREY MACE

Covenant Communications, Inc.

Cover image: Colorful Macaroons © Lecic

Cover design copyright © 2015 by Covenant Communications, Inc.

Published by Covenant Communications, Inc.
American Fork, Utah

Printed in the United States of America
First Printing: July 2015

21 20 19 18 17 16 15   10 9 8 7 6 5 4 3 2 1

ISBN 978-1-62108-621-5

For June Hartman,
who really did have a series of
teacup poodles that were all named Peggy.
You are loved and missed.

Acknowledgments

MANY THANKS TO

Covenant, for being so great to work with, and Stacey Owen, Awesome Editor Extraordinaire. I appreciate all your hard work and patience.

Billie Holiday, whose song titles I borrowed and whose music I sing loudly in the car in the summertime with the windows rolled down. Sincere apologies to anyone who might have heard me.

Tami Mowen Steggell, for generously letting me borrow her bakery, RubySnap. She is responsible for creating the most delicious cookies I've ever had and sabotaging my diet on numerous occasions. Check out RubySnap if you're in Salt Lake City—you'll thank me.

And beta readers. You know who you are, and I owe you big time, always and forever. A truckload of Godiva and a kitten for each of you.

Chapter One
"You've Changed"

I CAME OUT OF LAW school a bit too thin. Stress about finals and passing the bar and too many late nights can do that to you. Now, after six months of unsuccessfully applying for jobs, the scale is headed in the other direction. But I'm not too worried, especially since if I remain unemployed much longer, I won't be able to afford to eat.

Okay, that's a little dramatic, but you get the idea. If things got really desperate, I'm sure I could find a job *somewhere*. But I don't want just any job. I worked hard to get where I am, and I'm proud of what I've accomplished. I'm a lawyer. That's right—*a lawyer*. Ever since I was a little girl, I knew I wanted to have a career in law. I took AP classes and got A's, except in biology—I couldn't bring myself to cut into the poor lifeless frog. I started college as a sophomore, and I graduated from Stanford. *Stanford.*

I get that I'm repeating everything twice. I tend to do that when I get worked up about something, but I never realized it until my friend Shannon pointed it out. I'm working on weeding it out because a lawyer who says the same thing over and over doesn't exactly inspire confidence. Just when I think I have it under control, it creeps back in, like an accent you can never completely get rid of.

There I was two days after Christmas on a Thursday at two thirty in the afternoon, sitting in a café eating a chocolate croissant I couldn't afford. But I'd come from yet another interview that seemed promising but would probably never result in a job, so I felt like I deserved a treat.

I used my napkin to wipe away a trace of chocolate that had somehow migrated to my knuckle. I'd always figured that by this point I'd have a job in my chosen field and a decent paycheck to go with it. I'd be shopping for a not-too-big, not-too-small apartment with a view that would fill my friends with envy, an apartment I could afford to furnish however I liked. Instead, the only view I have is of a mound of debt that stretches to the skyline. A scholarship paid for some of it, but the amount still owed was nearly insurmountable. I had some money saved before school. I lived on that for a while, and when it ran out, my parents helped. After I graduated, my dad was always making jokes about how he could kick back and take it easy now while I took care of him. Lately, the jokes seem to have dried up, and he always slipped me some money when I saw him, which I really appreciated . . . even though it made me feel worse.

When I started school, the economy was just beginning to tank, but I never thought it would still be this bleak by the time I finished. So, despite numerous interviews for firms with great reputations, I remained empty-handed. Right now I was living in a smallish apartment in a sketchy part of town, and the rent was still more than I could afford. Unless I found a job soon, I wasn't sure how much longer I could reasonably expect to continue living there.

My croissant was gone. I glanced at the display case, longingly eyeing a fruit tart jeweled with a stunning array of raspberries. Raspberries are my favorite. It was probably thirty dollars' worth of posh dessert, but I imagined buying it, taking it home to the privacy of my crappy apartment, and consuming the entire thing. It was a ridiculous idea, broke as I was. Still, I considered it for a whole minute before my practical side took over.

I shook my head and said a mental farewell to the raspberry tart, promising myself that when I finally got a job, I would come back and buy one with my first paycheck to celebrate. I leaned down to pick up my briefcase. It had been a gift from my parents when I graduated—for good luck, my dad said, and I knew he was imagining me blazing into courtrooms with it, concealing documents guaranteed to win any case. He'd probably die if he knew the most important things it had ever concealed were my résumé and orange Tic-Tacs. I'm sure it cost a fortune; it was made of the kind of black leather that smells like power and tells the world you mean business. When I first started carrying it, I felt invincible, like a member of an exclusive club. But now I was embarrassed being seen with it, especially going back and forth to interviews for jobs I wasn't getting. It was as if even the gorgeous bag was mocking my failure. If my father wasn't so absurdly proud of it, I'd have left it in the closet until I had a job that made me feel worthy.

I shouldered the bag, which, despite its lack of contents, seemed heavier every time I picked it up. But before I could stand, a familiar voice caught me by surprise.

"Rachel, is that you?"

* * *

Two and a half(ish) years ago . . .

I rolled over and slapped at my alarm in my sleepy daze until I realized the ringing wasn't stopping. I opened my eyes to investigate. It was my cell phone. The fact that it was playing "Sixteen Going on Seventeen" should have been the first clue that it wasn't my alarm. I was constantly changing my ring tone to various show tunes, my love of which was a nerdy secret of mine. My CD collection of musicals was stashed on a shelf in the closet in my bedroom. I don't know who I was hiding them from.

I couldn't see who was calling without my glasses, but at this hour it had to be important. "Hello?"

"Rachel? Is that you?"

"Who is this?" The voice at the other end of the line was crackly, and I was having a hard time deciding what day it was or if I should be somewhere. Since it was dark outside, I guessed I was probably where I should be—asleep.

"It's Shannon, you goose. Are you asleep?"

"I can barely hear you."

"Wait a minute," she said, and then the noise disappeared. "Sorry, is that better?"

"Much." I yawned. "What's wrong?" I put on my glasses; the clock said 1:05 a.m. Everything was coming back to me. I'd been studying for a test I had in the morning and had gotten a killer headache, so I decided to go to bed early. I yawned again. If I woke up in the middle of the night, I always had a hard time going back to sleep. But the yawning was a good sign. I allowed my eyes to drift closed. As long as this was a short conversation, hopefully I'd be able to slip back into sleep without too much interruption.

"Nothing is wrong. Everything is wonderful." Her voice trilled.

"That's grand. You seem a little hyper. Have you been eating sugar after dinner again? You know we talked about that."

"Hey, sugar can actually be very beneficial under the right circumstances."

"Okay, so it was sugar."

"It's not sugar. I'm happy. Life is pleasant. Can't I be upbeat without some sort of external stimulant?"

"Did you actually use the words 'external stimulant'?"

"Maybe. You're kinda cranky. Were you asleep?"

"Yeah, I have a test in the morning," I said, trying to yawn. If I could yawn, it meant I was still sleepy.

"I'm sorry. Go back to sleep."

"It's okay."

"No, it can wait. Call me back when you're done with your test."

"Just tell me—it must be important."

"It *is* important."

"Well, I'm never going to get back to sleep if I'm lying here wondering what you called me about at one in the morning!"

She gasped. "Is it really that late? I didn't realize. I'm sorry. Go back to sleep."

"You're kidding, right?" A tiny bit of annoyance crept into my voice as I felt the chance of renewed sleep getting more and more remote. "Spill it already!"

"You're not going to believe it when tell youuuuuu," she singsonged.

"Shannon Sarah Fielding!"

"Okay, okay! NATHAN ASKED ME TO MARRY HIM!"

My eyes flew open, any thoughts of sleep gone. "You said yes, right?"

"I said yes!"

By this point we were both squealing like a couple of teenagers.

"That's the best news *ever*! I can't believe you didn't blurt it at me the minute I picked up the phone."

She laughed. "I was trying to draw out the suspense, like you do."

"Obviously, I don't do too well on the receiving end of suspense."

"It's okay. I didn't exactly time my big announcement very well."

"No, I'm really glad you called now that I know why you were calling! I'm dying to know—what does the ring look like?"

"It's gorgeous. I love it. I'm sending you a picture right now."

My phone beeped, and I saw a delicate ring with a square-shaped solitaire diamond surrounded by a row of smaller ones. "That is so you. Did you guys look at rings together?"

"No. I had no idea he was planning this. Nathan chose it all by himself."

"Well, he must have been paying attention; it's perfect."

"Yeah, I can't believe I resisted the idea of me and Nathan for so long. Sometimes I think he knows me better than I know myself."

"I don't mean to be a downer, but you've only been dating each other for a month. Are you sure?"

"I'm sure."

"Positive?"

"Rachel, Nathan and I have been friends for years! Besides, aren't you the one who's always saying we're perfect for each other?"

"I just want to make sure *you* know you're perfect for each other."

"I'm happy, I promise. This is what I always wanted."

"Always?" I questioned. There was a time in the not-too-distant past that Shannon was determined her relationship with Nathan would never progress beyond friendship.

"Okay, it's what I recently always wanted. Why are you questioning this? I thought you'd be happier for me than anyone else."

"You know I am. Marriage is forever—I don't want you to have any regrets."

"I will never regret choosing Nathan," she said. Her voice was firm and final.

"What are you going to tell Henry?"

"What about Henry?"

"As I recall, you were dating him too."

"I haven't seen him in at least a month. As far as I know, he's still off gallivanting in Europe somewhere."

"But you're going to have to tell him," I said gently. It was clear that in her excitement about getting engaged, Shannon had forgotten completely about this particular loose end. "You know how to get in touch with him, right?"

"I have his cell number," she mumbled. "But it's not really something you tell someone over the phone."

"You're telling me over the phone."

"You know what I mean. It's different. Maybe I'll wait until he comes back."

At least she realized he deserved to know, if not in a timely manner. "What if he doesn't come back?"

"Then I'll never have to tell him."

"Shannon . . ."

"I'm kidding. I mean, he has to come back eventually."

"What if he comes back to find you married with three kids? Don't you think that's a teeny bit unfair?"

"Obviously I'm not going to drag it out that long." She sighed. "I'll call him tomorrow, get it over with. I don't think it'll come as much of a shock to Henry anyway. He knew that my ultimate goal was to end up with Nathan."

"But he was still hoping for his own chance with you, even though he knew how you felt. That's kind of sweet, don't you think?"

"Rachel, this is supposed to be the happiest night of my life thus far. Are you trying to depress me on purpose?"

"Of course I'm not. I'm only trying to make sure you've thoroughly considered all your options."

"I have considered my options. I chose Nathan, and I will inform Henry of this decision tomorrow. Now, let's talk dresses. I promise I won't pick anything hideous if you agree to be my maid of honor."

I was kind of relieved that Shannon had dismissed the topic of Henry. I didn't want her to think I wasn't thrilled for her, but I also didn't want her to forget that halfway across the world, there was a handsome, wealthy man pining over her that any girl would be lucky to have. Obviously someone had to be the voice of reason. If Henry had paid one-tenth the attention to me that he had to her, I can almost guarantee my head would have been turned. I mean, I didn't know him that well, but he seemed pretty great. The thought flashed through my head how unfair it was that Shannon had two stellar guys competing for her, and I had zero. But since there was nothing to be done about it, I brushed it aside and moved on.

"I'd be delighted," I said.

Chapter Two
"Am I Blue?"

"Rachel, is that you?"

The voice was familiar, but I couldn't recall who it belonged to until I looked up. Towering above me was Henry, and although I hadn't seen him in quite some time, he wasn't exactly easy to forget. He was wearing an expensive-looking suit and a blank expression.

"Henry, how nice to see you." Although he was every bit as good looking as I remembered, there was something different about him. I couldn't quite put my finger on what it was. "Have you gotten . . . shorter?"

"I've never seen you here before, and I'm here quite a bit," he said, completely ignoring my comment.

"That's because I can't afford to come here."

"Really? Because you could probably feed a small third-world country for what you paid for that briefcase."

I glared. "It was a gift."

He just nodded, and I watched as his eyes skimmed my empty plate. "So what were you celebrating?"

"Why would you assume I was celebrating?"

"You said you don't come here much, so I figured you were treating yourself."

"It was more along the lines of wallowing."

His lips quirked upward in the first trace of emotion I'd seen from him. "Now you're speaking my language. I was going to grab a sandwich and go, but can I get you something?"

"Thanks, but I've reached my pastry quota for the day."

"Maybe a drink?"

I hesitated but only for a second. It was starting to snow outside. "Hot chocolate?"

"I'll be right back."

I watched as Henry placed his order at the counter. There really was something odd about him. He slumped a little, like he was tired. When he came back to the table, I noticed lines in his face that I didn't remember. I knew he was a little older than I was, but he looked like he'd put on a decade since I'd seen him last.

"How was your Christmas?" he asked.

"You know, same old. You?"

"Actually, I worked," he said.

"Oh. I'm sorry."

"No, it's okay. Didn't really have much else going on, so why not catch up on some stuff I'd been putting off, right?"

"Sure. Why not?" I tried to sound nonchalant. I didn't want him to think I pitied him. Christmas was one of my favorite holidays, and I couldn't imagine spending it by myself at work.

"What's it been, two years?" he said, quickly changing the subject.

"Two years and a bit, I think." He didn't mention the occasion of our last meeting, and I thought it unkind to bring it up.

"So I have"—he glanced at his fancy watch—"eight minutes. Tell me what you've been up to."

"Oh, you know. Graduating from law school, trying to placate the bill collectors and survive until I find a job. Just the usual stuff."

Henry frowned. "You must have graduated months ago."

Strange. How would Henry know when I graduated? Either he possessed a Rainman-like memory, or he'd made a lucky guess. "I did. In case you haven't noticed, the job market isn't the best right now."

The waiter brought Henry's sandwich wrapped up to go and a drink, along with my hot chocolate. Henry pushed it across the table, and I warmed my hands on the cup before taking a sip. It was heavenly.

"I didn't mean to be rude, but I'm surprised. I mean, you can never have too many lawyers, right?"

"Are you mocking me?"

"No," he said quickly. "I have the utmost respect for lawyers. They've gotten me out of some sticky situations."

I gave him a curious look.

"Work-related situations," he amended. "When you have as much money as I do, everyone wants a piece of you."

"I can imagine." *And it probably doesn't help that you're almost painfully handsome,* my mental voice added.

"So where have you applied?"

"At this point, it'd be easier to tell you where I haven't applied."

He winced. "That bad?"

"I just came from an interview. They all look very promising; 'Your schooling is impressive. You seem like you'd be a good fit here; we'll be in touch.' It's like they're reading from a script." I shrugged. "But none of them ever call. Honestly, a few more weeks of this, and I'm going to have to start looking for something just to pay the bills."

"I can't believe you've made it this long. Not many people your age have any savings to fall back on."

I couldn't help smiling. "People my age? You sound like my father."

He waved his hand. "I'm sort of a special case. Having money makes you ageless, gives you the authority to give advice and make critical judgments."

"That sounds like something you just made up."

"No, seriously. Whenever I open my mouth, people listen. It's like they think I have the secret to wealth and happiness."

I leaned forward a little. "And do you?"

"Maybe."

"Go on, then—enlighten me."

"The secret to wealth is easy."

"If it was easy, everyone would do it."

"Everyone *could* do it. All you have to do is decide what you want most of all and commit to that one thing 100 percent—all your time and effort."

I was skeptical. "And that makes you rich?"

"That's the secret." He gave me a half smile. "Well, that and a little luck."

"Aha! So you admit that hard work is only part of it."

"Hard work is *most* of it. But timing is important too."

I took another sip of my drink. "What about the secret to happiness?"

The brief smile fled from Henry's face, and he lowered his eyes to the tabletop. "The secret to happiness is very similar to the secret to wealth, but it doesn't work if the one person you want to commit everything to is already taken."

"I'm sorry. Maybe we should talk about something else."

"You probably think I'm crazy."

"Hey, love makes fools of us all, right?"

He gave me a mirthless laugh. "That sounds like a pretty accurate description. I know I made an idiot of myself at the wedding, but I was sort of hoping everyone had forgotten."

"Give it a few more years. I don't think anyone blamed you, if it makes you feel any better."

"You're just saying that because you're a nice person. I'm sure Nathan blamed me."

I gave him a tiny smile. "Well, that's understandable, don't you think?"

"Probably. I never thanked you, by the way, for dragging me out of there."

"I was only doing what any good maid of honor would."

"Whatever your reasoning was, thank you."

I desperately wanted to change the subject. "Wow, look at the time. It's been at least eight minutes. You're going to be late."

He sighed. "It wasn't that important."

I studied the gloomy expression on his face, wondering if there was anything left that was really important to Henry.

* * *

Two years and three(ish) months ago . . .

Shannon made a beautiful bride. As I sat and watched her and Nathan dancing, whispering, and laughing, it seemed that nothing could ruin this day. But something could, and he was in the audience watching as well. Once the bride and groom had finished their dance and everyone else drifted onto the dance floor to join them, he saw his opportunity and took it.

"Mind if I cut in?" Henry asked, tapping Nathan on the shoulder. I saw Nathan's jaw tighten, and I hurried onto the dance floor. If only I had seen Henry before he made this rash decision. But it was too late now—all I could do was damage control. I ran as fast as I could in my dress and heels.

"Henry!" I said brightly. "So good to see you. Imagine that, running into you at another wedding. We must have all the same friends. How about a dance?"

"Thank you, Rachel, but I think I'd like to dance with the bride first." He smiled at Shannon, but he looked . . . cold inside. There was no other way to describe it. It was as if all his wit and charm had been scraped out, leaving nothing but emptiness where his heart used to be.

"I don't think that's a great idea," Nathan said, and I noticed his grip on Shannon tighten. But looking at Shannon, I knew she understood. Henry was brokenhearted.

"It's okay, honey. It's one dance," Shannon said, trying to reassure Nathan with her eyes. It was so déjà vu it was almost creepy. The same thing had happened at the wedding reception where Shannon and Henry met, and I could tell the similarities weren't lost on Nathan either.

Nathan's eyes were dark, but he reluctantly surrendered his new bride to his one-time rival. "I'll be right over there if you need me," he said to Shannon, loud enough for Henry to hear. We started to walk back to the tables, but I had an idea.

"Hey, why don't we dance?" I said to Nathan. His face filled with gratitude. It was a good excuse for him to stick close to Shannon. We danced close enough that we could keep an eye on them and see that their conversation was civil but not quite close enough to hear what they were saying. I could tell that Nathan was going crazy. I couldn't imagine him putting up with this for much longer. When the dance ended and the next song began, Henry showed no signs of giving Shannon back. Nathan's thinly veiled attempt at goodwill disappeared. He started in their direction.

I stopped him. "Let me try first, okay?"

"I can't just stand here while another guy waltzes in and hijacks my wife on our wedding day!"

"Give me a chance. You don't want to ruin the day for Shannon, do you?"

"Of course not."

"I can fix this without a scene; I know I can. Just give me a minute, okay?"

Nathan finally waved me away, and I prayed I was as good at hostage negotiating as I thought I was.

"Where are you going on your honeymoon?" Henry was saying as I approached them. I was determined to stand there until he acknowledged me.

"Why?" Shannon asked. She looked uncomfortable.

"I'm curious," he said.

"St. George."

"Not very adventurous, is it?"

"Well, we can't really get away right now."

"That's too bad."

I was starting to feel ridiculous standing there while they danced around me, so I tapped Henry on the shoulder. He ignored me.

When Shannon didn't say anything, Henry continued. "I guess that means you won't be able to use the wedding present I got you." He stopped dancing and reached into his suit coat pocket, removing an envelope and holding it out to Shannon. She stared at it for as long as possible before finally, reluctantly taking it.

"Congratulations. Open it," he said.

She lifted the flap and looked inside. "You can't be serious," she said.

"What is it?" I asked, unable to be silent any longer.

"Plane tickets. For their honeymoon," Henry said.

"Do you have any idea how inappropriate this is?" Shannon demanded.

"I've heard Mexico is lovely this time of year," Henry said.

"I don't know what to say," Shannon said.

"I believe 'thank you' is the traditional response," Henry said.

"Henry, I think you need to leave," I said.

"What's wrong? We're only dancing. It's my last dance with Shannon. I think I'm entitled."

"Henry, let's go." I grabbed his arm, but he clearly wasn't going anywhere. "You shouldn't even be here. You're upsetting Shannon."

"I'm not upsetting her. You're not upset, are you, Shannon?"

"Yes," she said quietly.

"Oh."

I got the feeling he honestly didn't see anything wrong with this bizarre situation.

"Well, I'll leave then. I hope you'll be able to find the time to use my wedding present. You did get a passport, didn't you?"

Shannon's face went completely white, and I knew she was thinking of Henry offering to fly her across the world if she ever decided to give him a chance. I remembered the day she called me from the post office, where she'd been getting her passport, before she and Nathan started actually dating. "Just in case," she'd said, and I could tell by the look on her face that the memory haunted her now.

Despite agreeing to let me try to diffuse the situation, Nathan had obviously seen Shannon's face and was heading in our direction. I literally had seconds.

"Come on, Henry," I said again, tugging on his arm, but it was useless—like trying to move a stubborn six-foot-five giraffe.

"Did you get the passport before or after you and Nathan started dating?" Henry asked.

Nathan was close enough now for me to see his red, angry face.

"You're about to be clobbered by the groom!" I said, making one last attempt to impress on Henry the seriousness of the situation.

"I'm not worried about him."

"Henry," Shannon said. "Please just go."

Those words drained all the fight out of him. I quickly whisked him through the crowd, away from Shannon and Nathan. I looked back once and saw Shannon with a smile pasted on her face, trying to hide how upset she was in order to calm her new husband.

Outside, it was a beautiful August night. The crickets were chirping, the sun was disappearing behind a mountain, and Henry looked completely deflated.

"Why did you come here?" I asked.

"To say good-bye," he said.

"Maybe next time a card would be better," I said. I was trying to lighten the moment, but I could tell Henry wasn't really listening. He looked like a lost child, albeit a very tall one, and I suddenly wanted to comfort him. Even though it was a rotten thing for him to do, showing up there that night, he was the one who'd be going home alone. The pain on his face was startling. I wanted to hug him and tell him that everything was going to be okay, but before I could do anything, he managed to compose himself.

"See you around, Rachel."

But I hadn't.

Chapter Three
"I Wished on the Moon"

"ANYONE WITH EYES KNEW THEY belonged together," he said.

I nodded, smiling sympathetically. What was left of my drink was cold, and Henry showed no signs of going anywhere. His lunch stayed in the bag, forgotten. I figured the least I could do was listen if he wanted to talk.

"But Shannon was so oblivious," he continued. "I kept thinking one day this guy's patience is going to crack. He's going to get tired of this and give up, and that's when I'll make my move. Unfortunately, they finally ended up on the same page."

"It was inevitable," I said.

"I really loved her, you know."

I gasped. "You . . . loved her?" Why was he telling me this? I was practically a stranger—surely he must have someone else to bare his soul to.

"Well, I *think* I loved her. I'm not sure I ever loved anyone before that, so I can't be positive. But she was so perfect. I can't imagine it being better than that."

This was much worse than I'd thought. I knew Shannon had liked spending time with Henry, but she'd assured me they were just friends. Of course, she'd said that about Nathan, too, and look how that turned out. Obviously Henry had fallen much harder for her. Either he had been awfully good at hiding his feelings or Shannon really was clueless.

"I'm over it now."

I looked at him skeptically. "You don't sound like a guy who's over it."

"No, I am. Seeing you kind of brought everything back for a minute, but I get up every morning and go to work, and life is grand. Really."

"I hope so. You deserve to have a life, you know."

"A life," he mused. "I never claimed to have one of those."

"Me either. We're career people, you and I. Our lives have been forfeited."

"That's incredibly depressing."

"I know."

He smiled, maybe the first real smile since he'd sat down. "You're probably bored. I should go."

"I'm unemployed, remember? I have nowhere to be."

"Thanks for listening to me ramble." Henry stood and held out his hand to shake mine.

I took his hand. Shannon and I used to joke that if she ever ended up with Nathan, I should go after Henry, but now I couldn't imagine how I'd ever thought, even in my wildest dreams, that I might end up with him. He was an intimidating figure—almost six-foot-five; dark, messy hair; rich; fashionable in that gorgeous suit. I'm not sure how Shannon dated him for so long, but maybe he was different with her.

I realized I was still holding on to his hand. The look on his face was hard to read, but I guessed he was trying to figure out a way to extricate himself from the handshake without being rude. I dropped his hand and tried in vain to keep back the hot flush that was creeping up my neck. I tried not to think about how I had secretly coveted him a bit on dateless nights back when Shannon was going out with him.

"Good to see you again, Rachel. Tell Shannon I said hello." He strode quickly in the direction of the door before turning back. "On second thought, don't. That might be awkward."

While I was trying to come up with something to say in parting, he came back. He paused, studying me as if he were seeing me for the first time. If I'd had any hopes of burying the earlier blush, his close appraisal destroyed them outright.

"You look very nice," he said finally.

"Uh, thank you?"

He looked lost in his thoughts. "This interview you went to—were you excited about it?"

"I was nervous about it." I wasn't sure exactly where Henry was going with this.

"Are you hoping you get the job?"

"Well, yeah, it'd be nice to work—start paying off my loans and not have to worry about where I'll get rent money."

"Come by my office tomorrow. I might have something for you."

"Thank you," I managed. It was all I could do not to get down on my knees and kiss his immaculately polished shoes. He handed me his card and left without another word. I was stunned. This might be the best bit of luck I'd had in ages. Maybe it was true what he said; maybe timing had its place too.

* * *

I went to Shannon and Nathan's apartment. She usually got home before Nathan, and I hoped I would catch her alone. I needed some advice, and I didn't want Nathan to be around for this particular conversation. I wasn't sure Shannon would be home yet, so I was relieved when she answered the door.

"Did you get off early?" I said, putting my briefcase by the kitchen table.

"It was slow, so they let me go at four. How was your interview?"

I shrugged. "Fine, I guess. The same as every other interview."

"And the rest of your afternoon?"

Hmmm. How to go about this? If this job Henry was talking about came through, I wasn't sure how closely I'd be working with him, but I would definitely have to tell Shannon. And since she knew him a lot better than I did, I wanted to get an independent opinion on whether working with him would be a good idea. "It was . . . interesting."

"Sounds like there's a story there." We sat on the couch in the living room.

"Okay, I'm not sure how to say this and I'm not even supposed to mention it, but I need some advice, so I'm going to come right out with it. I saw Henry today."

Shannon stiffened a little. "Really? Did you talk to him?"

"A little."

"How was he?"

"Not great. Apparently you're pretty hard to get over."

She sighed. "I think about him every now and then, ever since the wedding. He was such a jerk that day. I get it, you know? I mean, I feel bad about the way things turned out, but I never led him on. He always knew I would choose Nathan if I had the opportunity. He even tried to help me!"

"Have you ever wondered why he might do that?" I said.

"Because, secretly, all guys are insane?"

"Just the ones who fall madly in love with you, apparently."

She rolled her eyes. "Thanks a lot."

"Seriously, I think he wanted you to have every opportunity to be happy. If you and Nathan didn't end up together, he wanted you to give him a chance, knowing you didn't have any regrets."

"But Nathan and I *did* end up together."

"I know. But I think Henry was a lot more invested in your faux relationship than you were."

"We weren't really dating. He knew that." Shannon fiddled with a loose string poking out of the couch.

"But it didn't stop him from falling for you. Hard."

"Are you trying to make me feel worse?"

"Of course not. He didn't even want me to mention that I'd seen him, but I need your opinion."

The relief on her face was immediate. "I totally don't mind if you go out with him. I mean, it would be weird at first, but Nathan and I could be civil if he was around. Well, I could, and we could always gag Nathan. You should date him—I want you to."

"Good heavens, no. Haven't you been listening to me? I doubt he'll ever date anyone again. He probably has a little shrine built to you in his closet."

"Hey! Not helping!"

"He told me to come see him at work tomorrow. He might have a job for me."

Shannon squealed. "Rachel Marie Pearce, that's awesome!"

"So you think I should go?"

"Absolutely. Henry is nothing if not a brilliant businessman. I think it would be a perfect place for you to start."

I was relieved. I still wasn't sure I wanted to work with Henry, but at least I knew it was an option. "I thought I'd run it by you—see what you thought."

"You don't need my permission, you know, to work with Henry or date him or whatever."

"And what would Nathan think?"

"It doesn't matter. Nathan is *my* husband, not yours, and you can do whatever you like."

"I don't want it to be awkward."

"We're adults, right? All of that is in the past now." She smiled. "Still, let's not tell Nathan until it's official. No use upsetting him unnecessarily."

"My thoughts exactly," I said, standing up. "I think I'll leave before he gets home. What are you guys up to tonight?"

"Apparently, Nathan is cooking."

"Wow, that's impressive."

"Yeah, or scary. I haven't decided which yet."

"Hmmm. Maybe you should go pick up some Maalox before dinner."

"I'm good to go on antacids. My tummy hasn't been so hot lately."

"Are you taking your pills? You know how your stomach gets iffy when you're stressed out," I said.

"Yes, *Mother*."

"Great. And then I come over and dump my Henry-sighting on you. I'm sorry."

"Sweetie, I told you it's no big deal. Henry's not even on my radar anymore."

"Are you worried about something?"

"Not that I'm aware of. Probably too much spicy food. Nathan showed up with buffalo wings last night."

I wrinkled up my nose. "Well, I think I'll go. Good luck with dinner."

"Let me know how it goes with you-know-who tomorrow."

"I will."

I went home to the crummy little apartment I could barely afford, changed into my flannel pajamas, ate a can of soup, and sat on the couch—the only piece of decent furniture besides the bed—to watch *Law and Order*. Shannon always teased me about my *Law and Order* addiction. We had this joke that between the original show and all the spinoffs and all the cable channels, there was always an episode playing somewhere in the world at any given time.

They were just getting to the big court scene at the end when I noticed something moving out of the corner of my eye. When I looked, there was nothing there. It must have been a trick of the light from the television. I went back to concentrating on the show, but a few minutes later, I saw it again. I peered around the room, finding nothing out of the ordinary. The third time I saw the flash of movement, I knew it couldn't be a fluke. I eased off the couch and crept to the edge of the room where the hideous green shag carpet faded into shadows, and there it was.

A mouse.

The tiniest little mouse I'd ever seen. If it wasn't so completely unsanitary, I would have scooped it up and petted it and kept it in a little cage with a wheel. It was that cute. It stared at me with its beady little mouse eyes, and I stared back at it until it got brave and dashed across the floor, disappearing under the couch. I took a big gulp of air. It was only then I realized I'd been holding my breath since my small friend had made its appearance.

I picked up my cell phone and dialed Shannon. When she picked up, I didn't even wait for her to finish saying hello before the words started spilling out.

"I have a mouse!" I said breathlessly.

"You have a *what*?"

"I have a mouse, and it's the littlest, cutest baby mouse you could possibly imagine. It was white and gray with big ears and a tiny little tail, and it actually looked friendly, like the kind of mouse in a children's book or something. It sat there and stared at me for a minute, and now it's gone and I don't know what to do about it. I mean, how long has it been here? Probably not long since it's a very small mouse, but still. I can't be living here with a mouse! I knew this was a terrible apartment, but I had no idea it was a terrible apartment that came with a mouse."

"Whoa, slow down for a minute and breathe!"

I paused and took a deep breath, letting it out slowly through my mouth.

"Feel any better?" Shannon inquired.

"Not really."

"Okay, where is the little mousey now?"

"It ran and hid under the couch, and it hasn't come out." Another episode was starting. The music was loud enough that I thought it might scare the mouse out of its hiding place, but no luck. I was kind of glad it hadn't reappeared; an out-of-sight mouse was somehow less threatening than one that was right in front of you. As long as it stayed where it was, I could avoid having to do something about it.

"Are you watching *Law and Order*?" Shannon asked.

"No."

"Don't lie! I can hear the theme music."

"I can't help it—it relaxes me before I go to bed." It was ridiculous that we had veered into this side conversation while there were more pressing mouse-matters to be discussed.

"I'm not sure how I feel about you finding murder and criminals comforting."

"Hey, I don't criticize you for watching *Hoarders*. That's much scarier than *Law and Order*."

"I don't even like *Hoarders*!" she argued. "I only watch it because Nathan likes it."

"Sure, blame it on the husband."

"You should try switching the channel. Maybe the mouse was attracted by courtroom drama."

"It's not funny," I said between laughs.

"It's really not. I was trying to get you to laugh so you'd stop wigging out."

"Thank you. I do feel slightly less hysterical now."

"Unfortunately, my rodent extermination skills are rather limited."

I gulped. "Extermination? You mean, kill it?"

"Unless you want to sew it a tiny pillow and get it a little bowl of popcorn."

"You make me sound like an idiot."

"So what was your big plan?"

I closed my eyes, but only for a moment. I didn't want to miss Mousey if it emerged from under the couch and made a run for it. "I didn't have a plan! That's why I called you."

"You did the right thing. Nathan will know what to do. He's busy teaching the Scouts how to tie knots or something, but I'll talk to him about it when he gets home."

"Couldn't we catch it and let it go outside?"

"It doesn't work like that. He'd be back in your apartment before you could say, 'Objection, Your Honor.'"

I couldn't think about trapping a baby . . . anything. Or poisoning it. "What about if we drove it up into the mountains and set it free?"

"Rachel, it's a *baby* mouse. You might as well be dropping off take-out for the first owl that swoops by."

"Wait until you see it. It has these big, sad eyes. You won't be able to kill it."

"I won't, but my big, strong husband will. You'll see."

"I don't want to be here when he does . . . whatever he's going to do."

"Okay, Miss Squeamish. I'll take you to a movie or for ice cream or something, and when we get back, it'll all be over."

"How can I eat ice cream when I know Nathan is murdering Mousey?"

"Rachel. Go to bed."

So I went to bed. There was nothing I could do about Mousey tonight, and watching television had somehow lost its appeal now that I knew there was vermin lurking directly below me, no matter how cute it was. I was afraid to even sit on the couch for fear of crushing the mouse. Besides, tomorrow might potentially be a big day. I imagined that Henry had connections all over the valley, and I really hoped that whatever job he had in mind for me would finally be the one that clicked.

Chapter Four
"Nice Work If You Can Get It"

WHEN I ARRIVED AT HENRY'S office the next morning, it was too early to go inside. It was 7:32 a.m., and while he seemed like the early-rising type, someone who would value initiative, I didn't want to look too eager. He said to come and see him tomorrow; he didn't mention anything about being on the doorstep at the crack of dawn.

I had tried to go back to sleep, but I was so nervous I couldn't stay in bed one minute longer. Instead, I got ready and took the bus to Shannon's. She didn't have to work until this afternoon, so she kindly let me borrow her car. Now I was here way before I dared go inside. I didn't want to bring the car back with no gas, so I turned off the engine and sat in the cold for about an hour, until I could see my breath. There was still no sign of Henry.

This was silly. I might as well at least go inside and see if he was there. Eight thirty is a reasonable hour to expect someone to be at work. Besides, no one wants their obituary to say that they froze to death in a working car in the middle of civilization. I got out of the car, and despite the fact that the weather was supposed to be mild and sunny, the air smelled like snow. I fished in my coat pocket until I found Henry's card. His office was on the third floor. I replaced the card and buried my hands in my pockets, trying to warm them.

Henry's office was in a nice brick building in downtown Salt Lake City. There was a little courtyard out front that was probably lovely in the spring and summer but very gloomy in December and filled with some scrawny birds that looked colder than I was, if that was possible. They scratched at the pavement, looking for a scrap of something edible, and I found myself wishing I had something to feed them.

Inside, the odor of coffee hung heavy in the air. At least I knew someone was there this early. There was a plaque near the elevator with suite numbers and their occupants. I got on the elevator and pressed the three.

"Going up," a mechanical woman's voice said, and I jumped. I hadn't realized how quiet it was in the building until the voice interrupted the silence.

"Third floor," she announced. I quickly got off the elevator, resolving to take the stairs when I left.

I stood in front of the door to Henry's office, looking for some clue that would tell me whether he was there. I could hear faint strains of jazz music coming from inside—a piano and what sounded like a trumpet, dueling for dominance. The tune sounded cheerier than I would have given him credit for, considering his gloomy mood yesterday. In fact, if his name hadn't been on the door, I would have thought I had the wrong office. I finally knocked lightly and waited.

Just when I was working up the nerve to knock again, the music disappeared. The door opened, and there was Henry, in yet another expensive suit. He probably had an entire closet of them.

"Rachel. Hi. I'm sorry. I wasn't expecting you this early."

I never should have come first thing in the morning. "No, I'm sorry. I didn't know what time you'd be here. I can come back . . ."

"Nonsense. Come in and sit down." Henry's office appeared to consist of two rooms and a closed door, maybe a bathroom or a closet. I wondered if the building had originally been apartments and later been converted into office space. The only items in the main room were a couch, a smallish copy machine, and a large potted tree of some sort. The room probably looked bigger than it really was because it was so empty. I could see a large desk, which I assumed was Henry's, in the other room. I tried to politely ignore the rumpled blanket and pillow on the couch, but there really wasn't anywhere else to sit. Henry seemed to realize this about the same time I did.

"Sorry about that. Let me clear those away for you." He grabbed the pillow and blanket and threw them through his open office door. From what I knew of Henry, money wasn't an issue. I was certain that he probably had a very nice house somewhere, so why was he sleeping on the couch in his office?

"Can I take your coat?" he offered.

"No, thank you." It was warmer in here, but it was all I could do to keep my teeth from chattering. "It's freezing outside."

"Did you walk here?"

"I borrowed a car, and I've been waiting outside. I didn't intend to get here so early. I wasn't sure if you were even here yet."

"Well, as you probably noticed, I crashed here last night, so you could have come up hours ago." He gave me a tiny smile. "You might have caught me sleeping though."

I said the first thing that came to mind. "A tall guy like you needs a longer couch."

"I'll admit I've slept in more comfortable places. Is the heater broken in the car?"

"No, I just felt guilty using up all the gas when I couldn't afford to fill it up." I wasn't usually the kind of person to admit how dire my situation was, so why was I telling a guy I barely knew?

He started wandering around the perimeter of the office. "I wish I could offer you a drink or something, but I'm fresh out of . . ." He rummaged through the cupboards as though he were expecting something other than reams of copy paper and boxes of ballpoint pens. Why would one guy need so many pens, I wondered? "Well, out of everything. I don't get many visitors."

I could see the pity in his eyes, and it made me angry. I was tired of people feeling sorry for me, and if we didn't change the subject, I might say something nasty and ruin this opportunity. Besides, he was sleeping in his office. As far as I was concerned, he was as deserving of pity as I was. "You mentioned yesterday that you might have a job for me?"

This seemed to remind Henry why I was here. "Yes. Of course. Just a minute." He disappeared into his office and returned with a stack of papers. He handed them to me, and I thumbed through them. I don't know what I was expecting, but it looked like spreadsheets of financial columns. I didn't want him to think I was dense, but if there was a position in a law office contained in these pages, I couldn't find it. Maybe he'd mixed up stacks and given me the wrong one.

"What is this?" I asked.

"A job. For you."

"Is this some kind of test?"

"Yes." He was looking at me as though I should know what to do next.

I studied them again, pages of columns of numbers. "Is this some sort of secret code?"

"Some people might say so."

"Can you give me a hint?"

He pointed toward the corner where the copy machine sat innocently.

My stomach sank. He couldn't mean what I thought he meant. Maybe it was some sort of personality test. I decided to play along. "Oh, I get it. You're trying to see how I would react in a situation where someone was patronizing me. No one wants a lawyer with a short fuse, right?"

"Actually, I'm trying to see if you're capable of operating the copy machine. My last secretary wasn't."

"Your secretary? Is that what your mysterious job opening is?" My voice was rising of its own accord.

"I thought I was pretty clear."

"Henry, I'm a *lawyer*. Where do you think I went to school—Kinko's?"

"How should I know where you went to school?"

"Stanford. I graduated from *Stanford*. I think I'm a little overqualified to be collating your copies and sending faxes, don't you?"

"Times are tough. Lots of people have to take jobs they're overqualified for. I thought you'd be grateful."

That was the last straw. "Grateful? You thought I'd be *grateful*?!" I spluttered.

He frowned. "Why are you repeating everything?"

I stood up. "I think I'd better go."

"Call me if you change your mind."

"Believe me, nothing in the world could persuade me to be your *secretary*."

He touched my arm, and I swear I could feel the heat of his hand through my coat. "Look, I can see that you think I'm a jerk, but I really was trying to be helpful. You have bills. You need a job; I need a secretary. I thought we could help each other."

"You thought wrong." The warmth wasn't unpleasant, but I still tugged my arm away. I didn't feel right about taking comfort from the enemy. I stormed toward the door while I still had some dignity intact.

"Plenty of people would love to have this job," Henry called after me.

I poked my head back around the corner and gave him my sweetest smile. "I guess you'd better call one of them."

Chapter Five
"Easy to Love"

BY THE TIME I GOT to Shannon's, I had calmed down a little, but as I sat in the driveway thinking of Henry's offer, it wasn't long before I was so livid again that my hands were shaking. I didn't know what made me angrier—the fact that I'd gotten my hopes up over a job that turned out to be so far below my expectations or that Henry seemed to think it was the best I could do.

Despite my outrage, a tiny voice reasoned that a girl in my financial situation—with mounting bills and who was soon to be homeless—couldn't afford to be quite so particular. Don't get me wrong—I have nothing against secretaries; they are competent, necessary people who fill necessary positions. But I had worked incredibly hard to get through law school, and I wasn't willing to settle. If that made me arrogant or prideful, well, I couldn't help that. I knew that the day was coming, probably sooner than later, that I wouldn't have a choice, but I would cross that bridge when I came to it. The little voice hinted that it might be tricky trying to navigate a bridge I'd so thoroughly burned this morning.

I hate it when the little voice is sarcastic. I hate it even more when the little voice turns out to be right.

Shannon's front door was unlocked, and she was inside halfheartedly lacing up her shoes to go for a run. I couldn't help noticing she looked a bit ill. I flopped down on the couch next to her.

"That doesn't look like the face of someone who landed the job of her dreams this morning," she commented.

"Do you know what the job was?" I realized I was gritting my teeth in an attempt to decrease the volume of my voice. I didn't give her time to answer. "He wanted me to be his secretary. His *secretary!*"

"You're doing it again."

"Doing what?"

"Saying things twice." Shannon was trying not to smile.

"That's what Henry said!"

"Well, he probably didn't get rich by being unobservant. Are you sure he wasn't teasing you? He always liked to joke around."

"He was completely serious. He said that jobs are hard to come by in this economy, and he thought I'd be grateful. *Grateful!*" I bit my tongue. I was going to have to work harder on that.

Shannon wisely didn't mention it. "Look, I know this isn't what you want to hear, and I'm not taking his side, but—"

"Don't say it."

"I think you need to prepare yourself for the possibility that you might have to take a job you think is beneath you, at least until you can find the job you really want."

"You make me sound like a stuck-up cow," I grumbled.

"That certainly wasn't my intention." She laughed as she put her arm around me and squeezed. "I know this isn't turning out exactly like you planned, but this is a temporary setback—a speed bump."

"I still have a little time to find the right job. I don't have to settle quite yet."

"The next interview could be the one." She paused for a minute. "I'm guessing from your response that you didn't ask Henry to give you twenty-four hours to think about it."

I winced. "I told him nothing on earth could possess me to be his secretary."

"O-kayyyy. So I guess if the time comes when you have to settle, it won't be with Henry."

"Probably not."

"Was that really wise?"

I glared at her. "Don't you have somewhere to be?"

"Well, I was headed out to work off a little excess energy. You should come with me. You look like you're carrying enough stress to power a steam engine."

"The only place you should be running is to the bathroom. You look terrible."

"Is it that obvious?"

"You are turning a rather alarming shade of green."

"Hold that thought," she said, disappearing down the hall into the bathroom. When she returned she was looking more like herself. "You sure you don't want to go running with me? It might make you feel better."

"You can't be serious. You were chucking up your breakfast two minutes ago, and now you're ready for a jog? I know you're hard core, but this is ridiculous."

She gave me a mischievous smile. "Can you keep a secret? I think I figured out what's causing my mysterious stomach issues."

My mouth dropped open. "You aren't."

"Just barely. About six weeks, I think."

"Ohhhh. Congratulations!" I said, giving her a big squeeze. "I'm going to be an auntie!"

"Yes, and I haven't even told Nathan yet, so you know nothing."

"Should you really be running?"

"I called my doctor, and he says it's fine. I feel horrible first thing in the morning, but once I throw up, I'm fine."

Suddenly I was really tired. "Well, you may be Superwoman, but I'm going home and back to bed for a while. I didn't sleep very well, and now that the adrenaline has worn off, I want to pull the covers over my head and pretend this never happened."

Her face lit up. "I almost forgot! I have a surprise for you." She disappeared down the hall.

"It'd be hard to top the surprise you gave me a minute ago."

"My mom thinks she has the solution to your mice problem."

"There are no *mice*. There is only *mouse*."

She poked her head around the corner. "Rachel, no one ever has just one mouse."

"Says who?"

"Says everyone. It's a well-known fact."

"Why didn't you mention this well-known fact last night?"

"You were already in a panic. I didn't want to make it worse."

"Thanks a lot."

"Okay, close your eyes."

I did as I was told, and I felt the couch shift when Shannon sat down next to me. "You can look now," she said.

I stared at the fluffy white little runt sitting on her lap. There were no words.

"It's a cat," she said. "Happy birthday!"

"My birthday is in July."

"Happy early birthday! Isn't he the sweetest cat?"

"That's not a cat. It barely even qualifies as a kitten."

"I'll admit he's a little on the small side."

"It's marginally bigger than the mouse."

"He'll grow. And he'll be fierce. Mice will fear him, you'll see." She scratched under his chin, and he yawned.

"Yeah, it's scary, all right."

"Who's a big scary mouse killer? You're a big scary mouse killer. Yes you are," she cooed at him. He batted at her finger and chewed on the end of it until he got bored. Shannon didn't seem to mind, but his teeth looked like sharp white needles.

"Where did you get it?" I asked. *I hope you can return him,* my inner voice added.

"My mom's cat had kittens. I can't believe I didn't think of it last night—it's the perfect solution."

"You do know how I feel about cats, right?"

"You spent all that time at my house, and I always had cats growing up."

"I know, and I hated them!"

She picked up the puffball and held it directly in front of my face. "How could you hate him? Nobody could hate him—he's just a kitten."

"Exactly! What do you expect a kitten that's 95 percent fur to do to the mouse? Cute him to death?"

She used her finger to show me his gums. "The other five percent is teeth." She grinned.

"Ugh, how can you put your finger in its mouth? That's disgusting."

"Oh, come on, he's a little cupcake. Yes, you are." He nuzzled Shannon's palm as if on command, but he eyed me cautiously. I knew he was waiting for her to turn her head so he could pounce on me. "Don't you want to hold him?"

My eyes widened. "Do I have to?"

She placed it gingerly in my lap, and I froze.

Shannon laughed. "It's not a nuclear weapon. Oh, and I got you some food and litter for him. I know you're a little short on petty cash these days."

"I'm short on non-petty cash."

"I'll go grab his stuff for you."

"Don't leave me here alone with it!"

"Honestly, you'd think I put a piranha in your lap. Be nice to him—you'll be old friends in no time."

This was really happening. Shannon expected me to take this creature home with me. I forced myself to pet his head very lightly, and he immediately began digging his claws into my skin.

"Help, I'm being attacked," I yelped.

She hurried back in to assess the situation. "That's how he shows he likes you."

"By shredding my leg?"

"Don't be silly. He's getting comfortable. See?" The cat curled up, and the claws retracted.

"He only did that because you came back in the room. He was moving in for the kill. I'm not sure this is such a great idea."

"Do you want to move?" she asked.

"I can't afford to move."

"Do you want to pay for an exterminator?"

"I can't afford that either."

"Then this is your best option. Give it a try—you might like having the company."

I motioned to the jumbo-sized bag of kitten chow she'd brought out with her. "I hope you're not expecting me to have all his little friends over for dinner."

"I got the biggest bag because I figured by the time that's gone, you'll have a job and money to buy more."

"By the time that's gone, I'll have children in college. He'll never eat all that."

"He needs lots of food so he can grow up big and strong, don't you?" She was talking to the cat while she smoothed its fur. Finally she turned back to me. "Come on, I'll drive you home. You can't exactly take all this on the bus."

There was no getting around this. I was at least going to have to give Shannon's idea a shot. Maybe if I was lucky, I'd be allergic, and I'd have a good excuse to give him back.

I stood up and put the cat down on the ground. "Come, Hannibal."

"Hannibal? As in Lecter?" Shannon asked.

I laughed. "I was thinking of the brilliant military strategist, but yours is much better. Come, Hannibal," I repeated. The cat scampered off toward the kitchen.

"He's not a dog. He won't come when you call unless he's hungry."

We spent ten minutes trying to catch the kitten, who obviously thought this was some kind of game. Either that or it sensed it was going home with me and immediately fled. Shannon finally coaxed him out from behind the fridge and handed him to me. I held it out in front of me awkwardly as it squirmed, mewing and trying to get away.

"He doesn't like that," Shannon commented.

"You think?"

"Here, hold him up close against you like this." She held the cat close to her neck, and it snuggled up to her, purring loudly. "Now you try it."

"You get the cat. I'll get everything else."

Once I got back to the apartment, I put Hannibal down on the floor. He sniffed for a minute and bolted in the direction of my bedroom. It was a tiny apartment consisting of a bedroom, bathroom, and miniscule living room/kitchen, but I wondered briefly if I'd ever see the kitten again or if it would exist lurking in the shadows, like Mousey. The two of them would probably bond over conspiring how to get rid of me.

I spent what was left of the day setting up all the cat stuff, which was depressing because the cat had more earthly possessions than I did. This was not my best day ever.

The more I thought about the way I'd exploded at Henry, the sillier I felt. I didn't know him that well, but on the few occasions I'd seen him, he'd always been friendly in an offhand sort of way. I'm sure when he saw me at the café, he felt bad and was only trying to help. That made me feel even worse.

After a few more minutes, I forced myself to shrug it off. I was on top of this. Today I tackled the mouse problem.

Tomorrow I would tackle the job problem. Sitting around moaning wasn't going to fix anything. Somewhere the perfect job for me was waiting to be found, and I was certain I wouldn't feel so guilty about the way I'd treated Henry once I found it.

Chapter Six
"I'm Just Foolin' Myself"

A MONTH LATER I WAS in the supermarket, wearing an oversized Stanford T-shirt and sweatpants. My hair was in braids, and I had twenty dollars in my pocket. My dad had given it to me the day before, and I was on a mission to find the maximum food at the minimum price. I never paid much attention to how expensive food was until I didn't have any money.

It was Saturday, and I'd woken with a feeling of impending doom, spending the first half of the day in bed. The night before, I had decided that I'd have to get a job on Monday—whatever I could find. I had to have some way of supporting myself while I was looking for the job I wanted. I was sort of ashamed it had taken me this long to surrender. I should have gotten something at least part-time months ago, but I had convinced myself that taking a lesser job was like admitting defeat. And I wasn't that kind of girl.

When I graduated, I had this picture in my head of how everything was supposed to happen. I'd be hired by a big firm who would offer me twice what I was expecting, a corner office with an amazing view, and occasional use of the company jet. This was my fantasy; I knew my real offer probably wouldn't be that amazing, but I had great expectations. After a couple months, my outlook shifted slightly. I decided that I would be hired by a medium-sized firm who would offer me a decent starting salary and a small office with only one window that would look out on a big tree, which would sprout huge pink blossoms in the spring and have a little nest with a bird family I could watch. The partners in the firm would go on and on about what a great fit I was and how they couldn't believe no one had snapped me up yet.

Fast forward to a month ago, right after the Henry debacle. It was getting down to the wire, and I was more nervous every day. But I still had faith that I'd find a good job—maybe in a small firm that was looking for young blood. The money wouldn't be great, but they'd be impressed by my schooling and willing to work with someone inexperienced. They would give me a small office where I'd be out of the way, but that didn't bother me. Once I had a chance to prove myself, I was sure I'd move up the ladder quickly.

Which brought me to the soup aisle, trying to decide whether chicken or beef Cup O'Noodles would have the most realistic flavor. I settled on beef and put a box of six in my cart. Then I noticed twelve packages of chicken or beef Ramen noodles were the same price, so I traded them out. It's pretty bad when even Cup O'Noodles is out of your price range. The little voice in my head reminded me that if I had taken Henry up on his offer, I could be buying real food right now. I ignored it. I couldn't believe things had gotten this desperate. I had never been this long without a job. I felt like such a slacker. I had the bizarre urge to tell everyone in the store that I was a law graduate, maybe hold a sign that said *Will Provide Legal Services for Food*.

Even when I was in law school with enough homework to keep me up all night, I worked part time as a hostess in a little Italian restaurant. It was run by a sweet grandmotherly Italian woman named Agnella, who always made sure I went home with an overflowing container of leftovers.

Everything in the store looked good, and I had a brief fantasy of filling my cart to the top.

I'd always hated carrying the groceries into the house and putting them away, but I promised myself that if I got a job where I could afford to purchase actual food, I would never again complain about it. In fact, stocking the shelves of my imaginary kitchen sounded like the height of amusement at the moment.

I threw some saltines and a couple of cans of soup in the cart and headed for the bread aisle. As I picked up an economy-size tub of generic peanut butter, I noticed a guy studying the bread choices. He was really cute—tall, dark hair, dressed in his workout clothes like he'd just come from the gym. In fact, he looked a lot like Henry. Now I was blushing at the idea of ogling someone who was basically a clone of my best friend's ex who I used to have a secret crush on. When the angle of his head changed, it was obvious that it wasn't Henry, and I was glad. I hadn't seen him since I blew off his job offer, and I was dreading the idea of running into him somewhere.

When gym guy reached up to grab a loaf of organic wheat bread, I automatically checked his ring finger, only to be rewarded with the gleam of a thin gold band. Of course he was married. I was surprised that the impulse to check still existed. It must be sheer instinct. Either that or I was attracted to the fact that he could afford organic bread. I was going through a bit of a social drought, but with my current job worries, having a date on Friday night was the least of my concerns. He glanced at me and smiled briefly before he took off. *Well, there goes another one*, I thought.

"That wasn't very subtle. You need to brush up on your skills," a voice said very close to my ear.

I jumped and whirled around. It was Henry. My heart was beating double time. "I don't know what you're talking about."

"Come on, you were practically drooling on his tennis shoes."

"If I was drooling, it was over the bread, not him," I sniffed. I glanced quickly in Henry's cart. He had cheese and pickles and deli chicken and ice cream and raspberries. *Raspberries.* In the winter. They probably cost a fortune. He must have caught me eyeing his selections because he took a peek at mine too.

"Are you buying food for the homeless?" he asked.

This was too embarrassing. I couldn't have Henry knowing that I still didn't have a job. So I said the first thing I thought of. "My ward is having a food drive. I thought I'd pick up a few things to donate."

"That's great. What can I buy to help?" Henry pulled out his wallet and started thumbing through bills.

I could see this very quickly escalating into a disaster. "I couldn't take your money."

"I insist. Come on, we'll pick some stuff out together. It'll be fun."

Well, on the bright side, he didn't seem to be holding a grudge about the way we parted before. I followed him wordlessly. On the next aisle, he crouched down and picked up a large can on the bottom shelf. "Look at this—it's an entire chicken in a can! How do they do that?" He got up and put it in my cart.

"What are you doing?"

"I'm getting this."

"Why?"

"For the homeless."

"You can't get that," I said.

"Who wouldn't want a whole chicken in a can?"

"Lots of people. That's probably why it's on the bottom shelf."

"Well, I think it's a great idea. I wish I'd thought of it." He grabbed a few cans of beef ravioli and two big bags of elbow macaroni and added them to the cart too. I couldn't seem to find the words to tell him the truth about my situation.

"How have you been?" he asked.

"Never better."

"How about tuna?" he asked.

I made a face. "I don't like tuna."

He rolled his eyes. "For the homeless."

"Oh. I'm sure tuna is great."

He picked up six cans and added them to the rest. I had to stop this before it got any more out of control.

"Henry, wait. You've got to put this stuff back."

"Why? Because you don't like tuna? Lots of people like tuna."

"Fine, buy a chicken in a can. Buy ten! But you'll have to take them to the food bank yourself."

"I don't understand. Why can't you add it to your stuff?"

I finally exploded. "Because these groceries aren't for the homeless—they're mine!"

He looked momentarily confused, but then a look of understanding crossed his face. "You still haven't found a job, have you?"

"Not yet," I said. My voice was defiant, but my Burning Cheeks of Shame gave my true feelings away.

"I'm sorry. It's none of my business."

"It's okay. There's no way you could have known. I certainly didn't expect to still be unemployed after all this time."

"I think maybe we started off on the wrong foot." He stuck out his hand for me to shake. "I'm Henry."

My face was still hot, but I was so glad he wasn't pressing the issue that I decided to play along. "I'm Rachel. Pleased to meet you."

"Likewise. So, Rachel, what is it that you do?"

"I'm an unemployed, wannabe lawyer."

"That's terrible. You're supposed to say that you graduated from Stanford and you're still weighing your options as far as job offers are concerned."

"Wow, you're good. When you said that, I almost believed you."

"You have to be upbeat. And patient. You're too smart not to end up somewhere great."

"Thanks for that, especially since you must think I'm such a jerk."

He laughed. "What, for turning me down? Not at all."

"Really?"

"I admire you for that—being willing to suffer while you hold out for something better."

"I'm not exactly suffering."

"Rachel, you're buying a case of Ramen noodles. Trust me; I know suffering when I see it."

Now I was laughing.

"And now my job is done." He started moving the stuff he'd picked out of my cart into his.

"What do you mean?"

"I made you laugh. Now we can part as friends."

"I'd like that. And you don't have to put that stuff back; I'll do it."

"Don't you dare. I'm buying it."

"Seriously, I'm pretty sure that whole-chicken-in-a-can thing isn't as cool as you think it's going to be."

"Not for me—for the food bank. You inspired me."

"But there is no food drive. I made it up."

"Doesn't matter; I'll drop it off myself. Anyway, your heart was in the right place."

"It wasn't. I just didn't want you to feel sorry for me."

"I don't feel sorry for you. I told you—things are going to work out fine. Good luck with everything."

"You too."

"I'll see you around."

I watched as he pushed his cart full of delicacies around the corner. I sighed. Either he'd already hired someone else or he was too busy admiring my previous unwillingness to surrender to notice that if he'd offered me the job again, I would have taken it in an instant.

Chapter Seven
"I Get Along without You Very Well"

On Monday I sat at the counter in the café, eating a pumpkin muffin I'd had to scrounge up loose change for, filling out a job application with shaking fingers. When I'd left my apartment that morning, I'd had no idea where I was going, but I was determined not to come back until I found a job, any job. When I walked by the café and saw the Help Wanted sign in the window, it seemed like a good omen. Well, that, and it was snowing. So I went inside and casually ordered the muffin, which made me feel better about my situation—like I really came in here for breakfast and decided on a whim that since I didn't have anything pressing going on today, I might work here, just for a laugh. If this was all pretend, I didn't have to face the fact that if I didn't bring home a check this month, I would no longer be able to afford even my terrible apartment.

When I was finished with the application, I handed it to the girl at the counter. She gave me a sympathetic smile, and I knew instantly that my muffin ruse wasn't fooling her. She had the brightest red lipstick I'd ever seen, and I wondered if she really enjoyed working here or if circumstances dictated that she swallow her pride as well.

"I'll give it to Blake. He's the manager. If you don't mind waiting, I can see if he's got a minute to interview you now."

"Sure," I said and tried to smile.

"Okay. I'll be right back." She disappeared into the back, taking my fake smile with her. She seemed nice, but she was only another part of the charade necessary to facilitate my survival.

"You know, for someone who can't afford to eat at this café, you seem to hang out here a lot."

Oh no. Smug Henry was the absolute last thing I could cope with at the moment. Maybe if I was nasty enough I could get rid of him before he found out why I was really here. "Are you following me?"

"I told you, I come here practically every day. What's your excuse?" He brushed snow from the shoulders of the overpriced trench coat that protected his overpriced suit.

So much for my good omen. I could have picked any random place to suffer, so why did I choose Henry's second home?

"I felt like splurging. It's a beautiful day."

"It's snowing."

"I like the snow," I lied. "It's invigorating."

"If you say so. Any good news on the job front?"

"I saw you two days ago."

"Well, it never hurts to be positive."

"Do you think I'd be lounging around in a café eating a muffin at nine-thirty in the morning if I had a job?"

He smiled shamelessly. "Hey, it works for me. That's one of the perks of being your own boss, I guess." His smile disappeared when he noticed my muffin. "Is that pumpkin?"

"Yes," I purred as I put the last bite in my mouth.

He frowned. "I don't see any more in the case. Is that the last one?"

"I can only hope."

Of course, counter girl picked this unfortunate moment to return. "You're in luck," she said. "Well, sort of. The bad news is that Blake's too busy to interview you now, but the good news is that he took one look at your application and said you're hired—as long as you don't feel the need to dispense legal advice to customers. You can start tomorrow." She placed a carefully folded white apron on the counter in front of me.

I wanted to die. Instead I managed to mutter a thank-you. She only nodded before grabbing a rag to tidy the tables. I knew I should be grateful, but instead I shuddered. Tomorrow that would be my job.

Henry had remained silent. I wouldn't look at him. I couldn't. It was too humiliating. And still he said nothing. If I didn't know any better, I'd say he'd slipped out to spare my feelings when he realized what was happening. The suspense was killing me. When I couldn't take it anymore, I barely raised my eyes to look at him. He was trying to keep a straight face and failing miserably.

"Really? My job offer was so terribly offensive to you, but you're willing to work here?"

"There's nothing wrong with working here. Being a waitress is an honest job!"

"Sure it is, but you're a lawyer. You can't tell me this isn't killing you."

"I don't have a choice," I hissed. "If I don't start somewhere yesterday, next month I'll be living in a box on the side of the road."

"Hey, you can't say I didn't offer."

Ugh. This was the hard part. I squirmed a little in my chair. "Yeah, about that. I shouldn't have been so angry with you. I realize now that you were only trying to help, but I was so excited about finally getting a job that when I realized what it was, I was really disappointed. I'm afraid my pride got the better of me."

"It's not too late, you know. You could still come work for me." He leaned down and whispered in my ear. "I'm pretty sure I can pay you more than they're offering. That is, if running my copy machine isn't beneath your dignity."

In that moment, I was torn between the impulse to kiss Henry and to burn that poor, innocent apron. I did neither, which was probably best.

"This is great! I can't believe you haven't hired someone already."

"Actually I did. She was terrible. I had to let her go."

"What if I'm terrible?"

"We'll cross that bridge when we come to it."

* * *

I spent the first hours of my new job stuck on the elevator.

I got up really early the next day and spent an absurd amount of time trying to decide what to wear, which was just silly. It's not like I was trying to impress Henry. I mean, he was cute and intelligent and all, but he had obviously taken himself out of the dating pool and wouldn't be interested in me even if he was available. Anyway, all of my stuff was either unemployed chic—T-shirts and sweatpants—or business attire. Shannon called it my *Law and Order* wardrobe. It was one extreme or the other.

I finally picked something and pulled my hair back in a twist that looked very professional. On the bus, I changed the ringtone on my phone to "Tomorrow" from *Annie*—for good luck. I got to the office with fifteen minutes to spare because I didn't want to be late on my first day.

When I got on the elevator that I had forgotten I didn't like, the woman announced we were going up. It almost immediately lurched to a stop between floors. For a minute I stood there, expecting it to magically start again. When it didn't, I pushed the emergency call button on the elevator. Nothing happened. That was the moment I started to panic. Not because I was claustrophobic, but because I was going to be late on my first day. I jabbed the call button repeatedly until I broke my fingernail. Then I started pounding on the door and yelling.

Okay, deep breath, Rachel. This isn't helping anything. Use your head. You have a cell phone. You can call Henry, and he'll send someone to come and get you out.

Great. Now where was the card with his number on it . . . ?

After a lengthy and exhaustive search of my briefcase, I had to admit to myself that the card wasn't there. I finally decided it was probably in the pocket of the jacket I was wearing the first day I'd seen Henry at his office. I pressed the button again with no response.

All you have to do is call Shannon! Shannon used to date Henry. She called Henry in Spain or Portugal or wherever to tell him she was marrying someone else and his life was over. Shannon will have his number!

Unfortunately when I dialed Shannon's number, there was no answer. I left her a desperate message telling her I was stuck on the elevator in Henry's building and to call me as soon as she could.

This was bad. What was I going to do? I mean, don't get me wrong, it could be worse. It's not like I was going to die in here. I had a cell phone. I could call 911. But the last thing I wanted to do was turn this into a drama fest, complete with a fire truck rescue. Henry would never let me live it down. There had to be another way.

Okay, you have a smartphone—at least for another week until they turn it off because you haven't paid the bill. You still have the Internet. Google Henry; his phone number is bound to be listed somewhere.

It is absolutely amazing how difficult it is to find a phone number for an Internet millionaire. For some reason, these people don't want to be accessible to everyone in the world. After a while, I gave up, but not before I changed my ringtone to "On My Own" from *Les Miserables*. Even in a tight situation, I was not without a sense of humor. But surfing the Internet was draining my phone battery, and I needed it for my last-resort 911 call.

I was forty-five minutes late now. I couldn't believe no one had found me yet. Didn't anyone else in this building ever use the elevator?! When my phone rang, I jumped.

"Hello?" I said, much too loudly.

"Rachel," Henry's voice answered.

"Henry," I said, sagging in relief against the elevator door. "You wouldn't believe the morning I've had."

"I hope you're late because you're at the café picking up a pumpkin muffin for me."

The surge of happiness I felt upon hearing his voice vanished. "If you must know, the reason I'm late is because I'm stuck in your stupid elevator!"

He laughed. The man actually had the nerve to laugh.

"Do you think this is funny?" I said, dangerously close to losing it.

"You're serious, aren't you?"

"Does this sound like the voice of someone who's joking?"

"The elevator does have a tendency to get stuck."

I sighed. "That would have been useful information to have yesterday."

"That's what I've heard, anyway. I always take the stairs."

"Still not helping."

I heard a whoosh of air come through the phone. "Well, push the emergency button." Quite possibly Henry was more upset than I was.

"I'm not an idiot. That's the first thing I did. Nothing happened."

"It's an old building. I'm not sure the button even works."

"Henry, I already know the button doesn't work. If it did, I'd be fetching your muffin by now."

"Just calm down. The worst thing you can do is panic," he said, the volume of his voice rising.

"I'm not panicking. You're panicking!"

"I'm sorry," he whispered. "I don't like to tell people this, but I'm really claustrophobic."

"I'll make you a deal—I'll keep your secret, but in return you have to do something for me."

"Of course."

"Get. Me. Off. This. Elevator."

This seemed to snap Henry back to reality. "I'll make some calls," he said before hanging up.

Twenty-five minutes later the elevator lurched to a start again, and when the doors opened on the third floor, I found myself staring at an elderly maintenance man in impeccable overalls standing next to an embarrassed Henry.

"Are you all right, young lady?" the maintenance man asked.

"I'm fine. I think the emergency button is broken though."

When he smiled at me, his eyes disappeared. He reminded me of a less caustic version of Waldorf, one of the heckler guys on *The Muppet Show*. "There's a trick to that button, miss. You have to hold it in for about a minute before the alarm goes off. That's how someone knows you're in trouble."

"Ah, that would explain it."

"So, now you know for next time."

"Oh, there won't be any next time. I'm a stairs-only girl from now on."

"Well, I'm sorry for the inconvenience. Henry said it's your first day, so I better let you get back to work."

"I'll let you in on a little secret. Henry doesn't know it yet, but he's going to give me the rest of the day off."

The Waldorf Muppet man laughed. "That's exactly what he needs—someone to put him in his place. Good luck, young lady."

Henry could barely look at me. "You really can take the rest of the day off if you want. I'll even pay you—think of it as compensation for mental anguish."

"I was kidding."

"Was it awful?"

"Not really."

He shook his head. "You're taking it very well."

"I'm fine, but I'm glad you found good old Waldorf there to get me out."

Henry laughed, a real laugh, and for the first time, he reminded me of the easygoing guy he used to be. "Waldorf from the Muppets, right?"

I gave him a curious look. "No one else I know would get that joke."

"I used to watch *The Muppet Show* with my grandfather all the time. Wow. I always knew that Syd reminded me of someone, but I never made the connection. I'll never be able to look at him the same again; they're like twins. That's brilliant."

This was weird, Henry and me sharing a moment. I didn't really know what to say next. "Well, shall we get to work?"

"I've got a better idea."

Chapter Eight
"Getting Some Fun Out of Life"

"Come on," Henry said, grabbing my hand and dragging me toward the stairs.

"I'm late enough already! Where are we going?"

"It's a surprise."

Henry's legs were much longer than mine, so I had to take two steps for each one of his to keep up. "Aren't there things you need me to do? Things *you* need to be doing?"

"This is what I need to be doing. I can't believe I didn't think about it before."

When we got to the parking lot, Henry led me to a silver sports car.

I whistled. "A Nissan Z."

He stopped. "You know cars?"

"A little."

"I'm impressed." He opened the door for me and closed it again after I slid inside. I inhaled the smell of leather. I was impressed too.

"Where are we going?" I repeated.

He flipped on the stereo, and a woman's voice wailed, trapped in the middle of whatever jazz song he'd left her in. "You'll see."

* * *

Thirty minutes later, we'd reached our destination.

"IKEA?"

"Sure. Why not?"

"Okaaaay." Well, maybe Henry wanted help picking out furniture—although I couldn't see someone with his money furnishing his house here. Not that IKEA wasn't great, but it had more of a utilitarian college student vibe than luxury mansion, which was where I imagined he lived. I followed him inside, and we wandered around until we found the office furniture.

"Here we are," he said. As though that should explain everything.

"Yes, here we are."

"Well?"

"Well, what?"

"What do you think?"

What did he expect me to say? "They're . . . nice."

"Yes, but which desk do you like?"

He wanted an opinion on a desk for his office? I'd only been in there once, but I definitely remember a heavy desk in some sort of very solid-looking, beautifully stained wood. He certainly wasn't going to find anything like that here. "I'm a little confused. Don't you already have a desk?"

"Of course. This desk is for you."

"Henry, you don't have to buy me a desk."

"But I do!"

"No. I'm not picky. I'll sit wherever your last secretary sat."

"See, that's where it gets tricky. My last secretary took the desk with her when she left."

I snorted. "You're kidding."

"Nope. I told her we weren't a good fit and that her services were no longer required. I had to leave early for a meeting, and when I came back, she and the desk were gone. Must have thought it was part of the severance package."

I couldn't help giggling. "That's the weirdest thing I've ever heard. Who steals a desk?"

"I told you she was terrible."

"Really, I don't need a desk. I'll sit on the couch or something."

"But what about when I have people drop by the office? It would look silly if my secretary was camped out on the sofa."

I couldn't argue with him there.

"Well, go on—pick one."

I spent the next twenty minutes choosing a desk. Henry disappeared to find a salesperson. This was turning out to be a very strange day. I was dying to text Shannon and tell her where I was. I was surprised she hadn't called me back after my desperate plea to be rescued from the elevator. When Henry returned, he was holding a card.

"I hope you weren't attached to this particular desk. Apparently we have to take the card back to the warehouse and find the box where your desk is waiting to be assembled."

I laughed. "How did you think this worked?"

"I don't know. My furniture sort of came with the house."

"And you probably think food only comes in take-out boxes that someone delivers to the door."

"Hey, I am a . . . nearly adequate cook!"

"I'm sure you are."

We started to walk in the direction of the warehouse with its aisles of rows and rows of shelves. Henry stopped suddenly. "I almost forgot. You need a chair too."

"But I feel bad."

"Why?"

"It's expensive."

He brushed it aside. "It's not a big deal."

"When you don't have enough money to buy a muffin, furniture is a big deal."

"Stop worrying about it. Besides, you shouldn't have to suffer because my last secretary was a klepto."

"I still can't believe she took the desk."

"And the chair, now that I think about it. Which one appeals to you?"

"I don't know. I guess I'd have to try them out."

"Huh. It would never occur to me to try several chairs before I chose one."

"Well, if you're going to be sitting on something for hours at a time, you want it to be comfortable."

"Yes, I suppose you would."

I stared at him, and I could tell it was making him nervous. "But that's not the most important thing you look for in a chair."

"It's not?"

I was an evil girl, but I couldn't help myself. This was really going to be fun. "The most important thing is speed."

"Pardon?"

"Oh, come on! You're a guy with a fast car. Haven't you ever played around on an office chair with wheels?"

"Never."

"Come on. I'll race you." I lifted one of the chairs off the display platform.

"We can't do that in the store!"

"It's eleven o'clock on a Tuesday. This place is dead. Who's going to care?" Okay, normally I'm not the girl who would be challenging someone to a chair race in IKEA, but for some reason, I wanted to shake Henry up a bit. Maybe I wanted to shake myself up a bit as well. Maybe part of me did it because it seemed like something Shannon would do, and I wanted to be as free-spirited as her.

"I'm not sure we should be doing this," he hedged.

"You better hurry and choose your vehicle, or you're going to lose by default."

"What if we get caught?" he said, even as he was taking down a chair of his own. He pushed it back and forth experimentally.

I was a little giddy with the idea that I was leading a straitlaced multimillionaire down the path to delinquency.

"It's not like we're shoplifting or anything—we're just messing around."

"Yeah, but we're not teenagers anymore. I think once you reach a certain age, this kind of thing is generally frowned upon."

"What are they going to do, throw us out?" I lined up our chairs side by side at the head of the aisle. I couldn't see anyone around, shoppers or staff, and I was relieved. I didn't really think Henry would let it get this far, and suddenly I was nervous. But I couldn't let him see that, or he'd never go through with it, and I wanted to feel the adrenaline pumping through my veins for a change, even if it was over something as silly as a race on a rolling office chair.

"Okay, the first one to make it to the bin of pillows over there is the winner." I sat down on my chair, and Henry took the one next to me. "And don't worry—if we get in trouble, I know a really good lawyer."

He threw back his head and laughed. That's when I knew that no matter what happened, this was a good idea.

"Ready, set . . ."

Henry was crouched slightly above his chair, poised for takeoff.

"Oh, crap, is that the manager?" I said, pointing to my right. When he turned his head to look, I took off. "GO!" I shouted, after my illegal head start.

Even with the distraction, Henry wasn't far behind, and it didn't take him long to push past me. I thought his height would make him awkward and slow in a chair that was made for normal people, but if anything, the extra inches made him faster. Shannon is one of the most competitive people I know, yet I remember her telling me once that Henry never lost. I always thought it was because he was as driven as she was, but watching him storm into the lead, I realized that maybe Henry never lost because he never had and didn't know it was even a possibility. What must it be like, I wondered, to be so good at everything that, no matter what you did, it appeared effortless to everyone else? But no matter how nice it must be to always come out on top, I imagined that Henry wasn't winning any popularity contests. I guess there's a reason people say it's lonely at the top—as far as I knew, the only thing Henry ever lost was Shannon.

When I reached the finish line, Henry was already there, out of his chair, cheering me on. I jumped out of my chair, and we started doing this bizarre little victory dance, at which point he must have been caught up in the moment because he picked me up off the ground, hugging me while my feet dangled. Even as I was scrabbling anxiously for the security of solid ground, I was laughing at the absurdity of the moment.

"Can I assist you with anything?" a voice said.

Henry returned me to my proper position. The voice belonged to a man wearing an IKEA nametag that said, *Conrad*. He was obviously not amused.

Have you ever had one of those moments where you did something crazy in public and when you look around, bystanders are smiling in an indulgent way, like, look at those crazy kids? Remember what it was like to be young and impulsive? For a moment, you feel wild and silly and incredibly *alive*—sort of like you're in a Target commercial or something.

Yeah, this was nothing like that.

When confronted with authority, Henry was all business again, which made me self-conscious. Then I imagined that my hair was probably doing something crazy, so I smoothed it. I already missed Impulsive Henry.

He pointed to the chairs. "We'll take them both."

* * *

The only bad thing about sports cars is that they're not exactly suited for transporting office furniture.

When we were once again barreling down the freeway at a speed that I was certain exceeded the limit, I said, "You already have a chair."

"Pardon?"

"You already have a desk chair, so why did you buy another one."

"I thought you might want a rematch one day." A tiny smile touched the corners of his lips. "That was quite possibly the silliest thing I've ever done, by the way."

"Me too," I confessed. "I'm not normally the silly type. Something must have temporarily possessed me."

"Now you tell me. So, where can I drop you?" he said.

"You can drop me where I work," I said slowly. "Which should be very convenient since you work there as well."

"I already told you, you're getting the rest of the day off."

"Henry," I started.

"You don't have to worry—I'll pay you for the whole day."

"It's not that. It's only noon. I'm sure there's something I can do to earn my keep for a couple of hours."

"You can come back tomorrow morning, once your new desk has arrived."

"I thought you were supposed to be difficult to work for."

"Oh, I am." He paused for a minute before continuing. "So you're willing to give it another shot tomorrow?"

"Do you really think your unreliable elevator is going to scare me away?" I teased. "I don't think you realize how desperate I am. In fact, I might get stuck in there again on purpose just so I can see Waldorf."

"He'd probably like that. Well then, I expect to see you at 8:30 sharp—not a minute past. Be prepared to work your little fingers to the bone."

Chapter Nine
"You Go to My Head"

"You did *WHAT*?" Shannon asked.

"We had a race on rolling office chairs," I said.

"In the middle of IKEA?"

"It was kinda fun, actually." I had Shannon on speaker phone while I was changing into my comfy clothes.

"I had to talk Henry into eating at Burger King. What you're telling me isn't possible. Maybe his mind has snapped."

"Hey, it was my idea."

"Maybe *your* mind has snapped."

I pulled my T-shirt over my head. "Thanks a lot."

"You gotta admit—it's a bit on the crazy side."

"It sounds like something you and Nathan would do."

She laughed. "Well, we're not exactly the poster couple for sanity."

"Where were you when I called, by the way? I could have died on that elevator."

"Let's just say I got into a bit of trouble myself."

I paused. "That doesn't sound good."

"It could have been worse."

"You're being awfully vague."

She paused—a very long pause. "I don't want you to freak out."

"Now I'm *really* worried." I went to the freezer and surveyed my dinner options. Hmmm, how many ways can one prepare ice cubes?

"There's no need to worry."

"The only reason anyone ever says that is to prepare someone before they tell them the thing they need to worry about."

"See, you're freaking out, and I haven't even told you yet," she said.

"Just tell me what it is."

Shannon gave a loud sigh. "Okay. I went running this morning, and after a few miles I started to cramp, so I turned around and went home. And then, once I got home, it kind of became apparent that things weren't exactly right. So I went to the ER."

I sucked in a breath. "Oh, sweetie. Is the baby okay?"

"The baby's fine, so far. But I'm going to have to stay down for a couple of days. And they want me to quit running for a while."

"But they think everything will be all right?"

"Yeah. It's still too early to hear the heartbeat, but I got to see it on the ultrasound." She sounded too excited to be worried. She wouldn't be able to sugarcoat it without my picking up on it.

"I'm glad you're both all right. I bet Nathan was so worried." I opened the fridge, where my choices were even grimmer than the freezer, if that was possible. Ketchup, mustard, ranch dressing, and soy sauce. The entire contents of my refrigerator consisted of condiments.

"He's fine. Everything is fine. No worries."

And there was the sugarcoating I was looking for earlier. I stopped mid fridge-scan. "Shannon . . ."

"Nathan still doesn't know." It came out in a rush.

"How could he not know? It's got to be pretty obvious something's wrong when you're camped out on the couch all day."

"Actually, I don't think he'll notice."

"Where is he?"

"He's in Arizona for a few days, doing some training for work. He left this morning."

"Why haven't you told him about the baby yet?"

"It's kind of hard to explain."

"Is it the money? I mean, kids are expensive."

"No, it's not that. I mean, we're certainly not rich, but we'll get by okay."

"Are you worried he isn't ready, and he'll be stressed out about it?"

"Are you kidding? He'll be thrilled. He wanted to be a daddy as soon as we got married."

"I don't get it. Why are you hesitating?" I went to the cupboard, but the cupboard was bare. I must have been weak from hunger; my mind was spouting nursery rhymes. I found myself wanting to laugh at the absurdity, but this wasn't exactly the kind of conversation you could giggle in the middle of.

There was another big sigh on the other end of the phone. "This is going to sound crazy. Can you handle crazy?"

"We've been best friends forever. I think I'm pretty much used to crazy at this point."

"I'm scared. Everything is going a little too well."

"The scenario you described hardly seems ideal."

"That's not what I meant. I mean Nathan and me, our lives in general. Everything is about as close to perfect as I could have ever imagined."

"Okay, I'm with you so far."

"Don't you see? It's a little too good."

"And that's where you've lost me."

"Haven't you ever thought about everything that's right in your life and what you have done to be so much happier than everyone else and wondered when it was all going to collapse around you?"

I didn't want to upset Shannon further by telling her that I was one of those unlucky people on the opposite end of the happiness spectrum. Don't get me wrong, it's not like I was *un*happy, but life wasn't showering me with the plethora of good things she had at the moment. "I think everyone thinks that from time to time."

"Maybe this is it. Maybe this is the bad thing I've been dreading."

The bad thing I was dreading stared back at me from the shelf—Ramen noodles. "Sweetie, you can't think like that. You should hold on to every little bit of happiness you get for as long as you can; don't waste it by wondering when a trial is going to come."

"I know you're right, but I have this sneaking suspicion that it's my turn to face something difficult for a change. I don't want to get Nathan's hopes up if this is a false alarm, you know?"

"You just told me you saw the heartbeat. I've got news for you—that's way beyond the false-alarm stage. You need to tell him. He deserves to be happy too. And if you're right and you can't keep this baby, you're going to need each other for comfort. You can't do this alone. That's what marriage is about."

"You are very wise."

I started heating water on the stovetop for dinner. "Yes, all the pearls of wisdom I know came from a fortune cookie."

She laughed. "Maybe those cookies are right. But I don't want him to find out something so monumental over the phone. I'll tell him when he gets home," she said, her voice a little lighter.

"So, little mommy, what do you need?"

"I don't need anything. I'm nesting on the couch with a giant bottle of water, some saltine crackers, and the remote. I'm good to go."

"You should have called me this morning. I would have taken you to the hospital."

"I didn't want to bother you on your first day at your new job."

"You didn't want to bother me, or you were afraid I'd show up with Henry?"

"Maybe a little bit of both."

"I knew it. Next time call me, okay? You're much more important than any job. Besides, I think Henry would understand."

She paused, and I could almost hear the wheels turning in her head. "You like him, don't you?"

"Yes I do, but not in the way you're suggesting. He's a nice guy."

She hooted. "A nice, rich, handsome guy. You *like* him. I knew it! Didn't I always say you and Henry would make a great couple?"

"You can forget about that nonsense right now. The man is never going to get over you. And I'm not saying that to hurt you or make you feel guilty—it's a fact."

"Say whatever you want if it makes you feel better, but I know the truth, Rachel Marie Pearce. And Henry or not, I think it's your turn to be happy for a change."

I smiled. Yet again I thought I was fooling my best friend, but she knew what I was thinking all along. "When does Nathan get back?"

"Friday morning."

"Let me know if you need anything, okay? I'm a phone call away."

"There is one thing I'm absolutely dying for."

"At last! Something I can do to feel useful!"

"Double Stuff Oreos."

"Really?"

"Yup. In the morning nothing sounds good. Everything I eat comes right back up. But later in the day, I need sugar. The baby needs Oreos. And maybe some ginger ale."

"Well, I fully intend to spoil the heck out of my little niece or nephew, so I might as well start now."

"Are you sure it isn't too much trouble? I know what a pain the bus is."

"Nothing's too much trouble for little Rachel."

She laughed. "What if it's a boy?"

"Pearce, of course."

"You get the Oreos for your namesake, and we'll discuss it."

"Done. I'll see you in a bit."

I hung up and turned off the boiling water, saved from yet another bowl of Ramen noodles. I spent a minute or two wishing that Oreos grew on trees.

Shannon wasn't being insensitive. She knew money was tight, but I'm sure she had no idea that I'd gotten to the point where my food budget came from a change jar. Unfortunately, the jar was empty. All I had to do was hang in there until my first paycheck. But desperate times called for desperate measures.

I went to the freezer and took out a large cottage cheese container. When I pried off the lid, I could barely see my VISA card, frozen in the middle of a block of ice. I got my blow dryer from the bathroom, put the container in the sink, and started the thawing process. It could be worse. Soon I'd have a check from Henry. Life would go back to normal, and Oreos would no longer be a luxury item.

Chapter Ten
"Don't Explain"

HENRY'S OFFICE WAS A LOT less threatening when I avoided the elevator. Now all I had to worry about was figuring out the copy machine. The door was open, so I walked inside. The telltale blanket and pillow were missing from the couch, so either Henry had planned ahead and hidden them someplace, or he had happened to be working late that night and fell asleep here when he really had a gorgeous mansion somewhere. My money was on the latter.

My brand new desk and chair were waiting. My mouth dropped open. Sitting on top of the desk was the biggest fruit basket I'd ever seen. After living on Ramen noodles and peanut butter for the last month, it was the most beautiful thing I could imagine. Henry was nowhere in sight. The door to his office was mostly closed, and I assumed he was in there. I sneaked closer to get a better look at the fruit selection. There were apples and bananas and pears and grapes and a mango, all nestled in a giant basket and swathed in cellophane.

My mouth was watering now. Even though it was sitting on my desk, I was trying not to get my hopes up. Maybe it wasn't really mine. Maybe Henry was in the Fruit of the Month

Club, and when they delivered his boatload of produce this morning, my desk happened to be the nearest surface available.

Still no sign of Henry. I wanted to rip into the basket and see what was under the stuff on top, treasures waiting to be discovered. There was no card, which could be good or bad, depending on how you looked at it.

"Good morning, Rachel." The sound of Henry's voice made me jump. It was probably too much to hope he hadn't seen me ogling the fruit basket. "I see you found my peace offering."

It was mine, it was mine, it was miiiiiine! "You didn't have to do that," I said as casually as I could.

"Oh, that's the standard welcome."

"Standard welcome, huh? You make it sound like this happens a lot."

"I told you, I'm not the easiest guy to work with."

"Are you grumpy?"

"I like things the way I like them. Besides, I still feel guilty about yesterday."

"It's not your fault the elevator in your building is sketchy."

I tried not to stare openly at the fruit basket, but I thought I'd glimpsed a fat kiwi under the banana, and now I couldn't concentrate on anything else. I finally tore my eyes away to find Henry smiling at me.

"Would you like me to leave you and the fruit alone for a while? Let you get better acquainted?"

"I'm sorry. I feel like Julie Andrews in *Victor/Victoria* when she's on the street, staring through the window watching someone eat spaghetti and meatballs."

"You like musicals?" Henry asked.

"I love musicals. I'm probably a little obsessed, actually." I felt my eyes straying to the elusive kiwi again.

"Just open it!" He laughed.

"I'm supposed to be working!"

"Breakfast first, and then work. I have a call to make anyway. I'll be in my office when you're ready."

I waited until I was sure Henry was on the phone before I pounced on the fruit. It wasn't pretty. Have you ever seen a lion tear an antelope apart on a nature show? I imagine if I could watch the video replay of me with the fruit it would be something like that—except, thankfully, the fruit didn't struggle. I mowed my way through a pear, a banana, and some of the grapes with almost frightening speed. Nothing had ever tasted so good. Unfortunately I had no way to peel the kiwi short of ripping off the brown, fuzzy skin with my teeth. I'd like to say I didn't consider it. I looked at it longingly and told it in a quiet voice that I loved it every bit as much as the other fruit, but I was saving it for later.

I must be worse off than I thought if I was talking to fruit.

Feeling much better (about my stomach if not my sanity), I went into Henry's office. He was looking at something on his computer.

"Okay, I'm ready. Put me to work."

He handed me a stack of papers. "Uh, I need six copies of this for a meeting I have tomorrow. And maybe you could staple them."

"No problem," I said.

He looked amused. "Really? I thought mastering the copy machine wasn't in your list of accomplishments."

"I have used a copy machine before. I'm not a complete idiot. The problem is they're all different, and running *your* copy machine isn't in my particular skill set. But I passed the bar, so I'm sure I can probably muddle through it."

I spent about ten minutes familiarizing myself with the handbook for the copy machine, which I found conveniently located in the cupboard where the extra reams of paper were. The pages were stiff and new—like the book had never been opened. I put Henry's papers in the slot, pressed the right series of buttons, and the copies were popping out in neat piles in seconds. I gathered them up and carried them triumphantly back to Henry's office, where I dropped them on his desk.

"Done," I announced.

"Really? You're finished already?"

"Affirmative." It was ridiculous, but completing this small task gave me an enormous sense of achievement—like I'd really accomplished something.

Henry was flipping through the pages as though he thought there was a punch line in there somewhere. "Amazing. And the machine didn't break?"

"The machine's fine. I might not be a secretary, but I think I can make a few copies without ruining the machine."

He frowned. "Remarkable."

"Why is that remarkable?"

"Uh, my last secretary said it jammed all the time."

I couldn't help feeling smug. "Maybe I have the magic touch."

"Well . . . good for you."

"What would you like me to do next?"

"Honestly, I thought that would take you all morning."

"Wow. I thought you were exaggerating, but your last secretary really must have been a mess."

"Yes," he said. His voice was distracted, and I could tell that his mind was somewhere else.

"I don't want to interrupt you if you're busy," I said. "I assumed you'd want me to answer your phone, but I can't seem to find one."

"There's no land line. I operate mostly through e-mail, but anyone who needs to reach me calls my cell phone."

"Henry, I'm not trying to talk myself out of a job here, but are you sure you need a secretary?"

"I do," he insisted. "I'm a very, very busy man."

"Okay, Mr. Busy, what can I do to help ease the burdens of your busy, busy life?"

"Right. Okay. I'm going to dictate a letter, and you can take it down, type it up, and e-mail it for me."

"I brought my laptop, so I can definitely handle the e-mailing part, but I'm afraid I don't have any paper. I'm sorry—I really had no idea what to expect today."

"Don't worry about it." Henry searched through the drawers in his desk and came up empty-handed. "I don't appear to have any paper either. All I ever use anymore is the computer. I can't remember the last time I wrote anything by hand, except my signature. I wonder if I can even remember how," he mused.

This was a little awkward. If I didn't know any better, I'd say Henry was making this up as he went along.

"There's paper in the copy machine," I volunteered.

"Brilliant."

I fetched a few pieces of paper from the other room. Who knew how long-winded Henry might be? Luckily I did at least have a pen. I wondered why I couldn't type it directly onto the laptop, but Henry was in charge, and if he wanted to assert his dominance by dictating letters like some boss from an old black-and-white movie, so be it. Anyway, it was better than sitting at my shiny new desk and staring out the window for the next seven hours, trying not to eat all the fruit at once.

I planted myself in the chair across from my new boss, pen poised at the ready. "Okay, shoot," I said. I wondered if I should call him sir. I felt a laugh bubbling up, and I bit my lip to hold it in. If Henry noticed my aborted outburst, he didn't say anything.

"Right. Subject line: *FYI*. Body of the letter is as follows. *I will be unable to attend book club this month—*"

"Excuse me, did you say book club?"

"Correct. Have you got it all so far?"

More lip biting. "I think so."

"*I will be unable to attend book club this month due to another pressing engagement. Please give my regards to everyone and tell them that I'm sorry I couldn't be there. I was really looking forward to discussing* Water for Elephants. *Sincerely, Henry.*"

"I have a question," I said.

"Yes?"

"Did you actually read *Water for Elephants*?"

"Can you picture me reading *Water for Elephants*?"

"Not really."

"Well, there you go."

I tapped my pen on the paper. "Who is this e-mail directed to, if I might ask?"

"My mother."

This time I couldn't help the laugh that spilled out so violently I nearly choked on it. "You want me to type *Sincerely, Henry* at the end of an e-mail you're sending to your mother?"

"What's wrong with that?"

"She's your mother! It sounds like a pen pal letter."

"I'm not sure what kind of relationship you have with your mother, but this is how we function."

"You and your mother are in the same book club," I said dubiously.

"She wanted us to do something together on a regular basis. She says she never sees me."

"And book club was the obvious solution?"

He shrugged. "It was her suggestion."

"It wouldn't hurt you to read a book every now and then."

"Hey, I like to read, but not the stuff they pick."

There was another laugh bubbling dangerously close to the surface. "Like what?"

"Let's just say that Nicholas Sparks and Jodi Picoult aren't my cup of tea."

"Doesn't everyone get a turn to pick?"

"Yeah. When it was my turn, I chose a Tom Clancy novel, which caused an uproar. Several of the ladies wanted to have me banned."

By this point, I was laughing so hard there was no use trying to hide it. "What happened?"

"They took a vote to dismiss me, and the motion passed. But my mother proposed an amendment stating that I would still be allowed to come but was never again allowed to choose the reading selection. It was reluctantly accepted."

"Why don't you take your mother to dinner once a month like any normal absentee son and abandon this whole pretense of book club?"

"It makes her happy. I only go to the meetings if the book has been made into a movie. That way I only have to waste two hours of my life instead of ten. And trust me, the movies are painful enough."

"Henry, they made a movie of *Water for Elephants*."

"Really?"

"Really."

"Okay, new e-mail. Tell my mother I'll pick her up for book club at six o'clock on Thursday night."

"*Sincerely, Henry?*"

"You're a fast learner."

I rolled my eyes. "And you want me to send this from my e-mail address?"

"Yeah, just put a line in there saying you're my secretary."

"It doesn't bother her that you can't take five minutes and e-mail her yourself?"

"She knows I'm busy," he said.

"Well, if I stretch this out it might keep me occupied until ten thirty. What would you like me to do after that?"

He unfolded his wallet and pulled out a twenty-dollar bill. "Could you go out and find me a *Water for Elephants* DVD?"

Chapter Eleven
"He's Funny That Way"

"*WATER FOR ELEPHANTS*, HUH?" SHANNON asked.

"And that was only the beginning! You should see some of the weird stuff he's sent me after."

"I can barely hear you. The connection is terrible. It sounds like you're in the middle of a windstorm."

"Well, the problem must be on your end."

"What makes you so sure?"

"Because I'm driving Henry's car, and it's as quiet as a mouse."

"Seriously? He let you drive the Z?"

"He didn't have much choice. He wanted a cookie, and I don't have a car."

"These are the kind of errands he's got you running?" Suddenly the line cleared, and I could hear her better.

"A cookie would be easy. This is way more complicated than that."

"It's a cookie—how hard could it be?"

"He doesn't want just any cookie. He wants Vivianna."

There was a pause, and I wasn't sure whether I'd lost the call or Shannon was attempting to decipher the information I'd given her. "Is that code for something?" she said finally.

"There's this bakery downtown called RubySnap, where all the cookies have women's names. Today he wants Vivianna—I think it's got mangoes and dark chocolate in it. That's his favorite one, but he likes them all. To be honest, I have a hard time keeping them straight."

"Cookies with women's names, huh? I'm getting a whole new insight into Henry's character. But it does sound incredible. What's your favorite one?"

"I never know how to choose. Each one is more delicious than the last. But if I had to pick, I think Lilly would be my favorite. It's lemon with this amazing glaze and crushed up lemon drops."

She groaned. "Stop, you're killing me."

"I'm sorry. I should know better than to taunt a pregnant woman with gourmet cookies."

"So, Henry's buying you cookies now, in addition to produce, huh? If you ask me, it's only a matter of time before he makes the natural progression to flowers, and after that it's a slippery slope. Diamonds can't be far behind."

"It's not like that."

"Are you sure?"

I signaled to change lanes. "It's a *cookie*. It's flour and sugar and egg—I don't think there's any deep underlying meaning. Besides, he'd be a pretty big jerk if he sent me out every day to buy him a gourmet cookie and ate it in front of me."

"And is he buying you fruit because he feels guilty eating that in front of you?"

There had been a bag of nectarines on my desk when I'd arrived that morning. I ate two for lunch, and I couldn't believe how perfect they were. Where in the world did he get a nectarine that actually tasted like a nectarine in January? "I think that's more of a joke."

"Because fruit is soooo funny."

I wasn't sure why Henry was going to the trouble to procure first-class produce for me, but I was fairly certain it didn't have anything to do with courtship. "He probably views it as a challenge. That's how he operates."

"Yes, I remember that particular personality quirk quite well."

While Shannon seemed to be at the point where we could talk about Henry without too much bitterness, occasionally I could hear it creeping into her voice. I wondered if she would ever be able to completely forgive him. I wondered if Henry would ever reach a place where he could say he was completely over her. It was funny how two people could end up resenting each other like that. However, since I doubted that the four of us would ever be making up a dinner party, the question was strictly academic. I decided to drop it.

"How are you feeling?" I asked.

"I've got another ultrasound tomorrow. If everything looks good, I'll finally be able to get up and do normal things."

"But no running?"

"No running." She sounded like someone mourning the loss of a beloved pet.

"You seem pretty down about it."

"Well, it's a huge deal for me, but when you consider a nine-month hiatus from running in the grand scheme of things, it's really nothing compared to what I'll be getting in return. I just want to do everything I can to make sure the baby is okay."

"I can't wait to congratulate the soon-to-be daddy."

"Um, you might want to hold off on that for a bit."

There was a momentary silence while I considered the implication of Shannon's words. "Tell me you told him when he got home."

"I was going to tell him. I really had no choice *but* to tell him. I mean, how was I going to explain being in bed all the time?"

I paused. While I was flattered that Shannon had told me, I couldn't help feeling uneasy that I knew her big secret when her own husband didn't. "What excuse did you give him?"

"I told him I had the flu."

"You can't be serious. Why didn't you tell him?!"

"We had this discussion, remember? I didn't want to get his hopes up."

"I thought we decided this was something the two of you need to face together."

"It sounded good in theory, but when he got home, I chickened out."

"Don't you think he's going to feel hurt when he realizes how long you knew before you bothered to let him in on it?"

"What if there's nothing to tell? Wouldn't it be better if only one of us has to be sad?"

The next light suddenly turned yellow. I was paranoid driving Henry's car, so instead of trying to race through it, I stepped on the brakes. "Shannon, that's not how it works. This is where the 'for better or for worse' part comes in."

"Don't you think I want to tell him? Don't you think I wish everything was perfect and we could both be excited?"

"I think you're only focused on the worst-case scenario. This kind of thing happens to a lot of women, right?"

"Yeah, the doctor said it's fairly common."

"And lots of them end up having perfectly healthy babies, correct?"

"But what if I'm one of the ones that don't?"

Someone behind me tapped on their horn, and I noticed the light was green again. "We're not going to focus on that until we absolutely have to. I think the best thing for you right now is to be optimistic. Let's operate under the assumption that this is just a tiny hitch in an otherwise normal pregnancy. Could you do that?"

"Why do I feel like I'm being cross-examined?" she grumbled.

I smiled. "They trained me well at Stanford—not that you'd know it from my current job prospects. But then, life doesn't always go exactly like we think it should."

"You're a good friend, Rach."

"And?"

She sighed. "I'll tell him tomorrow. After the ultrasound."

"No matter what?"

"No matter what. I promise."

I parked the car. "Good girl. I have to go in and procure the special cookie for the master now. Heaven help me if they're out."

"What happens if they're out?"

"Let's just say that you can purchase frozen dough from the store, and even though I have a really crappy apartment, it still has a working oven."

"He wouldn't."

"They were out of Virginia last week."

"You didn't."

I opened the car door and stepped out. The sun was peeking out from behind a cloud, and it almost felt warm. "It's not that bad. I mean, at least I'm getting paid. I can think of worse ways to spend an hour."

"Wow. I never thought I'd hear those words come out of your mouth."

"What can I say? Desperation makes us all reconsider our standards."

She giggled. "As long as you're only baking cookies."

"You can count on that. I'll secure the cookies, and you spend some time planning how you're going to tell Nathan your big news."

"I think I already have a pretty good idea. Maybe I'll have a nap."

"I'm trying not to be terribly jealous. Call me if you need anything, okay?"

"I will."

After I hung up, I went inside, got Vivianna for Henry, and spent a few minutes pondering my choices. A fat peanut butter cookie dipped in chocolate stared back at me from the glass case. Looks like Penelope was calling my name today.

* * *

When I got back to the office, Henry actually looked busy. He was bent over the computer, his face marked with deep concentration. Sometimes when I came back from running an errand, he'd be standing by the window, staring out. Sometimes he turned on jazz music, which had never really been my thing, but I was starting to develop an appreciation for it. I liked coming back and hearing some unknown horn solo when I was still at the top of the stairs. There was something . . . comforting about it.

"You look perplexed," I said. He startled at the sound of my voice. I guess he'd been so involved he didn't realize I was there.

"These numbers aren't adding up."

"Anything I can do?"

"A neck massage would be nice."

I scowled at him. "I will e-mail your mother. I will pick up your dry cleaning. I will make the pilgrimage to your favorite bakery every day. But I draw the line at massage."

"I never even thought about having you pick up my dry cleaning!" I could see him adding it to his Mental List of Things for Rachel to Do.

"Where's the ticket?" No use in postponing the inevitable.

"Actually, I picked it up myself yesterday. But don't worry— there's always next time." This was weird. He'd barely lifted his eyes from the computer screen the whole time we'd been talking. He looked concerned. I'd never seen Henry get worried about anything but Shannon. It was slightly unnerving. But I knew what would bring him out of his funk.

"I've got your cooookieeee," I said, waving the little paper sack in front of him. Usually he was like a little boy when I came back with his afternoon cookie, so excited.

"That's great, thanks." Eyes still on the computer screen, forehead full of lines, lips in a perpetual frown. No cookie love. This must be serious. I had to get his attention somehow.

"They were out of Vivianna though, so I had to get you something else."

"That's okay," he mumbled.

"In fact, they were out of cookies entirely. There's a scrapbooking convention downtown today, so they were completely sold out."

"That's understandable," he said, his finger tapping the same key over and over again. I wondered what he was scrolling though. It must be something important if the idea of a complete cookie sellout didn't even faze him. Time to get out the big guns.

"I stopped at the gas station and bought you a day-old doughnut instead."

"Yeah. Fine."

"Okay, who are you and what have you done with Henry?" I demanded.

His eyes finally met mine. He didn't look pleased. "Is there a problem?"

"I told you that RubySnap was completely out of cookies so I bought you a nasty, stale gas station doughnut instead, and you didn't even bat an eye! A *doughnut*."

"Rachel, it wouldn't be the end of the world. My life doesn't revolve around cookies, you know."

"Then why am I driving all over town every day to fetch them for you?" My voice was starting to get louder, and Henry must have sensed the impending explosion because he was finally paying attention.

"Because that's what I'm paying you for—to do the things that I don't have time to do. I know it's hard for you to accept that you're basically an errand girl, but I need a secretary or an assistant or whatever you want to call it, and you need the money."

I felt like he'd slapped me.

"Now, I need you to go out and get me some colored paper clips." He handed me some money.

Suddenly the ridiculousness of the situation was too much for me.

"Paper clips? *Colored* paper clips?"

"You're doing it again."

"Doing what again?"

"Repeating yourself."

I ignored him. "Why do you need paper clips?"

"Because I do."

"Henry, you don't have any *paper*!" I felt like my head was going to explode.

"If I say I want colored paper clips, that's what I want. And if I ask you to sort them into little piles according to color and size, I want you to do it. I have my own reasoning; it doesn't matter if it doesn't make sense to you. You're not entitled to an explanation."

I'm not *entitled*? "Picking up your dry cleaning is one thing, but I didn't graduate from Stanford to sort paper clips." In the heat of the moment, everything was blurring into one large, ugly mess. Five minutes ago, I was feeling nostalgic about jazz music, and now we were at each other's throats. Were we actually arguing about paper clips?

"Maybe you need to find another job then."

"Maybe I will." I grabbed the money out of his hand and stormed out of the office, slamming the door behind me. I couldn't resist one last parting shot though. I opened the door, and Henry looked up in surprise. "Now I know why you can't keep a secretary. You're an ogre!" I slammed it again before he had a chance to reply.

I was expecting to spend all afternoon driving to different office supply places, but they had colored paper clips at the first store I tried. I bought as many boxes as I could with the money Henry gave me, and if I'd had any money in my own pocket, I would have bought more. I was still seething when I left, but the idea of a tractor dumping a load of colored paper clips in his office and burying him up to the neck did afford me with a small giggle.

It was cold outside, but the sun was still making a cameo appearance. It was a nice day as far as winter goes, so I drove Henry's flashy car around until I found a sunbeam to park it in. Let him think I was scouring the city for his precious paper clips for an hour or two. I wasn't ready to go back to the office yet and face him. I lay back in the seat, closed my eyes, and let the warm rays perform their calming magic.

Chapter Twelve
"Love Me or Leave Me"

I WOKE UP.

In Henry's car.

I didn't know what time it was, but the happy sunbeam I'd fallen asleep in had vanished. In fact, it was almost completely dark outside. I fumbled for my cell phone. It was 5:36.

Great. After the argument I'd had with Henry, he'd probably reported the car stolen. Luckily I wasn't too far away. I drove back as fast as I dared, fully expecting to arrive and find three or four police cars in the parking lot. But everything looked normal. I climbed the stairs and saw that the light was still on in the office. When I went inside, Henry was sitting on the couch. I walked over and dropped the bag with the all the paper clips on the couch next to him.

He looked inside the bag. "Have you been out there all this time looking for these?"

I was tempted to say yes, hoping he'd feel bad or guilty or *something*. But the part of me that wanted to look competent outweighed the part of me that wanted to see Henry squirm. "I found those twenty minutes after I left. Then I parked your car somewhere so I could cool off and accidentally fell asleep."

He smiled and nodded. He looked tired, and I got the impression he would have gone home a long time ago if he hadn't been waiting for me to recover from my temper tantrum and bring his car back. I wondered if he'd been sitting there this whole time, trying to figure out how to tell me that I should start looking for a new job in the morning.

"Rachel, I'm sorry about what I said before. You caught me at a bad moment, and I was really stressed out. I snapped. You know I realize how insanely overqualified you are and that I don't think of you as an errand girl, right?"

"Yeah, I know. I appreciate you giving me this job when I was so desperate. And I shouldn't have called you an ogre . . . probably."

This whole conversation had the feeling of the awkward concession right before you get fired, but it was taking too long. I decided to make it easy for him. "Maybe this isn't going to work. Do you want me to pack up my stuff and get out of here?"

He looked alarmed. "Not unless you hate me and can't stand the idea of working here anymore."

"Well I did about three hours ago, but I'm sort of over it now."

"That's good. I'll try to be less condescending in the future."

"And I'll try not to scream at you and call you names— even if you deserve it."

"That sounds like a healthy working relationship."

I couldn't help laughing. "Well, I should go. I'll see you in the morning."

"Wait. It's getting late. Let me buy you dinner."

Bad idea, my inner voice warned. "Maybe another time."

"Do you have plans?"

"Not exactly."

"Do you dislike my company?"

"No, it's not that. When you're not being mean, you can be quite nice."

He stood up. "It sounds like you're out of excuses."

I actually had one really good excuse left. "I don't have any money for dinner." It was killing me to say this. I had such a sudden, sharp pain in my chest that I wondered if it was literally killing me. Hopefully it had more to do with my wounded pride than a previously undiagnosed heart condition.

"Dinner is on me."

"I couldn't."

"I insist."

I raised one eyebrow.

"To apologize," he clarified.

"I suppose we could be civil to each other long enough to get something to eat."

* * *

After my recent money shortage, actual restaurant food was unbelievable. Besides the fruit Henry had been plying me with, it felt like months since I'd eaten anything this good. We went to the Blue Iguana, and he suggested that we share the steak and chicken fajitas. Since I'd never been there, I took his advice. I wasn't disappointed.

I had a mild panic attack while we were waiting for the food to arrive. I stewed and fretted that I probably should have begged off and gone home to regroup, but by the time I was scooping up the last of the guacamole, it was hard to remember why I was worried. So far, Henry had been downright pleasant.

We talked about all sorts of things but nothing terribly personal. Stuff like what he thought of *Water for Elephants*, the best Italian food he'd ever had (which happened to be in Italy), why he liked living in Salt Lake, and how he ended up with his sports car. He asked questions about me, but I had become a master of deflecting the attention away from myself and drawing out the other person.

In college, I went on lots of dates. After a while, I got tired of sharing the same stories over and over with guys who didn't really care. One day I discovered I could have an entire conversation with someone and never reveal anything at all. I viewed it as a challenge, and I found I enjoyed being a mystery. It wasn't that I had anything to hide; I only knew I wanted to wait to open up to someone until I was sure they were genuinely interested.

Henry wasn't so easily deflected. Those guys in college liked to talk about themselves. All I had to do was distract them with a couple of well-placed inquiries and then sit back and listen to them ramble. Henry answered my questions but never got carried off on tangents. I thought I was holding my own until there was a lull in the conversation.

"Wow, you're good at this," he said.

"Good at what?" I knew he'd figured out my game, but I was determined to at least keep up the pretense of innocence.

"Getting people to talk while revealing nothing about yourself."

"Was I doing that?"

"I bet it comes in handy in court."

I smiled. "I wouldn't know."

"Tell me about all these lawyer interviews."

"What about them?"

"Well, you're Stanford educated. I know the economy's in bad shape, but I can't imagine why firms aren't jumping at the chance to hire you."

My temper flared. "You're saying it's my fault I haven't found a job yet?"

"Hey, calm down! That's not what I said. I just wondered if you might be somehow . . . unconsciously sabotaging yourself."

"I know my stuff, but you should see some of these lawyers. They're so intimidating!"

"I see. You go to an interview and feel inexperienced, so you shut down."

After the day I'd had, I didn't particularly want to discuss my inadequacies with Henry. "Can we talk about something else?"

He wisely let it go. "Sure. What made you decide to become a lawyer anyway, besides your uncanny ability to make people spill their guts?"

"Do you really want to know?"

"I wouldn't ask if I didn't."

I folded my napkin into a tiny square. "People do, you know."

"People do what?"

"Ask questions when they're not really interested in the answers."

"I've never understood that. Why waste time on things that don't matter to you?"

Over the years I'd answered the why-did-I-become-a-lawyer question a lot. I still didn't know Henry very well, but I decided to give him the benefit of the doubt. "I assumed you already knew this story."

"Now I'm really curious. Why would I know this story?"

I never brought Shannon up if I could help it, but with this particular tale, there was no way around it. "You know about Shannon's gypsy prediction, right?"

"Yes, I think I might be familiar with that."

"Did she tell you about my fortune too?"

He leaned forward across the table. "No, what was it?" Since he seemed sincerely interested, I decided to tell him.

"So Shannon was supposed to fall madly in love with a guy she met at a wedding reception before she turned thirty—you know that part already. I was supposed to be a rich lawyer."

"Wow."

"I know."

"You sound a little bitter."

By now, my napkin was impossibly tiny. I released it and watched it unfurl like a rabbit popping out of a hat. "I am. I think I always have been."

"What's wrong with being a rich lawyer?"

"Nothing, but I'd rather fall madly in love."

He grinned. "Wouldn't we all?"

"I guess the grass is always greener on the other side of the gypsy prediction."

"I hate to state the obvious, but you do realize that just because your gypsy aunt—who isn't even a real gypsy—tells you that you're going to be a lawyer doesn't mean it's going to happen, right?"

"Well it did, didn't it? And Shannon married a guy she met at a wedding reception." I sipped my water.

"Shannon met me at a wedding reception, too, remember? There are a million different ways you could look at that prediction and as many possible outcomes. I think you're reading too much into this."

"Why aren't you married?" I asked, regretting the question the minute it was past my lips. I was curious, but it really wasn't polite.

"I told you before—the only girl I ever wanted to marry didn't want to marry me."

"I'm sorry; I didn't phrase that question very well. Say we leave Shannon out of the equation altogether. What I meant was I'm sure you've had plenty of opportunities."

"Yes."

"And you've dated a lot of different girls?"

"A *lot.*"

I couldn't help wincing. "A simple yes would have been sufficient."

"Objection! I believe the counselor is leading the witness."

I smiled. "I'll return to my original question. Why are you single? You seem to have it all . . ."

"Everything except someone to share it with?"

I shrugged.

"I could never be sure that the people I liked really liked me for who I was and not the fortune that came with me."

"But Shannon wasn't like that."

"No, she was different." He gave me a nostalgic smile, and I wondered what particular memory he was thinking about to make him smile like that. "I never really figured out what she wanted, besides Nathan. I'm not sure *she* knew. But it doesn't matter now."

I couldn't decide what the next logical step in this line of questioning was. I wished I'd never brought it up. Whenever I mentioned Shannon, Henry's sadness seemed to seep out of him.

"I'm sorry. I know it's not polite to pry, but I'm trying to figure you out."

"I'm not that interesting, really."

"Of course you are. And you're funny and good-looking, and you know where to find a decent nectarine in January." He laughed, and I was glad that he didn't seem so somber anymore.

"Is the nectarine part important in a potential mate?"

"All I'm saying is one wonders why you haven't been snatched up yet."

"I told you; I'm fussy. I like things the way I like them."

"No comment," I said, draining the last of the water in my glass.

"Rachel?"

"Yes?"

"How would you like to go to dinner?"

I glanced around me. "Uh, we're at dinner."

"Not now. Another night. Maybe Friday."

My stomach did a strange twisty thing that either meant it wasn't at all comfortable with this idea or it was extremely excited for it. I couldn't decide which. "Are you asking me out? Like on a date?"

"Maybe."

"I think that's a pretty clear yes or no question."

"What if I was? Would you go?" he asked.

"Do you think that's wise? I mean, we work together."

"One date," Henry said. "It'll be very informal."

"Those sound like famous last words to me."

"Don't even think of it as a date if it makes you feel better. We're two people eating together at a nice restaurant, getting to know each other."

I wished I still had the napkin to fold, but my suddenly shaky hands would give me away if I picked it up now. "That's a date, Henry."

"It's only a date if you want it to be."

Did I want it to be?

I liked Henry—most of the time. Still, if I was honest with myself, I was probably still nursing the remnants of my earlier crush on him. He seemed like a nice enough guy when he wasn't issuing edicts about colored paper clips. But if we started dating and it went south, I'd have to see him every day at work . . . at least until I got a real job. That would be torture. Plus there was the teeny tiny hitch that he still wasn't over my best friend and I didn't know if he ever would be. I didn't want to be his rebound girl. But then, their strange relationship ended more than two years ago now, so I couldn't be the first one. Who knew how many rebound girls he had ploughed through since then. I wondered which number I'd be on that potentially long list, and I pictured us all in a line with numbers taped to our backs like marathon runners—The Girls Who Tried to Fix Henry. It sounded like the title of a sitcom, and it might have been funny, if it wasn't my actual life.

"Uh, Rachel? Where'd you go?"

Nice time to zone out, Miss Pearce. Now he knows you're contemplating the pros and cons of giving it a shot.

"I was thinking—if I agree to go out with you, how do you know that I'm not only after your money?" *Brilliant argument, Counselor.*

"Because you have your own money."

"That is the least logical statement I've ever heard you make."

"I have my reasons."

I laughed out loud. "Henry, I'm *poor*. I can't even afford a bag of oranges. This shouldn't be breaking news to you."

"I meant figuratively. You're a little off your game right now, but it's only a matter of time before things click and you'll be able to take care of yourself. You'll never need my money to fall back on, and that's an attractive selling point for me."

I leaned back in my chair and folded my arms across my chest. "Wow, you really have a way of making this sound romantic."

"Hey, you never know. It could be an advantageous match for both of us."

"Let me get this straight. You were hopelessly in love with my best friend, and now you're telling me that you think you might like to go out with me, but only because you're fairly certain I'm not a gold digger." I shook my head.

I wouldn't have thought it possible to ruffle Henry, but his cheeks were a little red. "I'm sorry. I used to be much . . . smoother."

I softened a little. "Maybe it's not lost forever. Maybe you're just out of practice."

"How about you agree to have dinner with me, and I'll agree to stop talking about it like it's a business arrangement."

"I'll have dinner with you," I said.

"Great!"

"But it's not a date," I said quickly. "I can pay for my half."

"We can call it whatever you want. And after we eat, if you still want to split the check, I can accept that."

"I will."

"We'll see. I'll pick you up at three on Friday."

"Three? In the afternoon? I'm pretty sure you're not old enough to qualify for the early bird special yet."

"You'll have to trust me on this one."

Chapter Thirteen
"I'm a Fool to Want You"

THE NEXT DAY AT WORK, everything was back to normal. Henry didn't hold a grudge over me calling him an ogre, and he didn't seem to think it was weird that we were going on a date in two days. I, on the other hand, was a bundle of nerves. Apart from anxiously waiting for Shannon to call and give me the post-ultrasound report, I couldn't stop imagining being Henry's actual date. Part of me wished I'd said no, and the other part wished we were going out tonight instead of Friday. So far I'd taken a card to the post office for Henry's friend's birthday and gone to the office supply store to buy a certain brand of pens and some stickers for color coding. I had no idea what he wanted to color code, and I didn't ask because I didn't want him to decide to foist his color-coding project on to me.

Shannon's appointment was at two o'clock, and I wanted to be out of the office when she called. I twiddled my thumbs until 2:38, and I couldn't stand the tension anymore.

"It's cookie time," I announced. My coat was on, and I was already halfway out the door.

Henry leaned back in his chair and stretched. "I'm not sure I want a cookie today."

"You're kidding. I've bought you a cookie almost every day since I started here."

"I know. I have to go to the doctor next month, and I'm a little worried. What if I've gained weight?"

Really? He was going to pick today to develop a conscience about his sugar intake? "Henry. You're practically seven feet tall. Half the time you don't eat lunch. I don't know how you maintain your weight as it is. You're not putting on weight, and a cookie in the afternoon isn't going to kill you."

"Maybe you're right. But if my labs come back all screwy, I'm going to tell them it's your fault."

Shannon could call at any moment, and I couldn't have that conversation with her in front of Henry. It wouldn't be fair to either of them. "You're impossible. What kind of cookie do you want?"

"Uhhhhh, Judy."

"Okay. Be right back." I had almost made it to the stairs when he bolted out the door after me.

"No, wait, I want Betty."

"Betty it is."

He put his hand on his brow and squinted. "Sorry, I should have gone with my first impulse. Judy."

"You're sure?"

"Absolutely."

"All right. I'll see you in a minute." I ran down the stairs as fast as I could before he had the chance to change his mind again.

I was just backing the car out when my cell phone rang. It had to be Shannon. Since I was preoccupied with trying to make sure I could get Henry's car out of the tiny spot he'd parked it in without scratching it, I hit the button to answer and put it on speaker.

"Well?" I said.

"Maybe I want Ricki."

Oh, give me strength. "Henry! Five minutes ago you didn't even want a cookie. Is it really that important? This is not the last cookie you're ever going to have."

"I'm sorry. I know it's silly. But I decided I was feeling a little . . . coconutty."

"You distracted me. You're lucky I'm a good driver—otherwise your car might be embedded in a dumpster right now."

"Just so we're clear, you know that would be grounds for immediate termination, right?"

My phone beeped. Shannon. "Henry, I have to go—there's a call on my other line. I'll be right back with Ricki, okay?"

"Yeah, I guess," he said. He actually sounded a little hurt that I wasn't going to blow off my other call to discuss cookie flavors with him.

"Bye." I switched over to the other line as fast as I could. "Well?!"

"So far, so good! The doctor said I could get up and start doing some things but nothing too strenuous. They want to check me again in a week unless something happens before then."

"Yay! That is excellent news, right?" My phone beeped again. It was Henry. I couldn't believe it. His newest cookie emergency would have to wait until I was finished talking to Shannon.

"It's great news. I'm really relieved. Except . . ."

"Except what?"

"What if I start having problems again when I try to go back to normal life?"

"I'm betting you're going to be fine," I said.

"But what if I'm not?"

"Well, you might have to stay down for a while."

"Stay down *more*? I can't stay in bed for the next seven months!"

I sighed. Shannon wasn't normally like this. She wasn't a worrier; she was someone who attacked her problems head on. Maybe it was the hormones making her act this way. Or maybe it was because she'd been stuck in the house and couldn't go running. She'd always said that running was how she relieved stress; maybe the stress had no outlet now, and it would keep building up until she exploded. I needed to find Shannon a hobby.

My phone was beeping again. Of course it was Henry. This was ludicrous. It's not like he was buying a house—it was a cookie, for heaven's sake, and I was in the middle of trying to manage a *real* crisis that wasn't bakery related.

"Rach? Are you still there?"

"Sorry, someone keeps calling on my other line, and it's distracting me."

"Go ahead and answer it—I don't mind."

"It's only Henry. He can wait."

"He is your boss, and technically you're on the clock. Maybe it's important."

"Trust me, it's not urgent. He's currently suffering from CRIS," I said.

"That sounds pretty serious to me."

"It does until you find out that CRIS stands for Cookie-Related Indecision Syndrome."

She laughed. "Somehow I don't think that's a real condition."

"I've just diagnosed the first case. I'm going to write a paper on it and become well-known and respected in the cookie community."

"Don't forget us little people when you're famous, okay?"

"I'll be sure to mention you in my Nobel Prize acceptance speech."

She laughed again.

"Okay, here's what I think. You need to be positive. You should do whatever the doctors tell you to do, but ultimately whatever is meant to happen will happen, and it won't do you any good to worry about something you have no control over. All this stress isn't good for you or the baby."

"I know. This is so strange for me. I'm used to being healthy and doing whatever I want, and this has completely sidelined me. I mean, it would be bad enough if it was just me that wasn't well, but now there's this other little person being affected as well. It's a lot to think about."

"You need a distraction. You and Nathan should go out and celebrate after you tell him the good news."

"That would be nice. I've been dying for a big fat cheeseburger with lots of onions. And French fries—no—*cheese* fries."

"Hey, you're the pregnant one, so you should call the shots as far as dinner is concerned."

"I'm not sure we should be celebrating this soon. In fact, I'm not even sure I should tell him yet."

"Shannon, you promised!" My voice was a little pitchy, but I couldn't help it. How could she possibly be changing her mind again?

"I know, but he's going to want to tell the world, and I'm not sure that's a great idea. I think we should wait until things are a little less up in the air, you know?"

"You need to tell him. Remember what happened when you didn't tell him you were in love with him?" The phone beeped. *Again.* "Aaarrgh, Henry! Come on, you have got to be kidding me."

"What did I tell you? He can't go ten minutes without talking to you. It must be love."

"It's not love—it's insanity," I growled.

"I think it's kind of cute, actually."

"Can you hold on for just a minute while I see what His Highness needs?"

"Sure. But be nice. Remember, you need this job!"

I switched over to the other line. "You better be bleeding, Henry, because if this is about cookies, we're going to have words."

"Did I catch you at a bad time?"

"I was on the other line. What is it?"

"It's not important."

"You called me four times in a row. It must have been a little important."

"The only reason I kept calling was because I was worried when you didn't pick up. Where were you?"

"I told you, I was on the other line. I'm still on the other line. What is it?"

"It's nothing. Get your other call."

"This is about cookies, isn't it?"

"It's not about cookies!"

"Just tell me!"

"If you hadn't already bought the cookies, I . . . wanted you to get some milk too."

I bit back the naughty word perched on the tip of my tongue. "Milk. Right. Got it."

"You're mad."

"I'm not mad. You're my employer, and it's my job to make sure you have milk if you need milk. So I'll get the milk. But I really have to go finish this other call."

"Go." His voice sounded so . . . dismissive.

"I'm sorry, but it's important."

"So go."

"Now you're mad." It suddenly struck me how much this conversation was more like a married couple than a boss/employee. If we argued over such petty things now, why even bother trying to date each other? The first time anything that actually meant something came up, the relationship would implode, and it would be over.

"I'm hanging up now, but not because I'm mad. Go finish your call," he said.

If it was anyone else on the other line, I'd call them back, but Shannon needed me. "I'll be back in a minute."

"Okay."

I switched back to the other line. "Unbelievable."

"Was the office on fire or something?"

"He wanted me to get him some milk to go with his cookie."

"This . . . is a little odd."

"Not really. They kind of go together, milk and cookies. I'm surprised he hasn't requested it before now."

"Not the milk, you dork! It's the situation that's weird."

"You mean that he's paying me enough to cover my rent and all I have to do is bring him cookies and send the occasional e-mail to his mother?"

"You're e-mailing his mother?" Shannon sounded horrified.

"I probably didn't mention that."

"See, this is bizarre. Henry was never like that when I knew him."

"Maybe that's because you never worked for him."

"No, that's not it. The Henry I knew was completely independent of everyone. The person you're describing sounds incredibly needy."

"I'm not sure the Henry you knew exists anymore."

"You're making me feel guilty again."

"It wasn't intentional. And we weren't supposed to be talking about Henry; we were talking about you. Now, repeat after me," I instructed. "I, Shannon . . ."

"I, Shannon . . ."

". . . hereby do solemnly swear to tell my husband, Nathan, that I am carrying his firstborn child the moment he walks through the door tonight."

"Uh, yeah, what you said."

"It doesn't count unless you say all the words!"

"You don't have to make me swear on a Bible, Counselor. I'll tell him."

"If memory serves, that's what you said last time."

"Yeah, well, I can't put it off forever."

"I don't know. They disguise pregnancy on television all the time. We just need to get you some props—like a big purse or a stack of empty boxes to carry, maybe a counter to hide behind," I said.

"I think Nathan might get suspicious if I was suddenly standing behind the counter in the kitchen every time he came home."

"Not if you started cooking."

"Very funny."

"I'm going to expect a breaking news bulletin on Nathan's reaction. In fact, if you could video it, that would be awesome." I pulled into RubySnap and parked in a normal-size space, one you could back out of without making a sixteen-point turn.

"It might destroy some of the shock value if I was waiting at the door with a video camera."

"I know you keep saying you're worried, but I bet deep down, you can't wait to tell him."

"He'll make a great daddy," she said.

"Well, I'd better go grab Mr. Indecisive's snack and get back before the CRIS reaches a critical stage."

"Hey, be nice to Henry, okay?"

"Wow. You're the last person in the world I would have expected to hear those words from."

"I'm serious. He deserves a little happy, and the only person who deserves a little happy more than him is you. Wouldn't it be great if you could do that for each other? Because if you combined your little happy with his little happy, you'd have a whole bunch of happy," she finished.

This would be the perfect opportunity to tell Shannon that Henry and I were going out on Friday. Because even if I was in denial about the actual terminology, there could be no denying that it was a date. But she would make too much out of what was probably nothing. "You sound like someone teaching a kooky seminar on positive thinking and how to get what you want from life."

"I do not!"

"Either that or someone desperately in need of a thesaurus—take your pick," I said.

"I bet I know a couple of words you wouldn't find in a thesaurus . . ."

"Shannon! Not in front of the b-a-b-y!"

She laughed. "Go be Cookie Girl."

"I will. You go be Pregnant Girl."

"Good luck with Henry."

"Good luck with Nathan."

By the time I got back, I was pretty much over the whole thing. Maybe Shannon was right—maybe I should be nicer to Henry. But that didn't mean I couldn't have a little fun at the same time. I walked into the office and set the cookie and milk on his desk. Before he could say anything, I launched into it.

"Do you know why what you did was wrong?" I said, sitting in the chair across from his desk.

"Uh, I interrupted your call?" he said in that cautious voice you might use to talk someone off a ledge.

"No."

"I nearly caused you to crash into a dumpster?"

"That *was* very naughty of you, but still not the right answer."

His face was blank now. "I give up. What did I do that was wrong?"

"You ordered milk."

"I'm sorry?" Clearly this was not the answer he was expecting.

It would be difficult to keep a straight face, but I had to persevere. "I can't believe you ordered milk. It's so . . . mean."

"What? Are you anti-cow or something?"

"No, I love milk."

"Here, take mine," he said, jumping up from his desk.

"I can't."

"Really, I insist. It was a whim—I don't mind at all."

"I can't because I'm . . . lactose intolerant." I was enjoying this way too much. It reminded me of the chair race I challenged Henry to at IKEA. I think it took doing something juvenile to realize how long it had been since I'd even thought about teasing anyone. I used to be such a fun person—what had happened to me? Maybe law school had burned out my joy gene. Or my mischief gene. Or both. Still, being around Henry seemed to bring out my dormant, slightly devious side.

"Oh," he said. "I'm sorry, I didn't know." He sat back down at his desk and set the milk carton slightly away from the cookie, like it was in quarantine or something. He took a bite of his cookie and snuck a quick look at the milk, but he seemed torn about what to do with it now.

"Go ahead and drink it," I said. "I'll be okay." I made a point of staring longingly at the milk before forcing myself to look away. I took a bite of my delicious cookie and cleared my throat like I was trying to choke it down.

Henry jumped up again, clearly guilt-ridden. "Can I get you some water?"

"It's not the same." I couldn't hold it in any longer. I dropped my head into my lap and started laughing, that silent laughter where your shoulders shake. Unfortunately from Henry's angle, grief and laughing were impossible to distinguish.

"Rachel, are you . . . crying?"

This made me laugh even harder. By the time I lifted my head up, there were tears on my face, but only because I couldn't stop laughing. Needless to say, Henry wasn't laughing.

"That's not funny!"

"It is a little," I said between wiping my face and trying to control myself.

"Why would you make something like that up?" he demanded.

"It was a joke. I'm sorry. I couldn't help it. You should have seen your face."

He shook his head, and I got the impression that he was trying not to smile, like when you catch a kid doing something naughty and you put on your serious face because you can't condone it, but really, it's hilarious.

"Now we're even," I said.

"Not even close. Wait until it's your turn."

"Oooh, I'm scared."

He cracked the milk open and took a sip. "You should be. I have endless resources at my disposal."

I gulped. Perhaps provoking my genius millionaire boss wasn't my best plan ever.

Chapter Fourteen
"Ain't Misbehavin'"

ALL DAY THURSDAY I WAS looking over my shoulder. Nothing happened. I tried to call Shannon to see how the big reveal went with Nathan, but she didn't pick up. Friday came, and everything seemed normal at work. I wasn't convinced. It wasn't bad enough I had the earliest dinner with Henry in the history of dinners to worry about; now I had to stew over whether he'd use the opportunity to exact his revenge. It was true what he said—he had his fingers in all sorts of pies. He could probably come up with ways to get even that I hadn't even considered, and now I was going to pay the price, all because I pretended to have dairy issues. It hardly seemed fair. Still, if he was planning something, he had an excellent poker face. When I asked him where we were going for dinner he smiled and said it was a surprise. Given the circumstances, that didn't make me feel any better.

There was nothing to do in the office, so I spent the hour from one to two obsessing over what a bad idea this was. I should never have agreed to go on a date with my boss, but it was too late now. At two, I put on my coat and scarf and walked into Henry's office.

"I'm going home to change, unless you need something else."

"Nope, I'm good. I'll see you in an hour."

Yikes. An hour didn't give me very long to pretty myself up. Then again, maybe I shouldn't make too much effort. I mean, it's not like I was expecting this to go anywhere. The last thing I wanted was to discover I was developing feelings for the man signing my paycheck, right? "Okay," I said, hoping my voice didn't betray how nervous I suddenly was. I dashed toward the door.

"Rachel, aren't you forgetting something?"

Was this it? Was he going to spring his payback on me now? "Am I?" I asked warily.

"I need your address."

"No doubt so you can send me a singing telegram or something equally embarrassing. Nice try, but it's going to be harder than that to get even with me."

He leaned back in his chair, folding his arms behind his head and smiling. "I need your address so I know where to pick you up."

"Oh, right." More like, oh, crap. My cheeks pinked up from a combination of feeling stupid for accusing Henry and feeling stupid about my living arrangements. It had never occurred to me that he would see the squalor that was my apartment. I knew that he knew I was in a tight spot financially, but I didn't think he had any idea of how bad things were, and I intended to keep it that way. I tore a paper out of the notebook I was carrying, scribbled down an address, and handed it to him. He tucked it into his pocket.

"See you in a minute," he said.

"You didn't even look at it."

"I'll look at it when I get in the car."

"How can you be on time when you don't even know where you're going? I could live in Iceland for all you know."

"If you do, you're making excellent time on the bus every day."

I shook my head.

* * *

Fifty-five minutes later I was pacing in front of the entrance to Shannon and Nathan's townhouse development, a stone's throw from their house. Shivering, I waited for one of them to appear and ask why I was lurking outside like some creepy, frozen stalker.

When Henry asked for my address, I knew there was no way I could let him see my apartment. So I thought I'd just have him pick me up somewhere else and pretend I lived there instead. I wrote down the first address I thought of—it seemed like a good idea at the time. Never mind that I led him straight to where his unrequited love and her normally-very-easy-going-except-around-the-one-person-I-sent-to-his-house husband lived.

There was a silent prayer going through my head, different variations on auto-repeat. *Henry seems like a punctual kind of guy. He has an expensive-looking watch, anyway. Please, oh please, let Henry get here and pick me up before Shannon or Nathan spot me and come out to see what's going on. Especially Nathan. I know it's the middle of the day and technically neither of them should even be here, but it would be my luck to get caught. This was a stupid idea, but if you can get me out of this tricky situation, I promise next time I'll think before I act. Henry will never find out where I really live because this is a one-time dinner. We won't get involved because dating your boss never turns out well. So we'll eat, and even if it's fun, I'll tell him we can't do it again because, really, the best-case scenario is that Henry and I fall madly in love and get married, which would be incredibly awkward for Shannon and Nathan, and they're my best friends! Who would we hang out with? I mean, Henry has a ton of money, so I guess we could buy some friends, but it's not the same. And that's the best-case scenario! The worst-case scenario is that tonight goes terribly, and we both realize what a huge mistake this was, only it's too late to go back, and Henry decides he has to fire me, and I can't even afford my rat-hole apartment, and Hannibal and I end up living in a cardboard box under the freeway overpass.*

The Z pulled up next to me, and Henry appeared through the window. "You look like you're arguing with yourself. Is something wrong?"

I was so relieved to see him, I didn't even care that he'd seen me mumbling to myself. "It was my teeth chattering. I'm cold!"

"It's freezing. What are you doing out here? I feel silly now. I would have come to the door."

"I'm sure you would have, but I didn't want us to be late."

"Late for what?"

"Wherever we're going," I said, as if it were the most obvious thing in the world.

"Are you sure you're all right? You're acting a bit odd."

"I think it's the cold. Once my brain warms up, I'll probably start making sense again."

Henry laughed. I think he thought I was joking. At least he wasn't still looking at me like I'd grown a third eye. "Those are for you," he said, pointing to a long, white box in the backseat.

Flowers. I couldn't remember the last time a guy brought me flowers. "You shouldn't have."

"Would you like to take them inside?"

"NO!" I said a little too loudly. I had a sudden vision of standing outside a door that wasn't mine, trying to explain why the key didn't fit. "Okay, here's the truth—I have a psychotic cat, and he's not very good around strangers. Actually, he's not very good around anyone, including me." *Anyone except Shannon*, I thought.

"I'm confused. If the cat is mean and no one likes it, why do you keep it?"

Because I'd rather have a cat that hates me than a mouse problem. "It's a long story."

"We've got plenty of time," he said. He was on the road now and moving toward the I-15 northbound on-ramp. I couldn't imagine where we were going. Salt Lake had lots of good restaurants, and he was headed away from all of them.

"I can't get rid of the cat because it was a gift."

"What kind of person gives pets as presents?"

"Someone who's only trying to help, I guess."

"They must not know you very well. I mean, we've only been working together for two weeks now, but I never would have pegged you as a cat person."

If there was any chance I was going to get serious about Henry, that would have been the moment right there. A guy who paid attention was a guy worth a second date in my book. But I couldn't—for lots of reasons, but mainly because it would be too weird for the people who were important to me.

"So what's your psychotic cat's name?"

Finally a question I could answer honestly. "Hannibal."

He threw his head back and laughed. "Wow, it really must be bad."

"Actually he's named after the famous military strategist . . . because he's so smart." *Not because he's a brutal, mouse-killing machine. Because of course, a nice girl like me doesn't live in a place with vermin.*

"I'm impressed. Did you study history as well as law?"

"Just the basics. But I love to read biographies. Or anything David McCullough. Most people's real lives are so much more fascinating than fiction, I think."

"Me too! Why can't they read something like that in my mother's book club for a change?"

I'd gotten so involved in the conversation I only now noticed that we were pulling into the self-parking lane at Salt Lake International Airport. The last time I was here I was picking up someone else from their trip and lamenting the fact that I never went anywhere. "Henry?"

"Yes?"

"Why are we at the airport?"

"It's a surprise."

"I thought we were going to dinner."

"We are."

"Uh, is there some new fancy restaurant at the airport?"

"The airport is only a stop on our way to dinner."

I paused to consider this bit of information when something finally clicked. "I don't believe this. You have your own plane, don't you? You can probably even fly it."

"I don't have my own plane. But I do have a ton of frequent-flier miles."

"You're joking. We're going to fly somewhere. For dinner."

"Surprise!"

My hands were suddenly clammy. "I can't drop everything and get on a plane!"

"Why? Did you have other plans tonight?"

"Well, no, but . . . well . . ."

"You're disappointed that I don't have my own plane, aren't you? Is that it? Because if flying commercial is a deal breaker, I can look into it."

"Stop being ridiculous. Okay, I'll say it. I've never flown before."

His eyes bugged a little. "On a plane?"

"No, with my invisible wings. Of course on a plane! What kind of a question is that?"

"But you went to school out of state!"

"I didn't come home much, but when I did, I drove. Stanford isn't that far."

"I don't believe this. How does someone get to be your age never having been on an airplane?" I'd never seen Henry gesture so wildly with his hands. It was kind of amusing. If we weren't in a parking garage, I might have been worried for my safety. It was like he'd temporarily forgotten how to drive.

"How many times have you been on a plane?"

"I don't know. Probably hundreds."

"*Hundreds* of times?! How old are you? How is that even possible?"

"My grandfather took me lots of places when I was a kid. And I fly a lot for work. I can't imagine never flying anywhere." He parked the car, and I let out a sigh of relief. Maybe flying wouldn't be that scary after the last five minutes in the car with Henry.

"It can't be *that* unusual. I'm sure there are plenty of people my age who have never been on an airplane."

"Yeah, in third-world countries maybe."

I gave him a dirty look. "I think you're the abnormal one, Mr. I-Grew-Up-in-an-Airport."

He got out, then came around to open my door. "You know, we don't have to do this if you don't want to."

"You changed your mind, haven't you? I can see it on your face."

"It's so much more pressure on me now because you've never flown before. If you hate it, it's indirectly my fault."

"Maybe you should stop thinking this to death, and we should just do it."

He looked surprised. "Really? You want to go?"

"The last date I went on, the guy took me to McDonalds. He even had a coupon. So there's really nowhere to go but up. This is a little more up than I was expecting, but it'll be an adventure, that's for sure. Where are we going, anyway? Should I have packed a bag?"

"Don't worry—I'll have you home in time to feed your demon cat, and tomorrow is Saturday, so you can sleep all day if you want."

I smiled. "What about my chores? I can't afford to pay someone to run all my errands, you know."

"I'm giving you permission to ignore your errands tomorrow."

"How very generous of you."

We went through security, and I was glad I'd worn socks with no holes in them. Call me crazy, but I couldn't have imagined a first-date scenario where I'd have to remove my shoes. Unless we went bowling, and Henry didn't seem like *that* guy. We walked to the gate where the flight information was posted. "San Francisco, huh? Or did you get them to alter the board to preserve the suspense?"

"Nope. That's where we're going."

I couldn't really grill him for more information because they announced they were boarding first class. Henry stood up. "That's us."

"You're kidding."

He shrugged. "It's the only way to fly."

"You really know how to treat a girl."

I sat down in one of the big plush seats at the front of the plane while Henry was talking to one of the flight attendants. That's when it really started to sink in. I was on an airplane that would be airborne in minutes.

"Are you scared?" Henry asked from the chair next to me. I realized I was gripping the arms of the chair a little too tightly.

"A little bit," I admitted. "But mostly I'm excited."

"Good."

There were people filing past us to the coach seating in the back. They all looked rather miserable, hauling their luggage and trying not to bang it into each other. "Do you ever feel guilty sitting in first class?" I whispered.

"Why should I feel guilty?"

"I don't know. I was watching everyone else going back into coach, and I wondered if they're jealous."

"You think about other people a lot, don't you?"

"I couldn't care less what people think of me." *Really? Which is why you deliberately misled Henry about where you live?*

"I didn't mean it in a negative way. I was trying to say that you're considerate. You're always thinking about how other people feel. It's nice."

"You barely know me. How do you know what I'm always thinking about?"

"I'm an observant guy. I notice things."

"I'm going to need an example."

"For one thing, some strange person gave you a cat as a gift. You obviously hate it, but rather than hurt that person's feelings, you decided to keep it."

I smiled. I wonder if he'd still say the person was strange if he knew who the giver was. "Some people would say that was spineless, not generous."

"I've always been more of a glass-half-full kind of guy."

"That's only one thing. I'm going to require more proof."

"Innocent until proven guilty?"

I nodded.

"Well, I remember when you tried to save someone bent on his own destruction. He was in a bad place and wanted to inflict his pain on other people who didn't deserve it. You kept him from making a big mistake—well, a bigger mistake, anyway."

Now I was feeling bad for deceiving him. Not that it wasn't nice hearing Henry sing my praises, but I figured I'd better clear up his misconception. "Before you start thinking I'm Mother Teresa, I think I better come clean about something. The address I gave you to pick me up today? I don't really live there. I was embarrassed because my apartment is in a bad neighborhood, and my reason for keeping Hannibal is only half as virtuous as you think. The reason my friend gave me the cat is because I have mice, and it seemed like the obvious solution—even if I don't like cats."

"You have mice?" I was afraid Henry would ask to be moved to another seat so as not to be contaminated by me, but his eyes were kind.

"Well, as far as I know, I only have *mouse*. But a reliable source told me that there's never just one."

He laughed. "I know you think things look pretty bleak right now, but I see great things in your future."

"Yeah, that's what Great Aunt Flora, the gypsy, said, and look at where I am."

"That's what Great Aunt Flora, the *non*-gypsy, said, and she was right. You graduated from law school. That's a huge feat!"

"Why are you doing this for me?" I waved my hand, gesturing around the cabin.

"Because you've had a rough time lately, and you deserve a little fun."

I closed my eyes and leaned back in the cushy chair. I thought about what Shannon said, how Henry and I both deserved to be happy. Wouldn't it be amazing if she was right? When I opened my eyes again, he was slouched down in his chair staring at me, bringing us close to eye level, which didn't happen very often. I'd never noticed before how nice his eyes were—sort of grayish, like the sea after a storm, which was a very romantic thought for a practical sort of girl like me. I wondered how many other people missed those eyes because of his height.

"I've never seen your eyes before," I said. I didn't know what was making me so bold, but I couldn't blame it on the altitude since we hadn't even left the ground yet.

"I wore them tonight just for you."

"I'm serious! They're sort of . . . pretty."

He smiled. "Wow, no one's ever told me I had pretty eyes before. Usually that's my line."

"It's not a line; it's an observation. I was wondering if no one ever sees them because you're so tall."

"Yes, generally the only other people my height are other tall men, and so far none of them have commented on the prettiness."

I smacked his arm. "I'm trying to give you a compliment."

"I'm sorry; I'm not very good at that."

"What—giving compliments or taking them?"

"Both. I told you before that I used to be smoother, but relationships, well, one relationship in particular, seems to have burned that out of me." He looked down at his hands. "And I tend to question any praise I get because I've gotten cynical. I always wonder if people are trying to butter me up because they want something."

"I don't want anything from you."

He raised his eyes to meet mine again. "I know. That's why I believe you."

Henry reached across the space between us and touched my cheek ever so slightly with his fingers. It was like the moment before you fall asleep, and you're drifting. You're almost there, but then you hear an unfamiliar noise and it jolts you back to awareness. Suddenly you're wide awake. It sounds corny, but it was like my eyes were never really open until Henry touched me. Everything was so much sharper. At that moment, I was much more scared about what was happening between us than I was about flying.

He blinked a couple of times like his eyes were coming into focus, too, and I wondered if he was thinking the same thing.

Before I could ask him, the captain's voice came over the intercom. "Good afternoon, folks. We'll be taking our place on the runway in a minute, so we need you to be seated with your seat belts on. We hope you enjoy your flight and whatever is waiting for you in the beautiful city of San Francisco."

I sat up a little straighter and fastened my seat belt. Henry did the same. Whatever was happening between us a minute ago had vanished. I was a little disappointed, but mostly I was relieved. This was all getting a little too cozy for a dinner with someone I'd promised myself never to date again. I had already told myself this was only one date, but if this was the kind of effort Henry went to on a regular basis, it was going to be harder than I thought to turn him down next time.

"Also, we have someone special on the plane today," the captain's voice continued. "Let's all give a warm welcome to Rachel—she's flying today for the first time." Henry started clapping loudly, and people around were joining in, smiling indulgently. I could hear cheering in the main part of the plane, and I slid down farther in my seat, trying to hide my red face. Fortunately only the people in first class knew it was me. I hoped there was a little girl named Rachel in coach who was getting a big kick out of this.

When the cheering died down, Henry folded his arms across his chest. "And now we're even."

"That was so much worse than what I did. You managed to share my humiliation with a whole airplane full of strangers!"

"Come on, it wasn't that bad."

"I'll get you back sometime when you least expect it."

"I'm looking forward to that. Oh, I almost forgot—these are for you." He reached into his pocket and handed me a pin with a pair of plastic gold wings attached.

I laughed. "So now I'm official?"

"They give those to all the first-time flyers."

"You mean all the first-time kiddie flyers."

"Hey, you shouldn't be deprived just because you're starting a little late."

"I still can't believe you did this. It will go down in history as the best first date ever."

"You don't even know where we're going."

"It doesn't matter. But I hope you're not going to hold me to my insistence that I pay for half of this date. I didn't know there was going to be airfare involved."

"So it's a date now, is it?"

"Dinner. I meant dinner!" I said quickly.

"Don't worry. Like I told you before, this one's on me. Do you want to know where we're going, or would you like to be surprised?"

The plane suddenly lurched forward, and I jumped. "Maybe I should wait and find out when we get there. I'm not sure I could process one more thing at the moment."

"All right. Next stop, mystery dinner!"

"Next stop? How many stops are there?"

He patted my hand, which was back to tightly gripping the armrest. "All in good time, my pretty. All in good time."

Chapter Fifteen
"Trav'lin' Light"

THE REST OF THE NIGHT was like a dream—the flight, the way the sun was setting when we flew over San Francisco, the bright lights of the city below. We took a cab to dinner at a gorgeous place called Gary Danko, which was terribly expensive but also the best gourmet food I'd ever had. (I Googled the restaurant after we got home and found it was listed as the number-one restaurant in San Francisco. I don't know why I was surprised. If nothing else, the date had reinforced that Henry didn't do anything halfway.) Every bite was more delicious than the last. We had the most amazing butter cake covered in apples and vanilla ice cream for dessert. Henry wanted to order the sorbet sampler with cookies, but I told him we ate cookies every day and we really needed to branch out.

At the end of dinner, I sat back in my chair and sighed.

"Are you pleased, or are you having trouble breathing?"

"A little of both. I was thinking that reality is going to seem even worse after being spoiled like this."

"Don't think of it that way. Think of this as a little bit of reality that you escaped from. Trust me, even this would get old after a while."

"I'll have to test that theory."

"No, really. If you lived like this every day, you wouldn't appreciate it. You might even start longing for a package of Ramen noodles."

I laughed. "I think it would take quite a while before I reached *that* point, but I see what you mean. This really has been wonderful. I'd like to pay you back, but my budget doesn't really stretch to five-star restaurants. I'm a pretty good cook though. I could make you dinner."

"Really? You would cook for me?" He looked so pleased at the idea.

"Sure," I said, already mentally planning the menu. Then I came back down to earth with a thud. "There are only two problems with that plan—my apartment and my grocery budget."

"Your apartment can't be that bad."

"It's a shoebox with rodents."

He laughed. "Okay, so you can cook at my house. And I'll provide the dinner budget."

"How is that paying you back exactly?"

"You don't have to pay me back. Believe me, a home-cooked meal is worth whatever I have to pay for groceries."

"Fair enough."

When the waiter brought the dessert out, Henry was starting to get fidgety. He only got more and more anxious until the last spoonful of cake was gone.

"Are you one of those people who can't stand to sit around when the meal is over, or are we late for something?" I said finally.

He glanced at his watch. "We should probably be going."

"What time is the flight?"

"Late."

"So where are we going now?"

"I don't think I should tell you until we get outside."

"Why not?"

"Because this is a nice restaurant, and I don't want you to disturb the other diners with your loud screaming."

I rolled my eyes. "Henry, in case you haven't noticed, I'm not really a screamer."

"Okay, we're going to see *Wicked.*"

I barely managed to clap my hand over my mouth in time. When I knew it was safe, I took my hand away, but I couldn't help bouncing around in my seat a little. "How did you know I love *Wicked?*"

"You said you were a big fan of musicals, so I figured it was a safe bet."

"And how did you know about the screaming?"

He grinned. "Lucky guess."

* * *

I couldn't stop smiling all the way home from the airport, even though I was sleepy. My eyelids wanted to shut so badly, and when I finally surrendered to this desire, I had a strange idea/fantasy/dream that Henry and I were married. We had been out late, and he was driving us home. I imagined falling asleep in the car, and when we arrived at our lovely, mouse-free mansion, Henry wouldn't want to wake me, so he'd pick me up and carry me inside. I'm guessing the carrying part was where it changed from a half-awake daydream to sleep because I've never been the kind of girl who fantasized that one day her prince would quite literally sweep her off her feet. I mean, I'd like to fall in love as much as the next person, but lately my wish list tended to include things like household maintenance and rodent removal, not happily ever after and glass slippers.

It was nice to let someone else take care of me for a change. So when I heard a voice calling me through the corridors of sleep, I tried to block it out for as long as possible. Somehow I knew that the voice was a part of the real world, and I wanted to stay in the much nicer fantasy realm for a little bit longer.

"Rachel," Henry said, his hand gently shaking my shoulder.

"Ssssh," I said. "The prince is tucking me in."

Henry laughed quietly, and it was one of those situations where you realize too late that you've said something in your sleep that you're going to regret. Suddenly I was all too awake, and I really hoped I hadn't said anything else embarrassing that I didn't remember now. I wished I'd never fallen asleep and let the unguarded part of my brain take over.

"I hate to wake you at the best part of your dream, but I have to know where to drop you off. I'm assuming you want to go to your real apartment instead of the fake one from earlier."

I stretched. "That would probably be best. I'd hate to end such a nice evening in jail when the real owners call the police."

"I hardly think Shannon would turn you in for breaking and entering."

I froze. "How did you know Shannon lived there?"

"It was simple deduction. You said you gave me the first address that came into your head. Your best friend was a pretty safe guess."

I buried my head in my hands. "I'm sorry. I'm sorry for bringing her up and putting that picture in your head. I'm sure you don't want to think about specific things like where she lives and what she's doing."

"It's okay—you don't have to apologize. Shannon picked Nathan. She's moved on, and so have I."

If only you meant that, I thought. No matter how awake I was, my brain was starting to feel foggy again, and I struggled to shake myself alert so I wouldn't drift off again and spout some other nonsense that might make things worse.

"So . . . your real address?"

I told him where I lived, and he didn't ask any more questions. I think he felt bad about waking me up in the first place. He'd been so nice tonight, but I wondered if his attitude would change when he saw where I lived. I must have fallen asleep again because the next thing I knew, Henry was waking me up.

"Is this it?"

I sighed. "So much for the fairy tale. This is the place. I'm sorry I keep falling asleep. I'm not usually such bad company. I'm going to blame it on all the excitement. When the adrenaline wore off, I passed out."

"It's okay. I did keep you out pretty late."

I reached into the backseat and grabbed the box of flowers. "Thanks again for everything. It was incredible, all of it. I'll see you on Monday, okay?"

"Let me walk you to the door."

"I'll be fine," I assured him. It's not like my house was dirty or anything. I was a good housekeeper, but there's only so much you can do to dress up something that needed to be bulldozed.

"Don't argue with me. I'm not leaving you on the street in the middle of the night."

"You mean in this neighborhood?"

"I mean anywhere. The world's not safe."

"Actually your Z is probably in more danger alone here than I am. You go inside with me for ten minutes, and when you come back, your tires will be gone," I warned.

"I'm going to walk you to the door."

He followed me to the front door of the building.

"Well, good night," I said again.

"I want to walk you to *your* door."

"It's up four flights of stairs, and there's no elevator. Don't worry, I'll be inside—nothing will happen to me."

"I think I can manage four flights of stairs."

I shrugged. "It's your funeral."

We finally made it to my door. "Okay, you've delivered me safe and sound. Now get back to your car before there's nothing left but the license plate."

He didn't seem concerned. Either it was well insured or he wasn't ready to go yet. "I had a really good time tonight."

"Me too. I can't believe we were in San Francisco a couple of hours ago."

"So when do I get to meet Hannibal?"

I smiled. "Probably not tonight. It's for your own safety. He's more of a morning cat, really. If you wake him up at night, your chances of getting your face torn off go up drastically. I'm a little afraid to go in there myself." The part about me being afraid was true, but as far as I could tell, Hannibal was the same level of cranky 24/7. Since we weren't even friends in the light of day when I'd had plenty of sleep, I couldn't imagine trying to be civil to him in the middle of the night. Also, I was pretty sure I wouldn't be able to keep up my side of the conversation with Henry for much longer, and I really didn't want to spoil the evening with a quarrel. I should have insisted on taking a taxi home from the airport, except for two tiny issues: (1) I had no money for a taxi, and (2) the idea of being woken up by the cabbie instead of Henry was a little frightening.

"Okay, another time then." He looked incongruous in the dingy, badly lit hall in his tailored clothing, and yet he still stood there. I could almost see the half-formed thought bubble over his head, like he was trying to say something but couldn't figure out how to say it. It was getting really late. Maybe he was a morning cat too. Whatever his sudden issue, it was getting awkward, and my brain was too tired to come up with something to diffuse the tension.

"Thanks again," I said finally. "It was more fun than I've had in a long time."

"No problem." And still he stood there, wearing his indecisive face. Could he really be contemplating which level of doorstep affection to go for?

My overtired, mushy brain was screaming now. *Why are you still here?! Are you honestly thinking of kissing me here in this nasty old hall? You could catch something that would necessitate a lengthy course of antibiotics in this building! Get out now while you're still relatively safe!*

Henry opened his mouth to say something, and then he closed it again. "Good night, Rachel," he said finally, heading down the steps without another word.

I'd wanted him to leave, been desperate for it even. So why was I disappointed?

Ugh. Curse my sleep-deprived inner voice. I turned the key in the lock and went inside, cautiously surveying the area for the angry cat I was expecting. He was nowhere in sight, which wasn't unusual. I went into the bedroom, and there he was, stretched out across the middle of my bed. He knew he wasn't supposed to be up there, but I was too tired to enforce the rule.

Out of the corner of my eye, I saw Mousey, gazing at me with his sad, soulful black eyes. "Hannibal," I hissed softly. "Hannibal, there's the mouse!" He opened one eye just a crack, gave me a touch-me-and-die glare, and closed it again. Mousey looked disappointed in me, like he knew I'd ordered his death and couldn't quite believe it. I felt like a villain. He gave me one last glance before scurrying off into the closet, and I wondered if he'd exact his revenge by chewing up all my best shoes.

I eased onto the bed, clothes and all—slowly, so as not to incur Hannibal's wrath. I scooted as close as I could to the edge and prayed that I wouldn't roll over on him in the night. I could only imagine the number of stitches I'd need after that little confrontation, and that's assuming I could get to the hospital before I bled to death. That was the last thought I remember before sleep took me.

Chapter Sixteen
"You're Driving Me Crazy"

"WHERE HAVE YOU BEEN? I'VE been calling you and leaving messages!" I said.

Shannon and Nathan were on their way into church on Sunday. I used to be in their ward, so I knew what time their meeting was. Since Shannon wasn't answering the phone or returning my calls, I was starting to worry that maybe something had happened with the baby. And since Nathan didn't know that I knew, I thought it would be easier to stalk them at church than stop by the house. She probably wouldn't be at church if something had happened, though, so why hadn't she called me back?

"Rachel, what are you doing here?" Was it my imagination or did Shannon look the teensiest bit uneasy when she saw me?

"I forgot it was our stake conference today until I got to the church and the parking lot was empty. So I thought I'd come to your ward instead."

"Hey, always room for one more, right?" Nathan said. "How've you been, Rachel?"

"Can't complain. Well, I could, but it wouldn't help."

"Any news on the real job front?"

Nathan knew that I had taken a crummy job but not the nefarious identity of my boss. "Not yet, but it's got to be any day now."

Nathan held the door open for us. "That's the spirit. And how's your evil cat?"

"I keep waiting for it to get bigger. Maybe I should get it stretched or something."

Nathan laughed, and Shannon . . . didn't.

"Rachel," Shannon said, "you have to be patient—he'll grow up soon enough."

"That's the thing. I'm not sure I want it to. It's scary enough as a kitten; when it comes into its full cat powers, I'll have no control over it."

"Didn't you read the manual?" Nathan asked. "The cat controls you, no matter the size. You exist merely to serve the cat."

"That's funny—mine didn't come with a manual."

He smiled. "It explains a lot, though, doesn't it?"

We filed into the chapel and sat down for sacrament meeting right as it was starting. Once the opening hymn started, I leaned over and whispered in her ear.

"Everything okay with the . . . chick?" With everyone singing, it was loud enough that I didn't think Nathan could hear me, but I wasn't taking any chances. Shannon and I used to make up code words for stuff we wanted to keep secret when we were young. I hoped she'd get the chick reference.

She looked confused. "The chick?"

"Yeah, you know. The *chick*," I said, looking pointedly at her nonexistent belly.

"Oh, right. The chick. Yup, everything's fine."

"I got worried when you didn't call me back. I thought maybe something had happened to the chick . . . or the hen."

"The hen feels pretty good. Ditto the chick, as far as I know. But there was a reason I didn't call you back. I didn't want you to judge me."

I frowned. "Why would I judge you?"

"Because I still haven't told the, uh, rooster."

"Oh, come *on*! Seriously?" I hissed. Nathan gave me a funny look, and I knew if we didn't tone it down, he would know something was going on. "What are you going to do— wait until the . . . egg hatches?"

"See, I knew it! There it is, right there—the judging. The hen knows what's best for the egg—and for the rooster, for that matter. And it's not for the . . . peacock to impose her opinions!"

"Peacock?! That's just mean."

"I know. I'm sorry. I was trying to think of something else in the bird family. It was either that or a goose."

I tried to hide a laugh behind my hand. "This isn't our most foolproof code, is it?"

"I'm afraid Nathan would crack it without even trying. So, how have you been?"

"I'm great. Except I'm still a little hurt by the peacock comment."

"I only asked because I happened to drive by and see the peacock freezing on the street near my house until someone arrived to save you, and by 'someone,' I think you know who I mean."

I could feel the blood draining from my face.

"That's right, I saw the . . . turkey show up in his fancy . . . feathers and whisk you away."

Everyone was bowing their heads for the prayer, so that's where the conversation ended.

Well, Relief Society should be interesting.

* * *

"Are you mad?" I asked.

"Of course not. I already told you I didn't care if you worked for Henry or dated him or married him. I just don't understand why you didn't tell me."

We were sitting on a couch in the foyer. It seemed mean to whisper through someone's lesson, so we stayed outside instead. People kept coming in and out of the main doors, and it was freezing out there.

I sighed. "I didn't know what to think. We got into this big argument at work about colored paper clips, and we were there late, so he bought me dinner to apologize."

"Colored paper clips? Are we still talking in code?"

"No, it was another one of the weird errands he sent me on. Anyway, dinner was nice, and he asked if we could go out one night. I said yes, but I never should have gone."

Shannon's eyes were full of sympathy. "Was it terrible?"

"It was pretty amazing, actually."

"I don't get it. Is that a bad thing?"

"Yes! He's my boss!"

"So?"

"What if I like him more than he likes me? What if everything goes perfectly for a while, and then we end up hating each other and I'm out of a job?"

"What if the two of you fall in love and live happily ever after and have lots of incredibly beautiful children?"

"What are the chances of that happening?"

"Well, zero, if you don't give it a chance. Where did he take you for dinner?"

"You wouldn't believe me if I told you."

"I'm probably the one person who *would* believe you."

"San Francisco."

Her mouth dropped open. "Shut. Up. So you finally left the no fly zone, huh?"

I nodded. "It was really fun. And after dinner, he had tickets to *Wicked*. It was like something out of a movie."

"I'm surprised you didn't ask him to marry you at the end of the night."

"That was the only awkward part—the doorstep."

"What happened?"

I rubbed my hands together in an attempt to warm them. "Well, nothing happened. He stood around for what seemed like forever, trying to figure out what to do, and finally he said good night and left."

"I wonder what his deal was. Did he seem nervous?"

"I don't know. It was really late, and I was so tired I didn't have the patience to go after him and hash it out. He seemed . . . indecisive."

"So I take it you told him where you really lived."

"Well, I didn't have much choice. There were no buses running in the middle of the night."

Shannon sighed. "It sounds like an adventure."

"Shannon Sarah Adams! You're not jealous, are you?"

"Of course not. I love Nathan, and I would never trade him. But when I was with Henry, I always had this feeling that there was the possibility that literally anything could happen."

"I know what you mean. I can see how dating someone with unlimited resources could be addictive."

"Does that mean you're going out with him again?" she squeeed. Well, as much as you can squee in church, anyway.

I shook my head. "I promised myself I wouldn't, no matter how fun it was."

"Are you crazy? You had a good time, right?"

"Yes."

"And you find Henry attractive?"

"Yes."

"And he would be able to take care of you in the manner to which you've become accustomed, right?"

I snorted. "You've seen where I'm living. I have absolutely no expectations in that department. Somewhere with no mouse would be heaven."

"Mice," she corrected.

"Whatever."

"Sounds to me like the right guy is right in front of you."

"It's not that simple."

"Or maybe you're making it more difficult than it needs to be."

I gave her an indulgent smile. "Enough about me—let's talk about you."

"One more ultrasound. I'll tell him after my ultrasound on Friday."

"I want to go on record as saying this is a bad idea."

"I know, but I need a little more time to make sure that the chick is a permanent thing before I get the rooster's hopes up."

"Remember how bad he felt when he found out you secretly had feelings for him and kept it to yourself?"

"Of course I do."

"This is worse."

She shook her head. "It is not worse, and when I tell him, he'll understand I had my reasons for keeping it a secret for a while."

"If I were you, I'd tell him."

"And if I were you, I'd take a chance on Henry."

"Guess we'll have to respect the other's right to make our own decisions."

"Guess so." I stood up. "Come on, let's go find the rooster and tell him we got out of class early."

Chapter Seventeen
"How Deep Is the Ocean?"

"So I have a little task for you today," Henry started.

"Wow. Nothing good ever started with those words."

"It's not as bad as it sounds. You might even like it."

"Hey, you're the boss. I live to serve."

This morning when I was getting dressed, I had decided that I was going to follow Henry's lead. If he didn't mention the date, I wouldn't either. And if he did, well, I'd wait and see how it played out. I'd had a great time and had decided I'd be willing to go out with him again, even if it would wreak havoc on the rest of my life. But I wasn't brave enough to be the one who brought it up first. So far he hadn't said anything. Maybe he'd had a terrible time and was trying to spare my feelings by pretending it never happened.

"I need you to go to the bookstore and find me a copy of *The Secret*."

"You mean that book about how all you have to do is wish for everything, and it will magically appear?"

"I think that's the general idea."

"Is life not turning out to be all you'd hoped?" I deadpanned.

"You're too, too funny, Miss Pearce."

"I don't know why you'd waste your time reading that. In fact, I bet you could teach the author a thing or two about wish fulfillment."

"It's the book club selection this month."

"Hmmm. As I recall, *The Secret* is nonfiction—so no movie." Actually there was a movie, but since Henry didn't know, I thought it would be funny to see him have to read something for a change.

"Yes, but it was my mother's turn to choose, so I thought I'd better make an effort to show up."

"You're a very good son to humor your mother like this."

"Thanks, but I'm not going to read it—you are."

I laughed.

Henry didn't.

"You're kidding." Well, that backfired. So much for making him participate.

"Oh, and there's one other thing I need you to do for me this afternoon. I need you to bring me something I left at home this morning."

Okay, getting to ogle Henry's house was an errand I might actually enjoy. But I couldn't let him know that. After all, I was only his secretary. Why should I care where he lived? Idle curiosity, that's all it was.

"I suppose I could be persuaded. What do I need to pick up?"

"There's a piece of paper with a web address on it—I think I left it on my kitchen counter. I have an online meeting this afternoon, and the password is on the paper."

"You're kind of overloading me today. I'm not your slave, you know."

"I'm a generous overlord—you can start reading the book tomorrow."

I pretended to hesitate. I knew that I was getting scandalously overpaid for something any minimum wage assistant could do for Henry, which was why I enjoyed teasing him about it. If I'd thought for one minute that he thought I was serious, I'd be totally embarrassed.

He sighed. "And I'll buy you lunch first."

"You drive a hard bargain."

* * *

"Where are we going?" I said as a shiver rippled through me.

"To eat our lunch in the park."

"It's February. It's probably only forty-five degrees out here." I was stumbling in my heels across the semifrozen grass. We'd stopped at Kneaders for sandwiches, and I'd assumed we were taking them back to the office, but somehow Henry ended up here.

"I know. Isn't it a beautiful day?"

I had to admit it was pretty nice . . . for February. The sun was trying to break through the clouds, but even when it made a brief appearance, it didn't give much warmth. Even with my coat on it was chilly. But Henry didn't seem to notice. He led us to a metal park bench and sat down. I sat gingerly next to him, springing off the bench again when I felt how cold it was.

"I can't sit there," I said flatly.

"Come on, it'll warm up."

"Nope. This is where I draw the line."

"Okay, we'll unwrap the sandwiches and stroll around. If we keep moving, you should stay nice and toasty."

"How am I supposed to eat a sandwich and walk at the same time?"

"Those are your two choices—walk and juggle or sit comfortably and freeze."

"Ogre," I said.

"Diva," he shot back.

My mouth dropped open. "Oh, you're gonna pay for that."

* * *

"I love birds," I said. "Why do all birds sound different?" Once I figured out how to manage the sandwich and stroll at the same time, it was kind of invigorating. Except now I was verbalizing bizarre thoughts that probably should have remained thoughts and never made the foray into the verbal arena. Obviously the cold was doing strange things to my brain again.

Henry cocked his head, listening. "There aren't any birds."

"I know! It was a general observation." Trust him to pick up on my random thought spewing.

"I don't know. Why do all people sound different?"

I ignored him. I wasn't done rhapsodizing about birds yet. "I mean, don't you ever wonder what they're saying?"

"My grandfather used to take me for adventures when I was little. We'd listen for bird sounds, and he'd tell me which birds they belonged to."

We were both quiet for a minute, chewing. "You talk about your grandfather a lot, but you don't really mention your parents much."

"I spent a lot of time with my grandfather when I was young." He didn't elaborate, and I wasn't brave enough to press him any further.

I heard a sudden loud bird noise, and I was glad for the distraction. I looked around frantically trying to find it, but I couldn't see anything. "Did you hear that? There's a bird! What kind of bird is that?"

Henry laughed. "Everyone knows what kind of bird that is."

"Well, I don't. What is it?"

"It's the bird people associate with the ocean . . ."

I stared at him blankly.

"It's a seagull."

"Oh, well that explains it. I've never seen the ocean."

He stopped walking, but it took me a minute to realize he wasn't following me. I finally turned around and came back to get him. "What?" I asked.

He just shook his head.

"*What?*"

"I can't believe you've never been to the ocean. You went to college in California!"

"I know, but the closest beach was about a thirty-minute drive, and from what I heard, it was cold and foggy."

"But still!"

"The only thing I did at school was school. I was always smart in high school, but college was different, and law school was . . . brutal. I had to work twenty-five hours a day to stay on top of it."

He nodded. "Well, that explains a lot."

I quirked my head to one side. "What does that mean?"

"I never understood why you weren't in a relationship. But when you have to devote so much time to your intended career, it doesn't leave room for anything else."

I started to walk away. I wanted to talk about this about as much as he wanted to talk about his absentee parents.

"Rachel, wait."

I tried to walk faster, but he grabbed the arm of my coat.

"No fair, your legs are longer than mine."

"I wasn't criticizing you. I think it's amazing how devoted you are and how much work you put into making your dreams reality."

"That's the thing—I spent all that time and trouble, and now I don't know if they are my dreams anymore."

"I told you, one day everything is going to click, and you'll wonder why you ever doubted yourself. Nothing worth having ever comes without effort, believe me."

He looked so earnest, and I could see that these weren't meaningless platitudes to him. He'd been there and paid the price himself. "Thank you."

"You're welcome." He was still holding my arm, and I was reminded of that first time we saw each other again in the café. I couldn't believe it had only been a little over a month and a half ago. "Don't take this the wrong way. You're one of the most intelligent people I know, and you're very educated and independent. You know what you want, but in some ways you're"—he struggled to find the right word—"childlike. It's kind of enchanting. I'm sure you know all sorts of things I don't, but there's something about you that makes me want to show you *everything*."

I was completely at a loss for words. Did Henry say what I thought he said? If someone else had called me childlike and inexperienced, I think I'd be offended. But the idea of Henry wanting to show me everything I'd never seen before didn't bother me. In fact, it was sort of adorable.

I couldn't believe I had been cold because I could feel the heat rising from my neck. It was only a matter of time before it reached my cheeks, which I hoped were already pink from the cold; otherwise, the jig was up. I wondered if he had any idea that his simple speech affected me more than anything any of the guys I'd ever dated had managed to come up with. As brilliant as some of those guys were, they had no idea who I was. But Henry did, and he'd just proven it.

I tried to tell him with my eyes. *Now, Henry. In case you were unsure, now is an infinitely better moment to kiss me than in the hall of my possibly soon-to-be-condemned apartment building. I'm more than willing, even if I'm not brave enough to say it in words. All you have to do is close that last narrow space between us . . .*

The peek-a-boo sun chose that moment to go behind the clouds again, and I shivered. Henry let go of my arm.

"Henry," I started.

"I think I've kept you out in the cold long enough. If you'll drop me off at the office, you can go run those errands for me."

"Sure," I said. He'd given me an opening, but I'd hesitated and now it was too late. Because as much as I thought Henry could read my mind, apparently there were limits to what he could see.

Chapter Eighteen
"I'll Never Smile Again"

THE RIDE BACK TO THE office was quiet. Henry went back to work, and I headed out to do his chores. I easily found the book he wanted and started in the direction of the address he'd given me. I confess I wasn't quite as excited to see Henry's house as I was this morning. Earlier it seemed like an adventure, but I felt like I'd blown it this afternoon, like he'd opened up to me and I'd panicked. I knew something like this was going to happen. I never should have taken the job with Henry in the first place.

I mentioned that when Shannon was dating Henry—or not dating him or whatever she wanted to call it—I was a little bit jealous. She had Nathan, who, for years, was in love with her and only waiting for her to say the word. Theirs was an ideal, ready-made relationship, the kind where you already know everything there is to know about the other person, good and bad, because you were friends first. So after the mutual admission of affection, the only thing left is to slide into that next stage.

Then there was Henry, who was only waiting for her to say that she'd given up on winning Nathan. Henry was new and exciting and different, and he adored her. Whether it was simply a matter of her being unattainable or he had true feelings for her I would never know. Nathan won, Henry lost, and everything else is history. The point was she had two really nice guys who both would have been thrilled to be chosen. I never even had one.

I used to imagine that Shannon and Nathan would live happily ever after, and suddenly the scales would fall from Henry's eyes—where he could only see Shannon before, he would finally see me. It was a silly fantasy because I never had any real feelings for him, just a crush. Looking back now, I think I was in love with the idea of being adored by someone more than the idea of Henry himself; he was just a face to associate with the abstract idea.

As I pulled onto the street where the house should be, there was a beautiful wrought iron gate. I could see several houses beyond it—it must be one of those. Henry had given me very detailed instructions on how to find it, but he'd failed to mention that I'd have to go through a security gate. I pulled up next to the gate and was dismayed to notice that even the guard shack was nicer than my apartment. An older gentleman stood up slowly and came around to greet me.

"Waldorf! I mean . . . Syd!" It took me a second to come up with his real name, and I hoped he didn't know the first name I called him belonged to his Muppet look-alike. "What are you doing here?"

"I'm here to let you in. There's not usually someone stationed all the time, unless there's a big party or something."

I was confused. "I'm sorry to take you away from your real job."

He laughed. "Oh, this is my real job."

"For some reason I thought you worked for the building doing maintenance or something."

"Only if something needs doing. My job is a lot like yours, really."

"What would that be?"

"I do whatever Mr. Henry needs done," he said simply.

I immediately pictured him at RubySnap, standing in line for Henry's daily sugar fix, and tried not to laugh. "Yeah, I guess that pretty much covers it," I said.

Syd/Waldorf opened the gate and pointed me in the right direction. "It's the big gray house at the back. You can't miss it."

I thanked him.

"Do you mind if I ask you a question?" he said.

"Go ahead."

"Are you going to be his girlfriend?"

That was the absolute last thing I expected him to ask, and I felt a sort of hopeful surge. Then I thought about our lunch in the park, and I deflated. "I don't think so."

"Oh." Syd looked a little disappointed as well. "I know it's none of my business, but I wondered because you're driving his car and everything."

"Nope, I'm like you—doing what needs to be done."

Syd's eyes sparkled. "Yeah, but he never lets me drive the car."

I laughed.

"I like you," he said. "You have a nice face. Like Snow White."

"That might be the sweetest thing anyone has ever said to me. You have a nice face too."

"Not bad for a Muppet, right?"

My face was immediately hot, and I hid it in my hands. "I can't believe I said that. I'm so sorry! I really meant it in a kind way."

"You're not the first one to notice. Don't worry about it. I might be an old guy, but my ears still work good. I'll stick around long enough to let you out again, okay?"

"Thanks, Syd."

"Please—call me Waldorf."

"Only if you call me Snow White."

He made an awkward sort of half bow, and I wondered how old he was. "Your wish is my command, Princess."

I waved as I drove through the gate. I spent the next two minutes with my mouth hanging wide open. There were some seriously large houses on even larger parcels of ground. I couldn't begin to imagine what living here would set someone back, much less paying someone to keep up the landscaping. Huge, beautiful trees, which had obviously been here longer than the homes, were in varying states of age. I passed a lovely old brown-brick home with vines completely covering one side. Even the mailboxes were elaborate. I drove for what seemed like forever until I came to the gray house at the end. Waldorf was right—you couldn't miss it.

Stately bare trees lined the long driveway that led to the monstrous house—and it was a monster. It was breathtaking, but in a foreboding sort of way. If houses were male or female, this one would be, well, an ogre. There was nothing delicate or feminine about it. There were still patches of half-melted snow in places under which the closely shorn winter grass peeked through. The gloomy walls sported numerous windows, which would let in plenty of light, but I had the feeling that even on a sunny day it would feel gray inside.

I let out a breath I didn't realize I'd been holding. I felt like Elizabeth Bennet when her carriage alighted at Pemberley for the first time and she realized she might have been mistress of the house. I parked the car in the drive, which was paved with loose rocks, and walked to the massive wood doors. I used the key to unlock them and stepped over the threshold. It looked exactly like I expected from the outside—dark stone floors, dark rugs, and windows that did little to admit any light. The whole place looked like it had been carved out of one giant rock.

I imagined Henry in this house after Shannon broke his heart, brooding, skulking around the rooms like Beast from the fairy tale, snarling at anyone who dared come too close. I expected Cogsworth and Lumiere to pop out at any moment and scold me for being here. I couldn't believe Shannon had never mentioned this incredible house.

I shook myself from the spell spinning its web around me. I shouldn't be dawdling when Waldorf was out there waiting to lock the gate after me. I wandered through the oversized main entry, past the huge stone staircase, and down a hall, which opened into the kitchen and a large family-style room. Everything in the kitchen was rough stone, sleek metal, or cool granite. It wasn't cold in the house, but I still felt chilly. It was so sterile; nothing looked lived in at all. I could have been touring a house that was for sale, from all the personality it had. The windows of the kitchen looked out onto a backyard that was overgrown, in a tasteful and cultivated way. Everything about this place screamed dark castle from a fairy tale.

The slip of paper was on the granite counter, where Henry said it would be, and I tucked it into the pocket of my coat. I wouldn't go upstairs—that would be too intrusive. But I couldn't help nosing around on the main floor. As far as I could tell, the living room was the only place that had anything of Henry in it. There were several big comfortable-looking chairs and a leather couch. Against the wall was a state-of-the-art sound system, but I couldn't see any CDs, only a wall with thousands of records organized alphabetically—Ella Fitzgerald, Glenn Miller, Etta James, and a bunch of others I'd never heard of; probably every jazz record in existence. But the biggest section was Billie Holiday—there must have been fifty records of hers alone.

I wanted to pick a random record and sit back in one of those cushy chairs to see what it was like to be Henry, but I didn't want to keep Waldorf waiting any longer than I already had. Besides, I should be getting back to work, even if it was going to be weird after the talk we had at lunch. I could spend whatever was left of the afternoon reading *The Secret*. I wondered if Henry was going to make me give him a book report or if he'd take me along to the book club and have me rehearse it like a trained monkey.

I was dying to go upstairs and see if the bedroom was as austere and impersonal as the rest of the place, but that really did seem inappropriate. So I got into the car and drove back to where Waldorf was waiting with the gate open. I waved and took off back into the real world. Now that I was no longer standing in Henry's fortress, it all seemed like a strange dream. I'd have had a hard time believing places like that actually existed outside of storybooks if I hadn't seen it with my own eyes.

On the way back, I stopped at RubySnap for Henry's cookie. He hadn't specifically requested one, but I prided myself on being a good employee who could always anticipate her boss's needs. The fact that I was craving sugar myself had nothing to do with it. I arrived back at the office to find Henry hard at work.

"Did you have any trouble finding it?" he inquired. Anyone else might have been waiting for me to gush over his mansion, but not Henry. I don't think he paid enough attention to where he lived to expect me to be impressed.

"Nope, it would be hard to miss. Tell me, does your house have its own zip code?"

He smiled. "Not yet, but I'm working on the zoning."

"You know, you might have warned me about the gate and the guard. I was afraid I was going to be fingerprinted or something!"

"You mean Waldorf didn't search you for weapons? He's slipping." He showed no signs of being upset about our earlier conversation, which made me feel better.

"I can't believe you live there. It's *enormous*."

"It's a place to live."

"It's a place for lots of people to live."

He snorted. "No one seems to be jumping at the opportunity."

I put Henry's cookie bag and milk on his desk, and the little dark cloud over his head vanished. He looked inside. "Yes, Virginia, there is a Santa Claus."

"You really do know all the names, don't you?"

"I'm closer to some of these cookies than actual people I know. How much do I owe you?"

"I had enough money left over from the book."

"Ah, the book. Well, you better get cracking. Book club will be here before you know it," he said with his mouth full of cookie.

"I have your mother's e-mail address, you know. What's to stop me from telling her about this nefarious plan of yours?"

"My mother likes you. Do you really want to break her little heart by telling her what a bad person her son is?"

"You're making that up. Your mother couldn't possibly like me—we've never even met."

"She says she can tell from your e-mails that you're very polite and much nicer than any of the other secretaries I've had."

Part of me was perversely pleased that Henry's mother liked me, but being classified as "the help" didn't exactly bode well for possible future family relations.

"Well, you can tell her that she seems very nice as well, even if she did raise a son who pays people to do his homework for him."

"Oh, and that reminds me—I have a bunch of copies for you to make," he said.

"I'll take the copies, please. The book can wait until tomorrow."

Chapter Nineteen
"My Old Flame"

I SAT IN THE OFFICE the next day, doing my reading assignment. It was actually kind of interesting—the notion that if you wanted something badly enough, you could will it into existence. I didn't believe it exactly, but it did give me something to think about. My cell phone rang. It was Shannon. I didn't want to answer her call while I was at work. I'd call her back later when I went on my cookie run.

But five minutes later, my phone rang again. I couldn't imagine her calling me at work twice in a row without a good reason. What if something was wrong? Henry had been in his office all morning—I was going to have to risk it.

"Hello?"

"Rachel, my dear. How are you today?" she asked. She didn't sound like anything was terribly wrong.

"Well, I'm kinda busy at the moment. I'm at *work*." I hoped she would get the hint that I couldn't really talk right now.

"Yeah? What's he got you doing this morning? Picking out names for his future children?"

I stifled a laugh while I peeked over my shoulder. There was no sign of Henry. "It's better than that. I'm reading a book for his mother's book club."

"You're in the book club now? Are you getting paid for that?"

"Oh no, I'm not in the club—I'm reading the book so I can tell him what it's about and he won't have to read it himself."

"You can't be serious."

"As a heart attack. I better go—he's in the other room, and he might come in here any minute," I said.

"Okay. I was just calling to make sure we're still on for tonight."

Tonight? What was tonight? I searched my mind for clues, but I was coming up blank. "Uh, I guess so. Refresh my memory—what are we doing tonight?"

There was a long pause. "You're joking, right?"

It wasn't her birthday, and it wasn't Nathan's birthday. "I'm sorry; I don't remember planning anything with you tonight."

"You're supposed to be coming over for that blind date."

"What?! When did I agree to this?" Of course, this was the exact moment Henry chose to saunter into the room.

"Anything wrong?" he mouthed.

"Apparently I forgot something important," I whispered, covering the receiver with my hand.

"I told you about it a week ago," Shannon said. "We were watching a movie."

"Well, I don't remember any of this."

Henry was still standing there, and this was getting more awkward by the minute. "Did you need something?" I mouthed.

"It can wait," he mouthed back, and he obviously meant that literally because he wasn't budging. Didn't he know it was rude to eavesdrop on a private conversation?

"We were watching *Castaway*, and I told you Nathan had a friend he wanted to set you up with, remember? I said I thought it would be better if we all went out together. Is any of this ringing a bell?"

"I'm sure I fell asleep. I always fall asleep during *Castaway*—you know this."

"But it's such a great movie!"

"There's only dialogue in maybe half of it. Are you sure I was awake during this blind date discussion?"

Henry was smiling now, and I couldn't imagine how this could get any worse.

"I'm, like, 75 percent sure you were awake."

"It seems like an important thing. I think I would remember if I was conscious. Anyway, I don't have anything to wear. I'm not going out tonight. Tell him I'm sick."

"Rach, you can't do this to me. This is one of Nathan's best friends!"

"Well, since Nathan has more best friends than anyone I know, I'm sure he'll get by fine with one less."

"It's too late to cancel now. Come on, you've been haunting your apartment like a ghost for months now. It'll be good for you!"

I sighed. There was no way out of this. I was going to have to suck it up and go, but I didn't have to like it. "Just so we're clear, I'm really mad at you right now."

"You can be as mad as you want, as long as you show up at my house by seven."

"You owe me big time. I don't even know this guy's name."

"His name is Jason. He's twenty-five, and he has gorgeous brown eyes. You really don't remember any of this conversation?"

"'Conversation' implies that we were both talking. Did any actual words come out of my mouth?"

"Come to think of it, you were unusually quiet."

"I rest my case. In the future, I will expect you to inform me of all blind dates in writing."

Shannon finally hung up, and Henry was still standing there, clearly enjoying my discomfort. "So, I take it someone has a date tonight."

"This isn't funny."

"If it makes you feel any better, I thought *Castaway* was boring too."

"I can't believe she did this to me."

"Oh, cheer up. It's one date, right?"

"I wasn't kidding when I said I had nothing to wear."

"What's wrong with what you're wearing now?" he asked.

"These are work clothes. Everyone else will probably be wearing jeans."

"I'll give you the rest of the afternoon off. Go buy some jeans."

"With what? My good looks?"

"I'm sorry; I don't mean to be insensitive. When you have enough money, you never even think about the fact that not everyone else can go out and buy whatever they need."

"It's not your fault. You're used to always having plenty. I was too, until recently. Not on the same scale as you, of course. I never had to worry about buying the things I *needed*—things I *wanted* were another matter. But I think pretty much everyone is like that, except you millionaire types," I said.

Henry took a hundred-dollar bill out of his wallet. "Here, take this. You need it more than I do. Go buy some jeans."

"I can't."

"You can. Think of it as an advance on your paycheck."

"Unfortunately I need that paycheck for rent and food. I really do appreciate the gesture, but I'll have to find something in my closet that will work."

Henry was still holding out the money.

"Put that away! I'm resourceful. I'll make do." I smiled to reinforce my statement, even if on the inside I felt anything but optimistic.

* * *

"I really like your sweater, Rachel," Nathan said. "In fact, I think Shannon has one like that."

"Almost exactly like it," I said.

"I'd almost be willing to bet that was the same sweater," he said, and Shannon kicked him under the table. He winced but covered it with a smile. "But you know me—I'm not exactly an authority on fashion."

I'd dug out a semi-decent pair of jeans and gotten to Shannon and Nathan's house early to borrow the aforementioned sweater. In Nathan's defense, he didn't get home until right before we needed to leave, so he didn't know about the sweater exchange program.

That was pretty much how it was going so far. Jason seemed nice enough—and he did have gorgeous brown eyes—but my heart wasn't in it. I was trying to have a good time because I knew Shannon meant well, but she did have this unfortunate habit of springing things on me at the last minute when she knew I would have no choice but to go along.

I twirled a forkful of spaghetti and wondered for the tenth time why I'd ordered it when I was wearing a cream-colored sweater that wasn't even mine to ruin.

"So, Rachel, what do you do?" Jason asked.

Here we go.

It was a completely innocent question, but it was like a storm cloud rolling in directly over our table. I could tell that everyone except poor, clueless Jason was holding their breath.

"I'm a lawyer."

"Wow, I'm impressed. And you're so young. What kind of law do you practice?"

"I don't. I mean, I specialized in family law, but I haven't been able to find a job yet."

"I'm sorry. The market's pretty rough right now, huh?" he said.

"Afraid so." There was a short, awkward pause, but it didn't take me long to expertly move the conversation away from myself. "So, Jason, how long have you and Nathan known each other?"

He brightened. "We met in the mission field. Nathan was my favorite companion."

"We had some pretty good times, didn't we? Remember when we tried to cook that chicken?" Nathan asked.

Jason laughed. "And we started the curtains on fire?"

This seemed to catapult them into "Remember When" mode, which was fine with me since it meant I wouldn't have to volunteer any more information about myself. All I had to do was smile politely and laugh occasionally, hopefully at something that was meant to be funny.

I was sipping my water after the waiter had taken the dishes away, and that's when I saw him—an unusually tall man sitting by himself at a table in the corner. He'd picked the perfect seat for someone who didn't want to be seen. I was the only one at our table who could see him at this angle.

Henry.

I couldn't believe this. I knew he'd always carry a torch for Shannon, but I'd hoped that by now it was more of a weak candle flame instead of a raging bonfire. I thought that after all this time he'd finally let her go. But following your ex-girlfriend to a restaurant where she was eating with her *husband* didn't exactly say "I'm over you." Even more than being worried about Henry's sanity, I felt sorry for myself. Obviously any hints of flirting I thought I was detecting from him were strictly imaginary.

It was a good thing I wasn't expected to participate in this conversation because I was completely distracted watching Henry watch us. I only glanced at him every now and then; occasionally he was looking in my direction, but mostly his eyes were on Shannon. I watched his waiter come and go with the check, but Henry showed no signs of leaving.

I had to put a stop to this before anyone else saw him. I was pretty sure Nathan would initiate World War III if he got even an inkling of what was going on. I wiped my mouth with my napkin, which was a little silly since we weren't eating anymore. "Would you excuse me for a minute?" I said as sweetly as I could. I stalked off toward the bathroom, walking as near

Henry's table as I dared without drawing attention to him. I saw that he saw me throwing dagger looks in his direction, and I walked into the restaurant lobby, waiting for him to follow. When he appeared, he looked like a little boy who'd been caught cutting all the hair off his sister's Barbie collection.

"This is really bad, Henry. What are you doing here?"

"Eating dinner. They have an excellent risotto. You look nice."

"Don't change the subject. You've got to stop this obsession. Shannon is married now, quite happily, I might add, and any chance you might have had with her has passed. I've tiptoed around the subject because I was trying to spare your feelings, but obviously someone needs to be blunt with you. You can't spend the rest of your life spying on her! It isn't fair to her, and it certainly isn't fair to you. You deserve to have a life, too, and you'll never be happy unless you learn to leave the past in the past and move on." I paused in my tirade because if I didn't take a breath, I'd be on the floor from lack of oxygen momentarily. "Now that I think about it, how did you know where we were eating dinner? I didn't even know."

Henry appeared to have developed an unusual fascination with the carpet. "I followed you home from work, and then I followed you here."

"See, this is not normal behavior! I'm sure you feel humiliated that I caught you, but isn't it better that someone found out now while you still have a chance to get a life of your own instead of ten years from now when you realize all your best years were wasted on someone who can never love you back? Aren't you glad it was me who saw you instead of Shannon or, better yet, Nathan? He would call the police if he knew you were stalking his wife! It's not too late to walk away with your dignity, but you have to *walk away and stay away*."

Still he said nothing. A couple on their way out of the restaurant passed us, and the guy gave Henry a look of pity. I needed to get back to the table before Shannon wondered why

I was taking so long and came looking for me. That would be a disaster. "Well, what do you have to say for yourself?" I said, arms folded across my chest.

"I wasn't spying on Shannon."

"Then what are you doing here?" I hissed.

He finally raised his eyes to meet mine. "I was spying on you."

It took me much longer than it should have to figure out what he was saying. "For someone who was spying on me, you were staring at her quite a bit," I said finally.

He gave me a little smile. "You won't be able to see it from your angle, but from where I'm sitting, the plant on the shelf behind her makes her look like Medusa. It was hard to look away."

Now I felt silly. "I'm sorry I assumed the worst of you, but you have to admit, it does look pretty suspicious."

"Only to someone who has as little confidence in themselves as you do. I've never understood that."

"Understood what?"

"How someone so intelligent and capable and beautiful could be so unsure about her abilities."

My head was spinning. Of all the things I'd pictured happening tonight, this was the least likely. It didn't even make the long list of possibilities. I was absolutely speechless, which, for someone who likes to argue and always has an alternate point of view, is a big deal.

Henry moved a little closer, until I could smell his cologne. He didn't wear it to work; the only other time I'd smelled it was when we went on the date that I insisted wasn't a date but really was.

"I wish you could see yourself the way I see you. The idea that you never even considered I might be here for you makes no sense to me; that I've stunned you into silence shows how little regard you have for yourself."

The volume in the restaurant of all those different people talking seemed loud before, but now it all just faded into the background. It sounded like the generic hum of bees in a hive, each individual voice blending into one single voice until they were indistinguishable—every one except the one whispering in my ear.

"I have plenty of confidence," I said, but I was surprised that my voice didn't sound convincing.

"See? You sound like you're trying to talk yourself into it."

I couldn't help being a little angry with Henry. He was my boss, not my shrink, and he had no right to go poking around in my subconscious, even if he was right.

"I have to get back to dinner. It's only a matter of time before someone comes looking for me."

"And that's another thing. Why do you let Shannon tell you what to do?" he asked.

"She's my best friend! She wants me to be happy, so she's trying to help."

"I get that she thinks she's helping, but just because she sets you up doesn't mean you have to go if you don't want to. You have a mind of your own, and you should use it."

"And I get that you think *you're* helping, but with all due respect, you should mind your own business."

Instead of being mad, Henry just laughed. "I like you, Rachel. I didn't know how much until I heard you talking on the phone about your blind date." He lowered his gaze to the carpet in front of him. "I couldn't believe how jealous I was."

And now I was speechless again. I wasn't sure how much more of this up/down I could take before my emotional switchboard short-circuited.

He was still staring at the ground. "All I could think about was this random guy who would buy you dinner tonight and drop you off at your doorstep and . . ."

"And what?"

"How he might find the courage I didn't." When he finally looked at me again, his eyes were hopeful. When I didn't immediately protest, he started to lean in toward me. He was mere inches from my lips when my common sense took over.

"If you don't mind, I'd really rather not kiss you for the first time when I'm on a date with another guy."

"Of course," he said, but he did grab my hand and squeeze it. Since I'd been working with Henry, we'd had some laughs, but it always seemed like he was surprised to find something that amused him. This was the first time in a long time that he looked genuinely happy.

"You better get out of here before someone sees you. We'll talk about this at work tomorrow." I tried to give him my best scolding look, but I couldn't help the perma-grin that had taken up residence on my face.

"Yes, ma'am." He disappeared into the parking lot, and I went back to the table.

"Everything okay?" Shannon asked.

"Fine," I said, unconsciously smoothing the tablecloth.

"Shannon got worried and went to the bathroom to check on you, but you were nowhere in sight. We thought maybe you went out the window," Nathan said. He winced as Shannon kicked him again. Poor Nathan—he was going to be a bruised mess by the time he got home if he kept this up.

"I wasn't feeling well for a minute, but I'm better now," I said. Jason smiled at me, and I smiled back, only feeling a little guilty. After all, I wasn't the one who'd set this date up. Apparently, he and Nathan had been reminiscing the entire time I was gone. When they were still going strong forty minutes later, I'd given up on paying attention. All I could think about was Henry showing up here tonight because he was jealous. I didn't want to get my hopes up, but at the same time, I wanted to stand on the table and tell the world.

Shannon looked strangely thoughtful, and I wondered if she'd seen Henry and me talking. Or maybe she was thinking about how to tell Nathan about the new addition to their family. I'd tell her about Henry later . . . maybe. Right now it was pleasant to be the girl with a secret for a change.

Chapter Twenty
"The Very Thought of You"

THURSDAY WAS VALENTINE'S DAY, A holiday I normally despised. There were so many things to dislike about it: the fattening food which everyone assumed you needed to make yourself feel better about not having a significant other, the cheesy greeting cards, the pressure to be able to claim that someone loved you, the open ridicule when you were unable to produce said someone. I'd never had a boyfriend on Valentine's Day—not once.

My roommates in college always managed to score these massive bouquets that looked like they cost more than the GDP of any number of poor countries combined, and they would collectively squee over the phone to their little friends, who would squee back about the flowers *they* got. It was all rather annoying when you were the flowerless girl with nothing to squee about. At least this year when I got nothing, I'd be in a less public environment. With any luck, Henry would forget it was Valentine's Day, and the subject wouldn't even come up— unless Hannibal happened to get flowers and feel the need to gloat/meow about it.

When I arrived at work, there was a flat of raspberries on my desk. An entire *flat*. I squeed like no girl has ever squeed before.

Henry came out of his office at mock speed. "What is it? Is something wrong?"

"Nothing's wrong."

"Then why did you make a noise like someone gutted your best friend?"

I pointed to the raspberries. "I'm sorry. It was a happy noise."

He suddenly looked sheepish. "Happy Valentine's Day. I thought you would like those better than flowers, but when I got here, it suddenly seemed like a stupid idea."

"No, no, no. These are much better than flowers. But how did you know?"

"That day I first saw you in the café you were ogling that raspberry tart in the case. It seemed like a fair assumption."

I gave him a big hug and immediately felt silly and backed off. Wasn't it improper office protocol to hug your boss in the workplace? "This is the nicest Valentine's Day I've ever had."

"Wow, if you act this way over raspberries, I shudder to think what your reaction would be to jewelry. It's just a little thing."

"Not to me. And now I feel bad—I didn't get you anything."

"I don't need anything. But you could hug me again if you like."

So I did.

"How was dinner last night?" he asked, once the hugging had ceased.

"You should know," I said, sitting down in my chair. "And for the record, normal people don't show up on other people's blind dates and then proceed to lecture them on their life choices. That was very naughty."

Henry sat on the edge of my desk. "Sometimes things seem like a good idea until you're there and it's already happening. By then it's too late to change your mind. It turned out okay though."

"Yes, but it could have been a nightmare. Do you know what would have happened if Shannon or Nathan had seen you there?"

"I know, I know. I did mean well. My heart was in the right place—it was the execution of the plan that was off."

"I really did think you were there for Shannon."

"Rachel," he started.

For one awful moment, I thought he was going to admit that he had been. When he didn't say anything, I took that as proof of my worst fears confirmed. "You were, weren't you? You only said you were stalking me to make me feel better and keep me from making a scene!"

Henry smiled. "Most people wouldn't feel better if someone claimed to be stalking them."

"You know what I mean."

"I already told you, I couldn't sit at home all night and wonder just how good a time you were having. It was about you, not Shannon."

Was he really interested in me, or was this just about acquisition? I go out with someone else, and that spurs him into action because he's used to having anything he wants and nothing piques his interest more than the unattainable? I suppose I shouldn't be so cynical, but it was hard not to be suspicious when Henry was flirtatious one minute and all business the next.

That's what comes of dating your boss, Rachel.

I shook off the thought. I knew it wasn't healthy, which was why I'd promised myself that first night that it would only happen once. I wouldn't go out with Henry again, at least not while I was still his secretary. But I still hadn't found the job I really wanted, and I liked Henry too much to give up on the possibility of us being more. It might be difficult remaining professional, especially since last night he'd admitted to following me because he was jealous and almost kissed me.

And now he was looking at me so earnestly that it was a little dizzying. So I did what I always do when I'm uncomfortable—I changed the subject.

"I can't believe those raspberries . . . in February. They're unreal. I'm starting to think you're some kind of a magician."

He laughed, and the earlier tension between us dissipated. I was relieved and disappointed at the same time. "A fruit magician?"

"Yes. You probably have a tall, black top hat at home, and you pull mangos and other out-of-season produce out of it instead of rabbits."

"Well, I used to use rabbits, but they kept multiplying. Picture your mouse problem, only bigger. So I switched to fruit—much less messy."

I laughed, picturing Henry's mansion crawling with bunnies. "I got a cat to take care of the mice. What do you get to fix a rabbit infestation?"

"Trust me, you don't want to know."

This was fun—Henry playing along with me. "I do feel bad about not getting you anything." Then I had an idea. "But I will fix you dinner one of these days, as long as you don't mind paying for the ingredients and allowing me to invade your kitchen. Just name the date."

"What are you doing tonight?"

Hmmm. Cooking dinner for a guy on Valentine's Day seemed like boyfriend/girlfriend territory at least, but if he was okay with it, I guess I was. "I don't have any plans, but I'd have to leave early, or we'll be eating at eleven."

"Today is a slow day. All I had was your reading assignment, and I was going to send you out later for some new shirts, but that can wait."

"Are you sure? With you paying for the groceries and me being on the clock to make dinner, I feel more like the caterer."

"I don't mind if you don't."

What did Henry want? Just when I was starting to think there might be a possibility of more, he muddied the waters with the money issue. Did he want a girlfriend or a personal chef? I shook my head. *Stop making this harder than it is, and just give it a chance!*

"Of course I don't mind," I said. "What time would you like to eat?"

"Well, let's see, I have an online meeting at four . . . maybe six?"

"Six it is. Would you like me to get the shirts before I get the groceries?"

"The shirts can wait. The place won't be open until later anyway." He handed me a hundred dollars out of that wallet that seemed to grow money. "Will this be enough for groceries?"

I couldn't help laughing. "I could buy enough groceries with that to last me a month. But you're right, special dinners are a little pricier."

"Is this going to be a special dinner?"

"Well, I don't really cook at the Gary Danko level, but I think you'll be pleasantly surprised."

Henry rubbed his hands together like a little kid and grinned. "I can't wait. Go on, get out of here!"

I laughed. "I don't have to leave right this minute. I could stay here and do something for a while."

"Nope. Nothing is more important than the special dinner. Go!"

I was putting on my coat when Henry reappeared. "I almost forgot—this is for you. Happy payday!" he said, handing me a check.

"Who gets paid on a Thursday?" I wondered aloud. Then I looked at the amount. "This is how much secretaries make?!"

He laughed. "Well, you're not just a secretary—you're an executive secretary."

"What's the difference?"

"About ten dollars an hour."

I whooped. "Well, hooray for executives! Now I can pay the rent *and* eat! Just so you know, this is so worth any ridiculous chore you choose to inflict on me."

"I'll remind you of that when you're writing the talking points for my mother's book club. Oh, and there's one more thing. I need to go to Houston tomorrow to meet some people, so you can have the day off, with pay. Sleep late, eat raspberries, evict your cat. Enjoy yourself. You deserve it."

This day was getting better and better. If someone had told me yesterday that I'd be enjoying myself on this most hated of all holidays, I'd have laughed in their face.

But by the time I got to the bottom of the stairs, I was worried. What if I'd built the dinner up beyond his expectations? What if he was disappointed? It would have been better if I had downplayed it and he'd been blown away; now I had the hype to live up to before I'd even started. I couldn't stay stressed out for long. I was headed to Harmons with a hundred dollars. I was the luckiest girl in the world.

I made a quick stop at the bank to cash my check, then to my apartment for recipes. I didn't have a large cooking repertoire, but the handful of things I could do, I did really well. Hannibal seemed surprised to see me. He tentatively rubbed against my legs in the kitchen, which was weird. It was almost like he was glad to see me. Maybe he just wanted a second breakfast. When I moved too quickly toward the door, he stepped in front of me and almost ended up mashed underneath my pointy shoes. He hissed at me and ran off in the direction of the bedroom. That was more like the Hannibal I knew. Still, I felt bad for ruining his brief overture at friendship, so I left him some extra food to apologize.

And now, for the fun part.

Harmons was my favorite grocery store, but I hadn't been in there for months. When all you're buying is stuff like cup of soup and saltines, you might as well go to Walmart. I'd only been to Harmons once since my grocery budget had become nonexistent. It was too sad to be around all that gourmet food and not be able to buy anything. But today was different. I had a hundred dollars to cook the most fanciful dinner I could imagine. Walking through the sliding glass doors felt like coming home. Not home to my crummy apartment, but home to a place I actually liked and felt I belonged.

I decided the main course would be prime rib because it's easy to make it look like you really know what you're doing. Some people are afraid of meat, but not me. My mom taught me how to pick and cook the right cut of meat for any occasion. I headed straight to the butcher counter. The butcher laughed when I told him I was making prime rib and needed a piece of meat for someone who was used to being impressed. After that, I got garlic and some beef stock and some fresh thyme. I was so excited. This was going to be spectacular.

I had plenty of time to make dinner, so I didn't rush, taking my time picking potatoes and green beans in the extensive produce section and finding a nice crusty loaf of bread. I hadn't had this much fun shopping in a long time, and I was going to get to cook in Henry's spacious, if gloomy, kitchen. Whatever enjoyment Henry gained from this dinner, there's no way it could rival the fun I was going to have making it. So I was back where I started—I still owed him.

While I was carefully placing my bags of groceries in the trunk, I got a text.

How's dinner coming? :) :) :)

I smiled at the enthusiasm. *It's only ten thirty! You have to be patient!* I answered.

I hoped I wasn't going to disappoint him.

I had one more stop to make before going to Henry's. I've heard famous chefs say you should never cook with a wine you wouldn't want to drink. Since I don't partake, I have no idea which ones are more drinkable than others. I'd heard that cooking wine was strictly for the birds, which meant Harmons was out. So I went to the liquor store and got a bottle of red wine to cook the prime rib in.

When I got to Henry's house, Waldorf was there to open the gate for me. We exchanged basic pleasantries before I drove through, and if he thought I was spending an awful lot of time here for someone who was supposed to be the secretary, he kept his observations to himself. I let myself in the front door, slipped off my shoes, and turned on some lights to try to brighten the place up a bit. I thought I might put some music on, but Henry's record player was mystifying.

I'd had a Fisher Price record player when I was a little girl, and this machine seemed to operate on the same basic theory—but that was where the resemblance ended. There were so many buttons and switches that it hardly seemed to be the same species. In the end, I decided not to risk it. Henry seemed pretty understanding. There were lots of things he could forgive me for, but breaking his fancy record player probably wasn't one of them.

My phone beeped again with another text message, but this time it was Shannon. *Are you out running errands for your evil overlord? Can I call you?*

She must be on her way to work. *Go ahead. I'm not in the office right now,* I texted back. My phone rang almost immediately.

"Hey," she said. "What are you up to? It's a little early to be fetching cookies, isn't it?"

"Not on cookie duty at the moment."

"Picking up lunch?"

"Nope."

"I'm intrigued. What weird errand are you off on today?"

"Well, I was supposed to be picking up new shirts," I started. Shannon snorted.

"But you'll never believe where I am at this moment."

"Did your destination require air travel?"

"Not this time."

"Uhhhh, Henry decided he wanted a zebra, and you're at the zoo trying to negotiate a price?"

I laughed. "That *is* the most bizarre guess you could have come up with."

"Yeah, but is it really more bizarre than colored paper clips?"

"I'm going to have to go with yes."

"I give up. Where are you?"

"I'm in Henry's kitchen, cooking his dinner."

"That is most definitely outside your job description. He can't force you to cook his dinner, you know."

"He didn't force me. I offered." I started looking through the drawers, trying to figure out where everything was.

"I'm confused. Was it a slow day at the office, or what?" Before I could answer, she gasped. "You're making prime rib, aren't you?"

I paused. "Maybe."

"You're making him prime rib on *Valentine's Day*! You're trying to ensnare him! Remember how we used to joke that no man could eat your prime rib and not make you an offer of marriage on the spot?"

"I'm not trying to ensnare him. I feel kinda sorry for him."

"You feel sorry for the man who has made a mockery of your professional life and sends you on demeaning errands that any sixteen-year-old with a license could do."

"Thanks a lot!"

"That came out badly, but you know what I meant. Why do you feel sorry for him?"

I busied myself peeling cloves of garlic. "Nobody ever takes care of him. After he went to so much trouble the other night, I wanted to do something nice for him."

"This is getting serious, isn't it? If you just felt a little sorry for him, you'd be making him a lasagna or something, but you're cooking the dinner no man can refuse. You like him."

"I do like him. I mean, he does tend to get on my nerves on a daily basis, but that's mostly in a workplace setting. You can't really not like him."

"So you're actually in The Sanctuary?"

"Yes, and I can't believe you never told me about it." I finally found the garbage can for the garlic skins and noticed with amusement that it was full of takeout containers.

"There wasn't much to tell. He never took me there."

My mouth dropped open. Okay, that was odd. I would have thought that if Henry was trying to lure Shannon away from Nathan, this house would have been a major weapon in his arsenal. I can't imagine he wouldn't have wanted to take every opportunity to show off, and it didn't get much showier than this.

"Rachel?"

"Sorry, my phone cut out for a minute there," I lied. "Maybe he never brought you here because it's gloomy, and he was afraid it would turn you off." *Yes, good. That sounds much better than saying it's a massive estate and it could have been yours if you played your cards right.*

"Really? So it's disappointing?"

"I . . . wouldn't say that. But it's not winning any awards for atmosphere." I didn't want to downplay it too much in case under some crazy set of circumstances Henry and I ended up together and we invited Shannon and Nathan to a dinner party. I had to bite my lip to keep from laughing at the very thought of the four of us sitting down at a table together. I'd have to make something harmless like soup that didn't require the use of knives.

"Who knows? Maybe he'll let you fix it up for him."

"I highly doubt that."

"You never know. You could be the lady of the manor someday."

"I'm pretty sure the closest I'll get to the manor is making dinner for the lord. What's going on with you? Are you excited about tomorrow?"

"What's tomorrow?"

I found a colander to wash the green beans. "You're telling your husband that he's going to be a father, remember?"

"Right, of course."

"Unless you want to wait until the baby is old enough to tell him."

"Ha ha. You're the funniest. I don't think I'd be able to put it off much longer anyway. Nathan mentioned that this was the longest he'd ever seen me go without running. So unless I tell him that I've given it up for Lent, I think it's only a matter of time before he figures it out."

"Oh, just *tell him already*! I can't believe you've waited *this* long. Don't you think he's going to find it odd when the baby is born a month early?"

"I'll say I thought it was the flu and it took me a while to figure out I was pregnant."

"I still don't understand why you didn't tell him in the first place."

"I told you, there was no reason getting his hopes up if I couldn't stay pregnant."

"I guess it doesn't really matter. Tomorrow he'll know, and you can stop keeping it a secret and start enjoying it. When are you going to tell me, by the way? I need to practice my surprised face."

"I'll be sure to give you plenty of notice."

Chapter Twenty-One
"These Foolish Things"

At five o'clock, I was starting to head into the final stretch of the cooking when I realized that I had Henry's car and he was basically stranded. I was annoyed with myself for not having realized this sooner. It really wasn't a good time to leave the food and go fetch him, but I couldn't exactly tell him to catch a bus either. I sent him a text.

Hey, stranger. It's almost time for dinner. Need a ride?

The message he sent me back solved one problem and created another. *Nope, Waldorf is going to drop me off.*

Uh, should we be feeding Waldorf? I replied.

I offered, but he wouldn't hear of it. He seems to be under the impression that he'd be interrupting something important.

A lump formed in my throat. That sounded promising and nerve-wracking at the same time. *Well, tell him I said he's welcome. There's plenty of grub.* As I waited for his reply, I contemplated the amusing picture of the three of us eating by candlelight this very romantic dinner I'd cooked.

There's no changing his mind. I told him I'd bring him some leftovers tomorrow.

I was relieved. Well, I was pretty sure I was relieved. I didn't know what was going to happen between Henry and me. I wasn't even sure what I hoped would happen, but I was almost certain that having Waldorf as a third-party would kill whatever potential romance might be in the air. Of course, I wasn't expecting anything—which was why I was touching up my lipstick in one of the many bathrooms I was sure I would find if I searched the house.

I lit the candles and turned out the lights, admiring the glow they cast in the cavernous room.

But suddenly I panicked. The whole thing looked like a big setup, and I realized I'd gotten carried away in the moment. I still had no idea whether Henry had any real interest in me, and this looked like a scene from a cheesy movie. Shannon was right; I should have gone with something neutral, like lasagna. I heard the front door open and close. This was a disaster. I began blowing out candles as fast as I could. It was too late to do anything about the menu, but I could at least get rid of the mood lighting.

"Rachel?" I heard Henry's voice getting closer. "Why is it so dark in here? And why do I smell smoke?"

I flipped on the main light and blinked as my eyes tried to adjust. Even the brightest light in Henry's house was dim, but after being in the dark with only the candles it seemed blinding. "Surprise!" I said. *Right—because this is a birthday party for a five-year-old.*

"As in surprise, you burned dinner, and we're going out?"

I laughed, but it sounded nervous and awkward. "Dinner is fine. I had the candles lit, but . . ."

"But what?"

"They all . . . blew out."

He smiled, and I knew he had probably worked out my little panic attack. But he didn't seem bothered by it at all. "I know it's a bit drafty in here, but freak windstorms have never been a problem before."

I threw my hands up in the air. "I know, it was really weird. I think it happened when you opened the door. Unless this place is haunted . . ." *Let it go, you sound like a basket case.*

He pointed to the half-empty bottle of wine on the counter and gave me a goofy grin. "Rough day?"

"That was strictly for cooking purposes!"

"Sure it was."

Wow, this kept getting better and better. If dinner went like this, I might as well leave now.

"How about I light the candles again, and you can take care of whatever you need to in the kitchen?" Henry suggested.

"That sounds like a great idea." I was grateful he wasn't going to tease me about the science behind my unexplained breeze/resident ghost theory and the suspicious half-empty wine bottle. I stood by the stove and pretended to be stirring something while telling myself that if I was going to panic I should have done it earlier without an audience.

"Should I put a record on?" he asked.

"Yeah, I tried to figure it out earlier, but it's slightly more advanced than my old Fisher Price player."

"I used to have one of those! The base was white and the arm was yellow and the records were—"

"—red," I finished. "That's the same one I had. I loved that record player. I played it to death. I'm not sure what happened to it."

"Me too. It was my favorite toy as a kid. You won't believe the sound on this one." He took a record out of a sleeve and put it on. The piano sounded somehow mellow and sharp at the same time.

"That's amazing. Definitely a step up from the Fisher Price model."

He laughed. "It's the one thing in this house I couldn't live without."

"The one thing in my apartment I can't live without is the cat, but don't tell anyone." When he laughed again, I was pleased.

"I knew it! I knew you secretly loved the cat!"

"I don't *love* the cat, but he's starting to grow on me. It's nice to have someone waiting for you when you get home. But if you ever tell anyone I said I was fond of Hannibal, I'll call you a liar. You've seen my place, from the outside anyway, and the inside isn't much different. I could leave there tomorrow, and I wouldn't miss any of it."

"There must be something."

"I have a few personal knickknacks; nothing that's worth anything to anyone but me."

"The difference is I have anything you could buy with money, but none of it's personal."

The timer dinged on the oven, interrupting the rather interesting turn the conversation had taken. "Are you ready to eat?" I asked.

"You have no idea. This has been the longest day ever. All I could do was think about dinner. My house has never smelled so good."

"I thought it smelled like smoke," I teased.

"Only for a minute. Can I help with anything?"

"You go sit down. I want you to be surprised. I guess I should have asked you if there was anything you didn't like before I planned the menu."

"I've never been a picky eater. Unless it's tofu or something weird like that, I'm sure it'll be delicious."

I gave him my best disappointed look. "You don't like tofu?"

He looked horrified and embarrassed at the same time. "Uh, I was totally kidding. To be honest, I've never given it a fair chance. But anything that smells this good has to be good, right?"

"We should have offered the prayer before I told you what you were eating. You might not be able to summon the necessary gratitude now."

"No, I'm ready to try something new. I'm excited. Bring on the tofu!" he declared.

I smiled. I knew it was wicked, but messing with him was so much fun. "You go sit down, and I'll get the food."

I already had the bread on the table, and I dished up everything else on two plates—prime rib and mashed potatoes with thyme gravy from the pan drippings and steamed green beans. I had to admit I was pretty impressed with myself. I took a deep breath and carried the plates to the table.

Henry groaned when I set the plate in front of him. "That's not tofu."

"I know. I wanted to see if you'd be a good sport about it."

"You are incredibly mean, but I'm so relieved that I'm not going to judge you." He stuck one finger in the gravy and tasted it. "Okay, which restaurant did this come from?"

"Everything on this table was made by me. Well, not the bread, but everything else!"

"I don't believe it. Do I need to go in the kitchen and search for takeout containers?"

"That doesn't show much faith in me. Besides, how would you be able to prove they were *my* takeout containers and not yours?" I dipped a green bean in the gravy and ate it.

"Spoken like a true lawyer."

I punched him in the arm, and he yowled.

"Watch out, that's the arm I need to eat with!" He cut a bite of the meat and tasted it. "This is . . . incredible," he said, chewing. "Your talents are wasted on Ramen noodles. Where did you learn to cook like this?"

"My mom taught me to cook when I was growing up. We only ate maybe five meals on a regular basis, but I can make them *really* well." After trying the meat, I didn't feel bad about bragging. It really was perfect.

"You ate prime rib on a regular basis? Is your dad a lawyer too?"

"My dad's a technical writer. We only had prime rib for Christmas dinner."

"You could open a restaurant."

"A restaurant that specializes in prime rib?"

"Well, that and the other four things you can cook." He took a piece of the bread and dipped it in the gravy. "You have really outdone yourself."

"I'm beginning to wonder what you were expecting."

"Uh, not this."

My mouth dropped open. "You thought my dinner was going to be crap, didn't you?"

"Of course I didn't. But sometimes very intelligent people don't have much in the way of . . . practical skills. They're too busy using their brains to tap into their creative sides."

"Think of me as a Renaissance woman."

"Oh, you are definitely the exception to the rule." He chewed another bite for a minute and started laughing.

"What? Why are you laughing?"

"I was thinking that there's no way I'm sharing this with Syd. I thought I'd be taking him a plate of mac and cheese tomorrow."

I wanted to join him with the laughing, but I couldn't decide if he was kidding or not. "Henry, you gave me a hundred dollars. Did you really expect me to serve you something that came from a box?"

"I'm mostly joking. But honestly, you're a surprising girl."

I glared at him. I wasn't mad—not really. But if he thought macaroni and cheese was the best I could do, he deserved to think I was.

"Surprising in a good way! This tastes like you went to Cordon Bleu instead of Stanford."

I grinned wryly. "I'm sure if I look hard enough, there's a compliment in there somewhere."

"And I'm sure you've been amazing all along, but I was too dense to see it. Every time I think I'm starting to figure you out, you change the game entirely."

I felt my face getting hot. *Didn't have to look too hard to find the compliment in that one, did you?* It was a very nice thing for him to say, but I tried not to read too much into it. "Glad to know I'm keeping you on your toes. Oh, and you should probably save room for dessert."

"You're trying to kill me, aren't you?"

I laughed. "You'll have to wait and see."

* * *

He ate every bite on the plate and asked for more. Maybe he was being polite, but I couldn't believe how happy that made me.

"I know you said to save room, but I'm going to have to wait for a bit before dessert if you don't mind."

"I don't mind at all. I can do the dishes while you recover from dinner."

"I'm sorry, no."

"I hope you don't think I plan on leaving your spotless kitchen in this state."

Henry stood up and took my plate. "My kitchen is incredibly happy right now. That is what a kitchen should look like, and mine never gets used. I may leave it like that for a week, just for the novelty."

"Absolutely not. It'll only take a minute."

"You cooked dinner—I should do the dishes," he argued.

"I made the mess—I should do the dishes."

"How about if I agree to let you help me with the dishes?"

I sighed. "I suppose that's the best offer I'm going to get. But I still think you should sit for a minute and let your food digest."

Henry started jumping up and down.

"Stop it! What are you doing? You're going to be sick!" I warned.

He kept jumping. "When I was a kid and I was too full but I still wanted to eat more, I was convinced that if I jumped around for a minute, the food would settle, and there would be more room."

I was laughing hard by now. "Only a kid could come up with logic like that."

He stopped and followed me into the kitchen. "I don't know. I think it's working. I feel better already."

"Really?"

"No, I feel terrible. I think that trick only works when you're eight."

Henry ran hot water into the sink and added some soap. The container looked brand new.

"I have the sneaking suspicion that these dishes have never been used before."

"You're not far wrong. I don't cook anything but toast, and since I'm the only one who lives here . . ."

I clicked my tongue disapprovingly. "Poor dishes—how neglected they must feel."

"I did have my mother over for Christmas dinner last year."

"And you cooked?"

"Not exactly." Henry put the rest of the prime rib on a plate and started scraping the gravy onto it with a spatula. He was biting the corner of his lip, concentrating so hard. I couldn't help smiling.

"Are you going to lick the pan?" I asked.

"Believe me, I'm not wasting one bit of this gravy. It's a masterpiece."

"So, did your mother cook Christmas dinner?"

He smiled. "Her cooking abilities are slightly less than mine, if that's possible. I had it catered, but we did use the dishes." He paused for a minute. "You know, if you could somehow figure out a way to incorporate food into these lawyer interviews of yours, you'd be hired instantly." He finally gave up on the gravy and put the pan in the sink to soak.

"That's incredibly sexist of you."

"I didn't mean it the way you're thinking. When you're cooking, you exude this level of confidence that I've never seen from you before. You keep going to these interviews, and every one that doesn't call you, your confidence falls a little further. I'm telling you, these law firms would be fighting over you, but because you feel defeated, you project defeat."

I didn't say anything. Henry had tried to tell me this before, but I wasn't ready to hear it then. I was ready now. In fact, I wondered if I should be taking notes.

"A big part of *being* successful is *acting* successful. No one wants to hire a lawyer who isn't convinced of their own abilities. Because if you can't convince them, how are you going to hook a client or sell a jury?" His eyes were bright and passionate, and he seemed so sure of himself.

"You would have made a better lawyer than me," I said.

"Nah, I hate arguing with people. And that's what I'm talking about right there. You need to believe that you're an excellent lawyer, or no one else will. Say it."

"Say what?"

"Say, 'I'm the best dang lawyer in Salt Lake City.'"

I laughed. "I'm not going to say that!"

"Why not?"

"For one thing, it isn't true, and it sounds ridiculous. I don't believe in that positive affirmation junk. You can't talk yourself into being good at something—either you are or you're not."

"I agree that you can't be a good lawyer if you don't have the skills to back it up, but I also believe that if you can't put on a good show, no one will ever give you the chance to prove if you've got it or you don't."

I didn't say anything. He was probably right. I mean, I'm guessing he didn't get to where he was by being wrong very often.

"You've got a job interview tomorrow, right?"

I nodded.

"Well, leave your insecurities at the door, and go in there like you own the job already."

"That's not who I am."

"Test it out once, for me. What have you got to lose? You went to Stanford. You're hot stuff. They'd be lucky to have you."

"I keep telling myself that."

"Well, why don't you try telling them for a change? You might be surprised."

By the time the dishes were finished, the record had stopped in the other room.

"You go fix the music," I told him. "I'll get dessert."

"Have I told you lately that you're too good to me?"

I started dishing up the strawberry pavlova—a light and fluffy, meringue-y sort of dessert with a crispy crust—perfect for when you've had a heavy dinner and want a bit of something sweet at the end. I could hear the music drifting in from the other room. I could tell it was Billie Holiday. I'd known nothing about jazz music before I met Henry, but she had a very distinctive voice. I licked a bit of sticky meringue from the serving spoon and left it in the sink.

When I came into the living room, I couldn't immediately see Henry, which was something when you considered his height. Anyone that tall couldn't exactly blend into his surroundings. There was one chair with a high back that faced into the room and away from the entrance. I guessed that was where I would find him. I could see him in here in his chair (I had decided that chair must be his favorite simply because of the size), listening to records late into the night and staring out the large windows.

I wasn't being intentionally quiet, but I must have been naturally stealthier without my shoes on because I got all the way to the chair without being detected. I peeked around the corner, and there was Henry, his head turned slightly to one side and his eyes closed. I hadn't been gone that long—could he actually be asleep? I quietly set the dessert plates on a little table and sat on the corner of the couch closest to his chair. If he wasn't sleeping, he was a very good actor.

I'd never had such a perfect opportunity to study Henry, and I decided, against my better judgment to take advantage of it. If you had asked me if he was someone who dealt with a lot of stress on a daily basis, I would have said no, but now that I could see his face at rest, I knew I must have been mistaken. It was remarkably unlined, much less so than when he was awake. I think I preferred the animated Henry with the crinkles around his mouth and eyes. They gave him character.

The slow song ended, and the next began with a trumpet/sax intro. A cheerful piano picked it up from there. This seemed to rouse him from his semi-napping state, and when he opened his eyes, I was brazenly staring at him.

"Sorry," I said, looking away and feeling self-conscious.

"I'm the one who should be sorry. I didn't sleep very well last night. I closed my eyes for a second after that delicious meal and drifted away for a minute."

"It's okay. I should go and let you sleep." Billie had begun singing about the foolish things that reminded her of someone.

"No, don't go yet. You went to all this trouble, and I don't want to ruin the evening," his lips protested, but his eyes still looked sleepy.

I left my perch on the couch and crouched down on the balls of my feet next to the chair, but Henry was so tall that I'd misjudged the distance this would put between us. I'd meant to come down to his level but ended up so far away that I felt silly now. "I don't mind. Most people are offended when they put someone to sleep, but I take it as a testament to my abilities." I paused to listen to the music for a moment. "Although I can't take credit for the beautiful serenade."

"I love this song," Henry said.

"Why do you like Billie Holiday so much?"

"My grandfather used to play her records all the time. He used to tell me that there were no real stars anymore—only famous people. With this faraway look in his eyes, he'd say that she had 'star quality.'"

"That's sweet. I never knew anyone who liked jazz music before, but listening to this, I can understand why you're entranced."

"Actually, the song isn't why I'm entranced." Henry sat up in his chair and started to slowly lean down toward where I was stationed in my ridiculous position, practically on the floor.

At this point I'd completely forgotten about dessert. I was lucky I even remembered where I was. Part of me was tempted to tell him it wasn't a good idea to kiss me when he was still half asleep and might not ever remember it in the morning. But that was probably more my sudden terror at the idea of kissing my boss. Besides, he looked pretty awake now.

This thing with Henry was dangerous and improbable and questionable, but there would come a time that I would have to be all in if I really wanted to see if it could go anywhere. After his admission in the park, I was pretty sure that this might be my last chance. I didn't know his history with relationships besides Shannon, other than the small tidbits he'd given me, but I couldn't see him repeatedly putting himself out there without some hint of reciprocation. I swallowed hard. Other than my awkward position next to the chair and the way the muscles in my thighs were protesting, I couldn't have engineered a more perfect moment if I tried. Maybe I'd take Shannon up on her offer to go running next time. I shook myself back to the present. Here goes nothing; time to reciprocate.

I closed my eyes just as Henry's lips pressed lightly against mine.

Once. For a millisecond.

That was it.

He stood up quickly, and I was so surprised I almost fell backward onto the floor.

"It's getting really late. I should take you home."

I glanced at the huge clock on the wall that could probably be seen from space. "It's five after nine," I said, but he was already halfway out of the room and headed toward his keys with the speed and accuracy of a stealth missile. And there was me, still holding on to the arm of the chair for security like it was the last Twinkie in the world, trying to make sense of what just happened. My brain told my legs that if they didn't want to walk home, they'd better stand up and follow Henry to the car. So I did.

I would have given anything for my own transportation at that moment. Henry tried to fill the weird silence in the car with lots of words, but I wasn't up for meaningless chitchat. I think I tuned out when I realized he was talking about how much snow we'd gotten this year in comparison to last. The whole situation was humiliating. I had my car door open before he'd even come to a complete stop in front of my apartment. "Good night," I said as I was already halfway out of the car.

"Rachel!" he called after me.

I stopped reluctantly and turned around. Now what? Was he going to quote me the rain totals in inches?

"Thank you for dinner. It was amazing. And I'm sorry."

"I'm sorry too," I said, immediately wishing I hadn't said it. What did I have to be sorry for? I guess I was sorry I finally had the proof that Henry and I weren't compatible. I could feel the tears burning behind my eyes, so I turned and ran toward the building. There was no way I was going to cry in front of him. Let him think I was made of stone if he wanted to; that was better than him thinking he had the power to hurt me.

When I got upstairs and looked out my small window, his car was still parked in front of the building. Tears dripped from my chin onto the windowsill, and I vowed that even if he came up here, I wouldn't answer the door. I left the window and started pacing around the tiny room. He could knock until his knuckles bled if he wanted, but I was done for the night. I couldn't believe I was being so silly. I never should have let myself get caught up in the atmosphere of romance, and whose fault was that? Mine. I could have kept it simple, but no! Stupid romantic dinner! Stupid light and fluffy romantic dessert! What was I thinking, making everything into some big proposition? Work was going to be impossible now. What had I told myself time and time again? Never date your boss.

But he was the one who kissed you, remember?

I couldn't help it. I had to know if he was still out there. I looked through the shades, and his car was still down there. Well, if he wanted to fire me, I wouldn't let him do it through my paper-thin door. He was going to have to wait until Monday and say the words to my puffy, red face. I went into my tiny room, kicked my shoes in the general direction of my hole-in-the-wall closet, and fell into the bed that took up 80 percent of the space. I had the sudden mental picture of the bed dropping upon impact, crashing through the floor and falling into the apartment below me. Despite the fact that I was still crying, I couldn't help the sputter of laughter. Maybe the guy in that apartment wouldn't throw me out after he kissed me. *He* kissed *me*—it's not like I forced myself on him or anything.

After a few minutes of raging, I wanted to go back to the window and see if Henry was still out there. The curiosity was killing me. But instead, I lay in my bed and tried not to imagine tiny mouse feet tapping on the floors, scurrying through the walls. I missed Mousey and his luminous eyes. Instead, I thought about Henry and that kiss and where it all could have gone wrong. I thought about his ashen face as he pulled away and how he almost looked haunted, like he'd seen a ghost.

I sat straight up in bed. *Haunted.* I was willing to bet that Henry had seen a ghost. And I was willing to bet my law degree that I knew who that ghost was. I needed to talk to the ghost in question ASAP, but it was too late to call her tonight. Nathan would be suspicious, but first thing tomorrow. I knew she was pregnant and I should let her sleep in, but this was an emergency. Life or death. Well, life or death of this fledgling relationship anyway.

I lay back down and wondered if I was ever going to fall asleep. I was a really good sleeper; hardly anything ever kept me awake. I was good at compartmentalizing. Hannibal must have sensed my somber mood and taken it to mean that I was vulnerable. He jumped up on the bed and walked over until his face was just inches from mine. If ever there was a good opportunity to take out the human, this was it.

"Go on, cat. Do your worst," I said. I held my breath and waited for him to claw me beyond recognition. On the upside, I couldn't be expected to go to work for weeks if I was in the hospital recovering from numerous skin grafts, my face wrapped like a mummy. But on the downside, I had no health insurance and couldn't afford to pay for the skin grafts. I'd probably end up one of those old cat ladies who never left the apartment, hiding my scarred face away in the shadows.

Hannibal nudged my cheek with his nose and snuggled up in the crook of my arm. Talk about a day for surprises. This was infinitely stranger than what happened with Henry earlier. If I didn't know better, I'd say the cat who despised me was being . . . protective. He was purring, for heaven's sake! I relaxed a little and thought a bit smugly that I wouldn't want to be Henry if and when he ever met Hannibal. I didn't know if he was still out there on the street, but I couldn't answer the door now even if I wanted. Hannibal had planted himself in a way that made it impossible for me to move.

Good kitty.

Chapter Twenty-Two
"Good Morning Heartache"

I DECIDED THAT HENRY WAS right about one thing—I should definitely sleep late. I still hadn't decided whether it was good or bad that I didn't have to go to work. I was relieved that I didn't have to see Henry for a few days, but on the other hand, it might have been better not to have so much time to build the tension. At least I knew he had the trip planned before we had dinner. If he'd texted me this morning and told me he was suddenly going out of town, I'd have known we were doomed.

Hannibal had disappeared, and I wondered if I'd dreamed the whole thing. That did seem more probable than my usually feral cat suddenly deciding to make friends with me. Guess I'd just have to wait until I saw what kind of mood he was in this morning. The fact that I had the same plan of action for the cat and Henry was pretty amusing.

I had a piece of toast (whole wheat, which I could now afford thanks to payday) with apricot jam, luxury of luxuries. It was a generic brand, but still. At least with the day off it would be easier to catch Shannon alone to grill her about Henry. I didn't know what time she worked and her ultrasound was scheduled sometime today, but it would be easier to ask her in person. I dialed her cell phone.

"Morning, Miss Executive Secretary," she said, yawning.

"Ah, I see someone else slept late this morning."

"What are you doing sleeping late? Shouldn't you be out buying multicolored Post-it notes or scheduling Henry's dentist appointment?"

"He had to go out of town, so I got the day off."

"Nice. So, how was dinner? Did the Rachel Pearce Prime Rib seal the deal?"

"I have to ask you something."

"Shoot."

I swallowed my bite of toast. "Do you want to go get a drink or something?"

"Is that the question?"

"No, but I thought maybe we could meet somewhere and have a hot chocolate and chat."

"I really wish I could, but I've got to get ready and go to my ultrasound. As long as everything's okay, I have to work after that."

Crap. I knew I should have started bugging her at the crack of dawn.

"This must be some question. Why can't you ask me on the phone?"

"It's kind of personal."

There was a long pause. "This is about Henry, isn't it?"

At least she wouldn't be completely blindsided when I asked her. I wished there was a more sensitive way to handle this, but I couldn't wait until tomorrow. Nathan would be home all day. "Did you and Henry ever kiss?" I blurted. I knew every detail of every guy Shannon had ever dated in high school, but since I went away to school, I only got the basics, and she was particularly evasive about Henry. I think I understood why now; she felt guilty.

"Wow, you weren't kidding."

"I know, it's none of my business, and I wouldn't ask unless it was vital that I know the answer," I rambled.

There was dead air on the phone for long enough that I almost asked if she was still there. "It was a mistake," she said finally.

"So you did kiss him?"

"Yes, but only once. And it was a mistake," she repeated.

I knew it. "Did you tell him that?"

"Not in so many words." I could tell from her tone that she still felt guilty about it. So many things were clicking for me right now—the reason it was so hard for Henry to let her go, Shannon being so upset when he came to the wedding—his attachment maybe hadn't been as one-sided as I thought.

"You did, didn't you?"

"I told him I loved Nathan, and it could never happen again."

"Right. So, how was it?"

"Rachel! We're not discussing this!"

"Humor me, it's important."

She hesitated. "You do realize this is a completely inappropriate question. If we weren't best friends and I didn't want Henry to find a way to be happy, preferably with you, I would hang up the phone and never speak to you again?"

"Yes."

"Henry is a really good kisser. And if you ever breathe a word of this to Nathan, I'll cut your tongue out and feed it to Hannibal."

"I won't say a word. Thanks for telling me." I was going to have to think about this in greater detail later, but right now I had an idea. "What are you doing tomorrow?"

"Nothing much. Probably just hanging out with the hubs."

"Celebrating your big news."

"Sure. Why?"

"Aunt Flora's in a nursing home now, and she's taken a turn for the worse."

"Aunt Flora's still *alive*?"

"I know. I haven't seen her in years. Anyway, I promised my mother I'd stop by and say hello. Would you go with me?"

"I don't know . . ." she hedged.

"Come on, do it for me. I really don't want to go by myself."

"I hate nursing homes. They give me the creeps."

"I'm not in love with them either, but wouldn't it be fun to see her again, for old times' sake?"

"Not really."

"I promise I'll never tell Nathan about you kissing Henry if you go with me tomorrow."

"Rachel Marie Pearce, that's blackmail."

"Think of it as an incentive."

"You drive a hard bargain, Counselor. What time should I pick you up?"

"Maybe fourish? I figure by the time we get there that will give us fifteen minutes at the most to visit before they bring her dinner in, at which point we say our good-byes and slip out."

"I suppose our friendship is worth fifteen minutes."

"Send me a message when you're on your way."

"Will do. And Rachel?"

"Yeah?"

"I wouldn't change my life with Nathan for anything, but I still have regrets about how things ended with Henry. Don't hurt him if you can help it. I think he's been messed up enough as it is."

"Got it."

I hung up and tried to process this new information. I—knew—it. I—knew—it! The reason Henry couldn't follow through with kissing me was because the last time he kissed someone he cared about, Shannon rejected him. Now he was afraid to put himself out there again. I wasn't saying he felt about me the way he did about Shannon, but I couldn't see him kissing me for the heck of it either. He didn't seem like that kind of guy. So now I needed to figure out if I really wanted to pursue this relationship.

It didn't take me long to decide. When I saw Henry again, I was going to put it all on the line, bet big and let the chips fall where they may. I was going to be the bravest I'd ever been. I'd tell Henry what a great guy he was and how anyone would be lucky to have him, and then he'd see that he wasn't the problem; he'd only been unfortunate enough to fall for a girl who couldn't love him back.

Of course, there was always the possibility that this had nothing to do with Henry's scarred ego and it had only taken him two seconds to decide that I was a bad kisser, and then all this speculation was pointless. I guess I'd find out soon enough.

I got out of bed and headed for the shower. It was almost time to see if Henry was right about confidence being the key to the job of my dreams.

* * *

"You ready for this?" I asked Shannon. We were standing outside a door marked *Flora S.* with a cheerfully colored red flower underneath the name. Compared to this, the job interview earlier had been cake. I sold myself until I was blue in the face, even if I didn't feel confident. Henry would have been proud.

Shannon was playing with the zipper on her coat. "Yup. We're doing a good thing, right?"

"Right."

"So let's get it over with."

The nurse who brought us to the room warned us that Flora probably wouldn't recognize us. She had dementia, which was sort of a precursor to Alzheimer's, as I understood it. She had good days and bad, the nurse informed us, but she loved to have visitors, even if she didn't always know who they were. I suppose it was comforting that she'd be happy to see us even if she didn't know who "us" was.

I opened the door a crack. She was sitting in a chair by the window and hadn't seen me yet. It was tempting to sneak away and tell my mother I'd seen her, which was true in the strictest sense. I had *seen* her, even if we hadn't spoken, and from the way it sounded, she wouldn't remember if she'd talked to me or not.

Don't be mean. Would you really use a poor old lady's faulty memory to get away with it?

I pushed through the door before I could change my mind. "Aunt Flora?" I called softly, not wanting to startle her.

She turned, and a huge smile lit up her face. "Sadie!" she said.

Sadie is my mom's name, so at least she was close. "How are you?" I asked, not bothering to correct her. Might as well let her think she was talking to someone she knew.

"Oh, I can't complain too much. I wish I was still in my own house, but they treat me really good here."

"I'm so glad to hear it."

"And who's this pretty girl you brought with you?"

"This is my friend, Shannon," I said.

She held out her hand for Shannon to shake, and I could see that some well-meaning person had given her glitter nails.

"Hello, Flora, it's nice to meet you," Shannon said. "Good heavens, your nails look prettier than mine."

"Isn't that nice? A little slip of a girl came in here yesterday and painted them for me. Or was it the day before? It doesn't matter. She was a very sweet girl."

This wasn't as bad as I thought it would be, even if she did think I was my mother. "It's a bit chilly, but the sun's shining. Would you like to go outside for a minute?" I asked.

"If you don't mind pushing me in the chair, that would be lovely. I can't walk very far on my own anymore."

"That would be fine."

She stood up and walked to the chair on her own, and I could see that, physically, she wasn't in such bad shape, even if her mind was gone. I tucked a blanket around her legs.

"Do you mind if we take Barney?"

Shannon and I exchanged looks. Barney? Surely her dog from so many years ago couldn't still be alive. Even if he was, I was pretty sure they would never let her keep a dog in this place. Maybe she only thought she still had a dog. Surely it wouldn't hurt to humor her and take her imaginary dog with us. "I'm sure Barney would like a little fresh air too. Here, Barney! Here, boy!" I slapped my leg and waiting for him to join us.

"He's over there in the corner, dear. He doesn't get around as well as he used to either."

I looked where she was pointing, and there was Barney. An actual dog. Except, as I got closer, I could see he wasn't quite . . . alive.

"Do you remember Barney?" she asked. "He was the best dog I ever had and such good company. When he passed on, I couldn't bear to live in an empty house without him. So I had him stuffed."

Shannon tried to cover her laugh with her hand. I carefully picked up Barney, afraid he might go to pieces in my hands, and handed him to Aunt Flora as quickly as I could. "Well, he looks great," I said. Shannon was almost in tears by now. She looked like she had a silent version of the hiccups.

"Now we're ready," Flora pronounced. "Tally-ho!" she said as I pushed her into the hall, Barney standing tall and proud in her lap like some sort of bizarre hood ornament.

* * *

Outside, the air was still and brisk, and the last of the sun warmed us as it started to go down. Shannon and I sat on a metal bench, which was not warm, and Flora waved to everyone that passed by. No one seemed surprised by Barney, and I guessed he was probably a familiar face around here. The taxidermist did a good job, I'll give him that. Barney was very lifelike—maybe even more than I remember him being when he was alive.

"You're not Sadie, are you?" she said suddenly. "You're Sadie's daughter, am I right?"

"That's right. I'm Rachel," I said. "You have a good memory, Aunt Flora."

"Sometimes things just come to me. And we've met before, haven't we?" she said to Shannon.

"That's incredible. We met one time at a wedding reception, when I was a little girl," Shannon said.

"Yes, it was Phyllis's wedding. See, I'm not as batty as they say!" she said beaming.

Well, she had the occasion right. I had to admit I was impressed, even if I had no idea who Phyllis was.

"You girls were so excited to be there. Do you remember I told your fortunes?" Flora asked.

Shannon and I both froze. This was getting downright eerie. I'd heard of moments of clarity, but this was crazy. I couldn't seem to find my voice.

"You did," Shannon said. "You told me that I would marry a guy I met at a wedding reception, and I met him that same night." She smiled. "Only he was a mean boy to begin with. It was a long time before we realized we liked each other."

"Ah, young love," Flora said. "Do you remember your fortune, Rachel?"

All the bitterness I'd managed to set aside came rushing back, washing over me like it was yesterday and I was ten years old again. It wasn't really Aunt Flora's fault. How could she have known I would take her pronouncement so seriously? All I wanted to do was wheel her back inside and get out of here. "You said I was going to be a rich lawyer."

"No, that's not what I said. I think you remember it wrong, dear."

No, you remember it wrong, you senile old bat. "I'm pretty sure that's what you said," I said as kindly as I could.

"I recall it like it was yesterday. You girls were wearing those little lacy aprons, and I told you that you would study the law and never have to worry about money," she said.

It was obvious she knew what she was talking about, and I couldn't believe in a million years that she would recall the event so perfectly. "Yes, that's what I just said."

"No, no, no," she said. "You've got it all wrong." She was getting agitated now, and I had a sudden vision of being the one who caused her to have a stroke or something and becoming the family outcast.

"Maybe we should go back inside," Shannon said. She stood up and started pushing the chair gently toward the door.

"Stop!" Flora said. "This is important, and I want Rachel to hear it."

I took a deep breath, summoning all the patience from my deepest reserves, and crouched down next to the chair. "What is it, Aunt Flora?"

"I said you would study the law, and you did, am I right?"

"Yes, I'm a lawyer now."

"So we agree on that part. But when I said that you would never have to worry about money, it wasn't because you'd get rich being a lawyer—it's because you're going to marry someone very wealthy."

Shannon and I gasped simultaneously, like we were watching a really bad soap opera and we'd just found out that so-and-so's third cousin twice removed was actually his evil sister, back from the dead. But it didn't seem to faze Aunt Flora at all. "Do you know anyone like that, dear? Someone with plenty of money?" Shannon was squeezing my shoulder so hard I was afraid she might snap my collarbone in half.

"Yes, I think I might."

* * *

Shannon and I took Aunt Flora back to her room and thanked her for the visit. Then we walked out to the car and just sat there in silence for what seemed like at least five minutes.

"Wow," Shannon said finally.

"Yeah," I added.

We sat there some more. I told myself that not only was Aunt Flora still a non-gypsy but now she was a senile non-gypsy. There was no reason to give this addendum to the original prediction any more reason to mess with my life, but I had to admit, she seemed pretty lucid for a minute there. And she was right about Shannon . . .

"Wow," Shannon said again.

"I know. Pretty amazing. You know its total crap, though, right?"

"What? How can you say that? She was exactly right about everything, and now she said you're going to marry Henry!"

"She didn't say I was going to marry Henry. She said I was going to marry someone with plenty of money."

"Oh, please. It couldn't have been more obvious if she'd given you his name, birthday, and social security number."

"I know she meant well and it was supposed to be a fun party trick, but this fortune of hers has already done enough damage. For years I've assumed that I'm going to be alone, and now I'm supposed to marry some wealthy guy? I'm done with it. I'm going to put it out of my head and get on with my life. I've managed to do just fine without any gypsy guidance for years, and I don't need any now."

Shannon didn't say anything, but I could tell it was killing her not to tell me how wrong I was. I didn't want to think about it anymore, so I changed the subject. "Could you believe that dog of hers? Barney? That thing was alive when we were kids! I was afraid it was going to be the same dog, still hobbling around!"

The laughing fit that Shannon had suppressed before was back. "It *was* the same dog—just without the hobble. I thought I was going to die laughing when I saw it! You should have seen your face when you had to pick it up!"

"Yeah, I noticed you didn't exactly race over there to grab it."

"I could barely even look at the mangy little thing. There was no way I could have touched it."

"Well, believe it or not, the taxidermist worked wonders. Poor Barney looked sketchier when he was alive."

"Oh, I'm so glad you blackmailed me into going. I haven't laughed that hard in a long time. It reminds me of this great aunt that my mother had—June. From the time I was a little girl, I remember going to her house and playing with her teacup poodle, Peggy. I loved that poodle. About a year ago, I mentioned to my mother that I couldn't believe Peggy was still alive, and she couldn't stop laughing. She said Peggy died years ago. I was kind of mad that no one ever told me, and I felt stupid that I'd been calling the dog 'Peggy' all these years, which made her laugh even harder. As it turns out, the dog's name *was* Peggy—they were all named Peggy."

"What?" By now I was laughing so hard I could barely get the word out.

"She had lots of poodles over the years, and every one of them was named Peggy."

When I could finally catch my breath, I said, "You made that up!"

"Cross my heart and hope to die."

"That is an awesome story." I shook my head. "Well, you better take me home. I'm sure you and Nathan have some celebrating to do."

Suddenly she wasn't laughing anymore.

"What? You said everything was okay with the ultrasound, right?"

"The baby is fine. Everything looks perfect."

"So what's with the sad face?"

Shannon busied herself with putting on her seatbelt and fiddling with the rearview mirror.

"*Shannon.* This is beyond belief. Why didn't you tell him?"

"You were right. I've put it off too long, and now I feel stupid. I should have told him at the beginning."

"Well, there's no time like the present."

"What if he doesn't understand?"

"Tell him what you told me—you were scared, and you were trying to protect his feelings in case it didn't work out. I'm sure he'll see why you didn't tell him."

"You think?"

"You kept the fact that you had feelings for him a secret forever, and he forgave you for that."

"You're not helping. Am I a terrible person?"

"Not at all," I soothed. "You're a considerate person . . . and maybe a little neurotic."

She laughed, but now she was crying at the same time, which only helped to reinforce my theory.

"So this is what they mean by pregnancy hormones, huh?" I said.

"Shut up. One day it'll be your turn, and then we'll see who's laughing."

"And crying."

"Exactly."

I leaned across the seat and hugged her. "Go home and tell your husband the good news."

"I will," she said.

I gave her my best cross-examining-the-suspect stare.

"No, really, this time I will for sure."

Chapter Twenty-Three
"Stormy Weather"

THE DAY IS MONDAY. THE time—7:58 a.m. The place—the hall outside Henry's office. The mission, should I choose to accept it, is to ascertain the subject's feelings on relationships and try to engage him in another kiss, preferably outside the office where I won't have conflicted feelings about it.

I told myself I had this completely under control, but the truth was I was scared to death. Henry was probably expecting me to still be angry, but I wasn't even going to bring up dinner unless he did. Onward and upward! I was going to project confidence. I may have lost the last battle, but I was not going to lose the war. I squared my shoulders, opened the door, and walked onto the battleground. The subject, I mean, Henry was sitting at his desk.

"Morning, boss. How was Houston?"

"Uh, great." He looked disoriented, so I took it as a sign that I was handling this the right way. "How was your weekend?"

"It was fine; I slept in and everything. Although in the end, I decided to let the cat stay."

"Rachel," he started. He looked serious, and all my big plans to be uber confident went right out the window.

"You're going to fire me, aren't you? Because you shouldn't. I can do better! I'll wash your car! I'll polish your shoes! I'll address your Christmas cards!"

"It's February," he said, but at least he was smiling now.

"I'll start early. You seem like a guy who needs to send a lot of Christmas cards."

"I'm not going to fire you, Rachel. And the Christmas cards aren't a bad idea."

Whew. "I'm sorry, I interrupted you. What were you going to say?" He looked exactly like he had that night in my hallway, like he was trying to figure out how to say something. I waited as patiently as I could. Now that it wasn't the middle of the night after an exciting but long day, I wasn't in any hurry.

He opened his mouth and closed it. Then he did the same thing again. Now I was getting worried. This seemed important. I had this unfortunate habit of putting ideas into his head, so maybe he really was thinking about firing me now. Either that or he was having a stroke, his tongue paralyzed, and all he could do was hope I would piece it all together before he collapsed to the floor. "I need to tell you something," he said.

"Go on," I said, trying my best to ooze patience. He was. He was going to fire me. He had decided I was more trouble than I was worth, and he was already thinking about his new secretary and whether he could find one that was willing to cook *and* wear a maid's uniform. Maybe he'd force me to give him the prime rib recipe in exchange for a good severance package.

"I . . ."

"Yes?"

He sighed. "I have a job for you."

I'd have bet my entire flat of raspberries that wasn't what he was originally going to say, but what could I do? Openly accuse him of chickening out? What if he had? That was his call. Whatever it was, he would tell me when he was ready. "You always have a job for me," I said, trying to lighten the moment. "What is it today?"

"Well, this is a slightly bigger job than normal."

"That sounds intriguing." I was having a hard time figuring out how Henry's brain operated. One minute he was flirting with me, and the next he was all business. Was he OCD? Schizophrenic? Or was he just shy?

He hesitated again.

"Wow, this must be bad. Don't tell me, let me guess—you found out that next month's book club selection is the Bible, and you need me to read the whole thing this week."

He gave me a small laugh. "That's not it. But it's sort of along those same lines."

"Book of Mormon?"

"I think I already know how that one ends. Guess again."

"I can't imagine what it might be, so I guess you'll have to tell me."

He handed me a thick manila envelope. "I need you to take these papers and deliver them."

"That doesn't sound too bad. Where am I taking them?"

"St. George."

"What?! That's four hours away. Why can't you just fax them? Or e-mail them? That's what technology is for, right? Isn't this supposed to be the paperless age?"

"I can't. They have to be originals."

"Why?"

"They're notarized."

"So I'll overnight them for you."

"They really have to get there today. I'm sorry, if there was any other way, I'd never ask you to do this. But you can take the car, and I'll give you gas and food money."

I didn't say anything, but I was relieved. At least he wasn't firing me . . . yet. "Well, I suppose there are worse ways to spend the day than on a road trip in a sports car," I grumbled.

* * *

After I put gas in the car and got over my fear of mangling Henry's beautiful vehicle, I was kind of excited. I plugged my phone into the charger, put on *My Fair Lady*, and sang along at the top of my lungs. Even if it would be a long drive, it was an adventure, which was something I didn't have much of lately—with the exception of my impromptu plane ride. It would be more fun if I wasn't going by myself, but it would still be a nice break. I liked to drive. I had music and scenery and a 44-ounce Diet Dr. Pepper—what more could you want in life?

By the time I got to Nephi, it started to rain, not a light sprinkle of rain either, a huge downpour of drops, like the heavens had decided to punish me for something. I pulled over to the side of the freeway for a minute to wait it out. The sound of the rain pounding on the roof was so loud it completely drowned out Eliza Doolittle. I might have forged ahead in my own car, but I wasn't about to risk wrecking Henry's Z in an unfortunate hydroplaning incident. I couldn't help being paranoid. This car probably cost more than I had left in student loans, which was a pretty hefty amount. The thought of doubling my debt in one day was crippling.

When it slowed down enough that I could at least drive, I pulled back onto the road, but I crept along until the rain was more manageable. Forty-five minutes later, the outlook was improving. I switched to *Into the Woods*. The sky was still cloudy, but there was blue at the edges and a rainbow that was struggling to break through. With every mile marker I passed, things were looking up.

Until I got to Cedar City, where it was snowing. Just a little snow, nothing sticking to the road yet, but it was still enough to unnerve me yet again. I stopped to take a potty break and wait for the weather to make a decision one way or the other. As I ate my turkey sub in the car, *very carefully*, multiple napkins protectively covering every available surface, I glanced at the envelope on the seat next to me. I hoped that whatever was in there was worth all this trouble.

When I got to St. George, I drove to the address Henry had given me without too much trouble. The roads here were wet too. It must have been raining earlier, but luckily it had paused, and the sun was trying to make an appearance. I got out of the car and stretched before retrieving the envelope and starting toward the building, which was about the moment I stepped in a puddle that was really a deepish hole in disguise, filled with muddy water. (I know that's the definition of puddle, but this particular puddle was deep enough to justify the hole description.)

I managed to regain my balance but not before the envelope went flying out of my hands, landing in another puddle/hole conveniently located nearby. I cursed and grabbed the package as soon as I could, but when I picked it up and shook it off, it was soggy and black in spots. The damage was done. I couldn't believe I'd gotten this close just to ruin things at the last minute. And there were no do-overs—these papers needed to be in someone's hands today.

Maybe the envelope was thicker than I thought. There was always a chance that the papers could still be safely nestled inside. I wiped my dirty, wet hands on my dress pants—at least they were black—opened the metal fastener, and lifted the flap, hoping against hope that they weren't wet and unreadable.

The good news was the papers weren't entirely ruined.

The bad news was the pages were blank.

I thumbed through them three times to be sure, but they were just normal, blank copy paper.

Someone was going to pay for this.

I didn't bother going inside. I got back in the car and drove in an angry red haze until I reached the entrance to northbound I-15. I was no longer concerned about what condition I returned the car in. Right now hydroplaning was the least of Henry's worries. I didn't know what the blank pages in the envelope meant, but I knew it couldn't be anything good. I thought about calling to warn him, but he probably had money all over the world and I didn't want to give him the opportunity to flee the country.

Chapter Twenty-Four
"Detour Ahead"

By the time I reached the top of the stairs that led to the office, I had calmed down a little. Might as well give Henry a chance to explain himself before I pronounced his sentence. As far as I was concerned, he was already guilty, although I wasn't sure of what. Deception. Cruelty. Insanity. Perhaps all of the above. But I wanted to at least let him *attempt* to explain before I condemned him. I wondered how many other secretaries he'd lost, pulling a stunt like this. The elation of finding those raspberries on my desk seemed like a lifetime ago, and all my goodwill toward him had vanished. I was starting to get angry again.

The door to Henry's office was partly opened, and I went in without knocking. He didn't look up.

"You made pretty good time. Did you find the place okay?"

"Yup. You give very good directions. But I did have a little weather trouble." I was long since dry, but my pants were dirty and my coat was water-spotted. When Henry looked up, he seemed alarmed. I must have looked even worse than I thought.

"Are you kidding? The weather was supposed to be fine today. I checked!"

"Well, you know what they say—even a broken clock is right twice a day."

He cocked his head to one side. "Are you okay?"

"Aside from being confused and angry, I'm fine. Maybe you can explain this to me." I pushed the dirty, open envelope across his desk.

Henry pulled out the pages and stared at them for a minute. "Uh, right. No wonder you're mad. But I can explain."

"When you say that so confidently, I want to believe you, but I can't imagine how you're possibly going to come up with a reasonable excuse for this."

Henry tried to interrupt, but I wasn't finished venting yet.

"You sent me across the state during a storm to deliver an envelope full of blank paper. Who does that? I've had four hours to think about how you're going to put a positive spin on this. In fact, I've been debating over whether you're mean or crazy. So go ahead and explain it to me. Tell me you gave me the wrong envelope. Was that it? Because that's the only excuse I can think of that's even remotely plausible."

"It wasn't the wrong envelope."

"Did you want to get me out of the office for the day? Because that would make you kind of a jerk, but at least it would make sense."

"You're getting closer to the truth, but I promise the reason has nothing to do with whatever you're thinking."

"Right. So you wanted to get rid of me."

Henry rubbed his face tiredly. "No, the reason I sent you to St. George is because I wanted to keep you."

"Listen to yourself! That makes absolutely no sense at all."

Henry stood up from his chair, came around the desk, and pushed me gently but firmly into the chair across from him. He returned to his own chair and sat down again. "Since I don't see any way around this, I'm going to tell you the truth."

"That would be lovely."

"I don't have a secretary."

I realized that I was blinking three times as much as a normal person. I probably looked psychotic. "I've got news for you. You do have a secretary, and she's sitting right in front of you. Are you delusional?"

"What I meant was I've never had a secretary before. Not before you."

"I don't get it. What about all those stories about how terrible your last secretary was and how difficult you are to work for?"

"I made it up."

"Why would you do that?"

"How can I explain this without making it sound insulting?" He paused for a minute. "When I saw you at the café and you were so down, I felt sorry for you. I wanted to help, but I knew you wouldn't take money, so I invented a job for you."

"You invented a job," I repeated, feeling numb as the explanation started to sink in.

"You needed a job; I needed a secretary."

"Except you didn't need a secretary."

He grimaced. "Not really. I'm sorry, I couldn't think of any other way to help, so I had to get creative. When you mastered the copy machine in fifteen minutes, I knew I was in over my head. So I came up with all sorts of errands I could send you on. I thought of everything I could that an eccentric millionaire might need and a few things they wouldn't, but yesterday I officially ran out of ideas, hence the great paper chase today."

I closed my eyes. "I feel like such an idiot."

"Don't feel bad. You couldn't have known."

"No, not for that. Well, not *only* for that. I feel terrible for accusing you of sending me on a fool's errand because you were mean. But you have to admit, I was half right on the crazy part."

"Only if you think it's crazy to buy a copy machine so your new secretary would have something to do."

I wouldn't have thought it possible, but I actually laughed. "Tell me you didn't buy that copy machine just for me."

"If you'd gotten here any earlier that morning, you'd have caught the guy who delivered it. I'm surprised you didn't see him."

"And what would you have said then?"

"That my last flaky secretary ruined the copy machine, and I had to get a new one." He shook his head. "She really was completely incompetent, you know?"

I don't know how he managed to say that with a straight face, but once I burst out laughing, he wasn't far behind. We both just sat there in near hysterics, and every time I looked in his direction, we both started howling all over again. I was wiping away tears from the corners of my eyes. When I could finally get myself under control enough to speak, I said, "I don't know why I'm laughing. I mean, even if it is funny, this rotten day has just gotten worse."

"What do you mean?"

"Well, I'm sort of out of a job now."

Henry looked stricken. "You don't have to go."

"I can't stay here when I know you got along fine without me before."

"You can! I'll come up with new things for you to do, real things! I promise!"

"That's just it—you shouldn't have to create tasks for me so you can justify paying me." I had a sudden thought. "I bet you invented a job for Waldorf, too, didn't you?"

Henry sighed. "Syd is an old friend of my grandfather's. When I was little, they used to do all sorts of crazy things and drag me along. A kid couldn't ask for better guardians. Syd was your typical old bachelor, never married; my grandfather was widowed early. When my grandfather passed away, Syd was all alone. He'd fallen on hard times financially, so I hired him to do odd jobs for me. He thinks he's the one taking care of me and not the other way around. He's not as quick as you, and if you ever enlighten him, I'm afraid we couldn't be friends anymore."

I closed my eyes briefly. It all made sense now. "I'll never tell. You're a good man, Henry. I always knew you were a nice guy, but I had no idea . . ."

He looked away. "Stop, you're embarrassing me."

"You described them as your 'guardians.' Was that a term of endearment, or was it a legal thing?"

"I'd really rather not talk about it."

"I'm sorry. I didn't mean to pry."

Henry smiled. "Don't be sorry. I had a wonderful childhood, even if it was unconventional."

I was curious about where his parents were when he was growing up. He never talked about his father, and going to your mother's book club every now and then didn't exactly sound like your traditional mother/son relationship. At least I knew she was alive. I wondered if he'd been raised exclusively by his grandfather and why his parents weren't in his life.

I stood up. "Would you like me to pick you up one last cookie before I go?"

"Come on, stay, at least until you find something else. It's been nice having someone around. I knew you wouldn't be my secretary forever, but I figured that when you went, it would be because you found a great job not because I chased you away."

"You didn't chase me away, but I can't stay here and take your money when you don't really need me."

Henry got out of his chair and came around to where I was standing. He walked behind me and leaned down until his face was almost in my hair. "And what if I did need you?"

My heart ramped up, and I tried to surrender myself to the moment, but it wasn't right. "Then I really couldn't stay. Not like that. If you want to explore that avenue, I probably shouldn't be working for you anyway."

"What will you do now?" he said, completely ignoring the last part of my answer.

"I'll figure something out. Do you mind if I ask you a question?"

"Go ahead."

"Why did you really offer me this job?"

"Isn't it obvious?" he said.

"Not really. I mean, maybe I'm dense, but the day you ran into me in the café we hadn't seen each other for years. Why go to all that trouble for someone you barely knew?"

"I already told you. I liked you."

"Even then, when I was practically a stranger?"

"You were very kind to me once, and I wanted to—"

"—return the favor?" I finished.

"Maybe that's how it started. But it's more than that now."

"Is it? Because I can't figure out what you want from me. One minute I can almost imagine that you're flirting with me, and the next minute you're all business. I can't keep up." I couldn't believe I was actually saying these words, but now that I was jobless, I felt like I had nothing to lose.

"*You* can't keep up? I'm the one who keeps putting myself out there, only to get shot down. For a guy with an intense fear of rejection, I'd say I've been pretty brave!"

"What? When did I shoot you down?"

"The night we went to San Francisco, the day we had lunch in the park," he said, ticking them off on his fingers.

"You have to admit you sprung that San Francisco thing on me."

"That was kind of the point. It was supposed to be a *surprise*."

"And it was incredible. I loved it. No one has ever done anything like that for me before. But it was confusing."

"Why was it confusing?"

"Well, we had this really fun night—at least, I thought it was really fun."

"It *was* fun. I had a great time," I said.

"But when you dropped me off, you completely froze."

"I wasn't the one who froze. You were the one that froze!"

"Did you expect me to make the first move?"

"Of course not, but you weren't exactly giving me any signs that you were interested. You looked so uncomfortable," he said.

"It was hard to be at ease when you were seeing exactly how desperate my situation was. In case I wasn't clear enough before, I'm embarrassed about where I live."

"Where you live is only temporary. Besides, I don't care about things like that."

"Well, I do, and it didn't help that you stood there in the hall forever looking like you wanted to speak or kiss me or something until you changed your mind. And then you ran away with no explanation," I added.

"I didn't change my mind, and I ran away because you couldn't get inside fast enough."

"It was two o'clock in the morning! I couldn't exactly invite you in. Besides, I wanted to give you an out since you were obviously having a major moment of indecision."

"Okay, forget about the hallway. What about the day in the park? Who was the one that panicked then?"

"I'll admit, I hesitated—"

"A-ha!" He looked so triumphant that I momentarily wanted to smack him.

"But only for a millisecond. And when I tried to explain, you ran away again!"

"I didn't run away. It was obvious you weren't as interested as I was, so I dropped it to preserve what little dignity I had left."

"Is that what you were doing when you kissed me at your house? Because that seemed more like fear to me."

There it was again—that same haunted look; I knew immediately that I was right. "You still have feelings for Shannon, don't you? That's why you couldn't kiss me. You were thinking of her."

He looked absolutely mortified. "You must think I'm the worst person who ever lived."

"I think maybe you didn't understand how wrecked you still were, and I don't blame you for that. But I can't try to build anything with you when you're still rooted in the past."

"I had no idea you were even onboard with the idea of a relationship until now. You're not exactly an open book yourself."

"Look who's talking!" I said. "You're always so hot and cold. What am I supposed to think when you seem interested for five minutes only to cut me off five minutes later?"

"I wouldn't pretend to be interested if I wasn't. I don't play games. I'm not that kind of guy."

"Well, I'm not the kind of girl who leads someone on to keep her job."

"I never said you were. But when the chips are down, sometimes we all do things we wouldn't normally do."

My eyes narrowed. "That's low. I would rather starve than work for someone I didn't respect. I can't believe that's what you think of me."

"I can't help being suspicious. I've been burned in the past."

"And I'm sorry you've had such bad luck with people, but we're not all out to get what we can at whatever cost. I think you're jumping to conclusions, and I don't deserve that."

"And I don't deserve the predatory boss label. I wouldn't take advantage of you because you're my employee and I know you need the money."

"I never said that. Stop putting words in my mouth!" I shouted.

"You said you shouldn't be dating me and working for me at the same time, which implies that you think it's a bad idea."

"That's just common sense. Everyone knows you shouldn't date people you work with, and you certainly never date your boss because when you break up, working together becomes impossible and one of you ends up having to find a new job. I'll give you two guesses which one of us will be going."

Henry took a deep breath. "I think we should back up a minute to where this started to get ugly. I said I liked you and I didn't want you to go, remember?"

"And I said you were a good man. But obviously we've each got some deeper issues."

"I shouldn't blame my commitment issues on you. You can't be held responsible for what my life was like before or people who deceived me. You're not Shannon, and you never will be."

"I think that's been the problem all along. I'm not Shannon."

He was silent for a minute, and I think he realized how awful what he said sounded, even if he hadn't meant it that way.

"And just so we're clear, she never deceived you. You knew exactly what her situation was, and you hung around anyway, knowing that if she ever got the chance, she would take Nathan over you in a minute. There's nothing wrong with picking a lost cause. It's your right as long as you understand that when your bet doesn't pay off, it's your own fault. You need to stop blaming your choices on her because until you do, you'll never be able to move on. I'm sorry if that sounds cruel, but it's the truth." Now that I'd started, the words just kept spilling out.

"Just so *we're* clear, I never expected you to be Shannon."

"I know. You were willing to settle for the next best thing. But I'm not anybody's second prize, and I'm not willing to settle."

He didn't say anything, and I figured I'd finally pushed him too far.

"Good-bye, Henry."

It was already late, so I went home, fed Hannibal, and climbed straight into bed.

Chapter Twenty-Five
"You Can't Be Mine"

So, that was that. I'd played a hunch and lost. It happens. Only now I'd lost my job too. I kind of thought if I lost my job it would be because I won Henry; instead I lost both. I felt curiously detached from the whole situation, but maybe I was just in shock. Once the numbness wore off, the pain would set in. I know it sounds ridiculous, but when Aunt Flora said I was going to marry someone with money, I really thought it would be Henry, despite the way I brushed it off to Shannon. Since he hadn't called after I left his office last night, that was looking less and less likely.

It was ten o'clock Tuesday morning, and I was sitting on the couch in my living room petting Hannibal . . . and he was letting me. I think he could tell I wasn't well. The television was on in the background, but I wasn't paying enough attention to even know what was on. Hannibal and I played a little game now. When it was my turn to choose, we watched *Law and Order*. When it was his turn, I switched through the channels until he meowed, and that's what we watched. I think he appreciated me consulting him on our viewing selection. He seemed to be a big *Baywatch* fan, but he also liked CNN on occasion. At least

Shannon had the sense to give me a cat who liked to stay up on current events.

I hadn't seen Mousey again, or any other mice, for that matter. I was afraid Hannibal had finally done his job and gotten rid of him/them, and the guilt over the look Mousey had given me was wearing on me. I know I should be relieved that there was no sign of my previous rodent inhabitant, but I'd kind of gotten used to the idea of the three of us living here together, like a bizarre little family.

My phone rang. I didn't care who it was, I wasn't answering it. I couldn't even form a sentence, so there was no way I could carry on a conversation. I picked it up and stared at it in disinterest. The caller ID said Stratton. That sounded familiar and somewhat important for some reason. My brain suddenly switched on. Stratton, Whitby, and . . . crap, what was the last one? The law firm I interviewed with last week! Without even thinking, I picked it up. "Hello?"

"Is this Rachel Pearce?"

"Yes, it is." Hannibal was standing at attention now, his ears perked up. Even he could tell this was important.

"This is Angela from Stratton, Whitby, and Beckett. I'm calling to let you know that the partners would like you to come in for a second interview, if you're interested."

"Yes, thank you, I'm definitely interested."

"On Friday I have a ten thirty, an eleven thirty, or a three in the afternoon."

"I'll take it. Thank you."

"Which one would be most convenient for you?" she asked, and I could tell she was smiling.

Idiot. "The ten thirty would be perfect. Thank you." I wished there was one even earlier in the day. The last thing I wanted to do was sit around all morning stressing over it.

"Ten thirty it is. We'll plan on seeing you then, Miss Pearce."

"Thank you. Thank you so much." I hung up the phone and sighed. It was official—I was going to be the first person in the history of the world who blew the second interview before she even got there. I bet no one else they called neglected to choose an appointment or said thank you seventy-six times.

Hannibal was looking at me, his head cocked and his eyes all questions. He really was a very intelligent cat. I rubbed his head as enthusiastically as I dared.

"That's right, buddy. If I get this job, you'll be eating gourmet cat food and sleeping on silk sheets from here on out!"

My phone rang again. Ugh. It was probably them calling to tell me that if I couldn't even pick an appointment time they had changed their mind and had no desire to interview me again.

It was Shannon.

I really wasn't ready to talk about Henry yet, but now was probably as good a time as any. I picked up the phone.

"Maybe I'll wait until the baby gets here and then act surprised," she said. "Isn't there an entire show on cable devoted to women who didn't even know they were pregnant? I could be one of those women."

"I'm not even going to ask why you didn't tell him this time."

"When I got home from going to see Aunt Flora with you on Saturday, I was all psyched up to tell him."

"And?"

"I forgot he was going to see a movie with one of his friends. He claimed he told me about it, but I have no memory of that conversation. Must be pregnant brain syndrome."

Hannibal pushed up against my hand, which was now resting on his back. Apparently he was getting annoyed that the petting had ceased. I started scratching his ears. "Now you know how I feel. So why didn't you tell him on Sunday?"

"Well, we were having dinner at his parents' house that night, and I knew if I told him, he wouldn't be able to wipe the grin off his face for the rest of the day. I'm not ready to tell everyone yet."

"Couldn't you have told him when you got home from dinner?"

"I was going to, but when we walked in the door, he planted himself on the couch like a lump and flipped through the channels for two hours. I couldn't. The timing was terrible."

"And Monday night?"

"The game was on."

Hannibal was purring so loudly Shannon could probably hear him through the phone. "Which game?"

"I don't know. Does it matter?"

"Okay, so you can tell him tonight when he gets home from work, the minute he walks through the door before he has a chance to switch on the television."

"Well, that's the thing. He sent me a text saying that his boss wanted to see him about a complaint."

"Who complains about Nathan?" I wondered. "Everyone loves Nathan."

"I know! And now he's in a really bad mood, and he'll probably be in an even worse mood after this meeting with his boss. I can't tell him if he's angry about something—it'll totally ruin the moment!"

"Seriously, Shannon, you couldn't make this stuff up. What are you going to do? This is exactly like when you met at BYU and you never told him you were the girl from the corsage incident when you were kids."

"I know! That was silly enough, but this is even sillier. I'm happy about the baby, and he's going to be ecstatic, so why can't I just tell him?" she said.

"I think it's because you're trying to turn this into a big production. If you try to manufacture the perfect moment, you really will be telling Nathan while you're getting the epidural. You don't have to have fireworks and a band because this is something that's big enough all on its own. A pregnancy announcement doesn't need any artificial enhancement."

"I'm sure you're right. I wish I'd told him as soon as I found out, trouble or no trouble."

I smiled. "Well, there's always the next baby."

"Yeah, give me enough chances, and I'm bound to get it right eventually."

"Don't drag it out any longer. Tell him when he gets home tonight. Everything will be fine, you'll see," I said.

"I'll make something he really likes for dinner, and then I'll tell him."

"Good girl. Let me know how it goes."

I guess I didn't need to worry about giving her the Henry news. She hung up the phone without ever asking if I was at work. Lucky for me she had bigger worries at the moment. Hopefully by the time she noticed that I was no longer Henry's secretary, I'd have a shiny new job doing what I should have been all along.

* * *

I wanted to text Henry. Or call Henry. Or visit Henry. And I wondered why Henry didn't seem to feel the need to text, call, or visit me. I really thought we were making some progress, but obviously we weren't on the same wavelength if he was willing to let me go so easily. When I said I had to quit, he didn't really even argue with me even though he knew that without a paycheck, I was basically destitute. Then again, I was the one who insisted on going, so maybe he assumed I had some sort of backup plan. After all, reasonable people don't leave their jobs when they have nothing to fall back on—unless they're terribly noble. But it's hard to feel noble when your stomach is empty.

Even if he was willing to let me sacrifice my job for my principles, what about the other part? The budding romance part? Was he really going to let me leave without even giving us a chance?

This was getting me nowhere. Henry would do whatever he would do. Right now, I had the tiniest bit of positive energy from the prospect of the second interview, and I would do whatever I had to to hold on to it. Right now, that consisted of obsessively cleaning my apartment so I wouldn't have to think about anything else.

You might wonder how long it could possibly take to clean an apartment the size of a hatbox. The answer is as long as you need it to. I already keep my apartment very clean and tidy, but there's a difference between regular cleaning and deep cleaning. I scrubbed and polished and dusted and shined until my knuckles were raw. Hannibal moved from one place to another, always in close enough proximity to keep an eye on the proceedings but far enough away to avoid being swept into a dustpan. I think he was alarmed by the intensity of the sudden scouring.

I was working on the bathroom sink with an old toothbrush when my doorbell rang. For the briefest instant, I wondered if it might be Henry. I glanced at myself in the ultra clean mirror and snorted. My hair was pulled back in a bandana, but that hadn't stopped sweaty tendrils from curling around my neck. I was in my grubbiest sweats. There wasn't enough out-of-season produce in the world to get me to open that door looking like this.

After the doorbell rang several more times, whoever it was started knocking. I wondered who could want to see me bad enough to keep this up.

"Rachel?" I heard a muffled voice say through the thin door. "Are you in there?"

I peeked through the peephole. It was Nathan and Shannon. Great. Now I'd have to answer it because they had a key, and it was only a matter of time before they would use it and find me cowering in here. I'd given Shannon a key when I moved in because I had this fear that if I died, no one would ever find me. She said I was morbid, and the only way she would agree to take the key was if I promised I would never die and leave her with the responsibility of being the one to discover me. I brushed my hands off on my pants before I opened the door, as though I could magically fix my appearance.

"Rachel. Finally! What took you so long?" Nathan asked.

"In case you didn't realize, that was me not answering the door," I said.

"See? I told you," Shannon said. Her eyes strayed to the bandana on my head in concern. She had this theory that when I was wearing hats, my life was all but in ruins. A bandana wasn't exactly a hat, but I'm sure it was close enough for her to worry.

"Why wouldn't you answer the door?" Nathan asked.

I smiled at Nathan because he was the kind of person who genuinely couldn't understand pretending to not be home. "Would you answer the door dressed like this?"

Shannon frowned. "Why are you dressed like that? Shouldn't you just be getting home from work?"

"I had the afternoon off. I'm *cleaning*," I said, hoping that my tone told her to leave it alone. Nathan was still in the dark about my job, or ex-job, and something told me this wasn't a good time to bring it up. Something told me it would never be a good time.

"Your place already looks spotless enough to win a prize. Maybe you should come over and clean our house," Nathan said. He ducked away just in time to avoid Shannon slugging his arm. At least he was learning.

Hannibal walked in the room, sniffed Nathan and Shannon, and walked over to stand by my feet.

"Okaaaay, that's weird. Since when does the cat like you better than me?" Shannon said.

"We've bonded," I said. "It's a delicate process."

"Are you sure you're Rachel and not someone who looks a lot like her?" Nathan asked.

"I'm as Rachel as it gets." Why were they standing there by the door like we were strangers? "You wanna come in and sit down?" I asked.

"Only for a minute, and then we'll let you get back to your cleaning frenzy," Nathan said.

Shannon and Nathan sat on the couch, and I walked over to the tiny bar. "Can I get anybody anything? Glass of water? Peanut butter sandwich?" I held up the bottle sitting on the counter. "Windex?"

"We're fine. We had some big news that we couldn't wait to tell you. We're pregnant," Nathan said casually.

I froze, but not before I shot a desperate look at Shannon. She told me she was going to tell Nathan, but it was like the girl who cried wolf. Somehow, I didn't think she'd actually do it. Even if she did, I assumed they'd want it to be their secret for a while. The least she could have done was text me and warn me they were coming. I realized too late that there was something wrong. Shannon looked at least as surprised as I did.

"Looks like I was right. I really am the last to know," Nathan said.

"But *how* did you know?" Shannon said, not even bothering to deny it.

"I saw the itemized bill from the ER in the mail. You had a pregnancy test, but you didn't mention it. You were throwing up, you quit running, you were more indecisive than usual. I put the pieces together. The question is, why didn't you tell me?" he asked.

"Honey, I feel terrible that you found out this way. I wanted it to be special," Shannon said. I was afraid she was going to start crying, and this was already awkward enough.

"Is that why you told Rachel before you told me? Because you wanted it to be special?" Nathan didn't sound particularly angry, but it took a lot to ruffle him. The only time I'd ever seen him really mad was around Henry. *Henry. I haven't thought about you for hours. If only I hadn't quit my job so impulsively yesterday, I might still be at work, and I would have missed this whole confrontation.*

"I'm sorry! I had to tell someone. You were out of town, and Rachel is my best friend—"

"I thought I was your best friend!" he said, voice slightly louder than normal.

"You are! Of course you are!" she said.

"I don't know if I believe that. And you!" he said, turning his death stare on me. "My wife is obviously flooded with crazy baby hormones and doesn't know what she's doing, but you have no excuse. You should have told me!"

"It wasn't my secret to tell. It's up to Shannon how and when to dispense her secret information!"

"I notice she didn't waste any time telling you," Nathan said. This was so strange. I felt like I was on one of those talk shows where they put people that shouldn't be within miles of each other together in a room and wait for the explosion.

"Nathan," Shannon started again.

"What?" he demanded.

"I . . . I . . ." Shannon really was near tears, and I knew I shouldn't be here for this. Even Hannibal had deserted me and galloped off into the bedroom, the traitor.

That was when Nathan couldn't keep his straight face anymore and burst out laughing. Shannon sat there stunned.

"Shut. Up. What was that?" I demanded.

He could hardly get the words out. "That was me giving the two of you a little grief for keeping secrets from me. You should have seen your faces."

"You're not mad?" Shannon said.

"I was a little, at first. I figured you'd tell me eventually, but I got tired of waiting and decided to get even."

"You decided . . . to get even," Shannon repeated. "You . . . Jerkface! Do you have any idea what I've been going through the last few weeks?"

"Maybe I would if you'd decided to share it with me," he countered.

"The reason I didn't tell you is because I've been really sick. I almost lost the baby, but I didn't tell you because I didn't want both of us to be disappointed," she shouted. "I was waiting until I knew everything was going to be okay!"

"You almost lost the baby?" he said, his voice so quiet that I barely heard the words.

Shannon was crying now. There were so many tears on her face I wondered if she'd been saving them for a special occasion.

"I'm so sorry," Nathan said, and I could tell that he was truly contrite. "I never would have teased you if I knew something was wrong." He gulped. "Is something wrong?"

Crap. Now I was afraid that *Nathan* was going to cry. I really had to get out of there. I crept into my bedroom, determined to hunker down with Hannibal and wait out the storm. I closed the door halfway and sat on the bed, wishing I had something fun in there to do. I resolved to make myself an emergency box in case I ever got trapped in my room again—maybe nail polish, fruit snacks, a deck of cards—that sort of thing. *A worthwhile investment, since you get stuck in here so often,* the little voice commented.

I'd been in there about fifteen minutes when I heard Shannon laugh. That sounded like progress. Then I heard her scream. I flew out of bed and down the hall and saw Shannon . . . standing on the couch.

"I think I found your mouse!" she yelped. Nathan was busy trying to untie his shoe so he'd have something to smack it with, and I caught barely a glimpse of large, beady, triumphant black eyes before the rodent ducked behind the television.

"Mousey! You're still alive! I knew it! Run, Mousey! Run!" I cheered.

Nathan stopped and stared at me, shoe in hand. "You do know you're seriously mental, right?"

That's when the three of us started laughing, and I knew everything would be okay.

Chapter Twenty-Six
"All of Me"

I SAT ON THE COUCH and stared at the blank television screen. Hannibal sat next to me, and I could tell he was wondering why we weren't watching something. There was nothing else to clean. I contemplated starting over again, but I was afraid if I polished and scrubbed anymore, my shabby apartment would be worn down to nothing. It was 2:35 p.m. on Thursday. If I was at work, I would be going to get Henry's daily cookie fix right about now. I wondered what he would say if I showed up at the office with Vivianna like nothing was wrong.

Rain pelted my window, but the weather barely registered. I missed him. Why hadn't he at least called to check on me? Didn't he miss me even a little bit? I don't know what I was expecting—it was doomed from the start. I never should have brought Shannon into it. I'm sure he didn't like me telling him how he felt, but wasn't it better to be honest about everything up front? I liked him—a lot more than I'd expected to. I really could see us as a couple. But he obviously still had unresolved feelings, and there was no point trying to start a relationship if he couldn't let go of the past.

I wanted another chance. I wanted to go back to that walk in the park and not panic. I wanted to go back to that night in his living room, when he gave me the shortest kiss ever and immediately fled the scene like a criminal. I wanted to chase after him and kiss him back until he couldn't think about anything but me and my lips and how it could be different this time.

I could throw my pride out the window and pursue this. I didn't like the idea of being the one who made the first move, but the idea of never seeing Henry again was one I liked even less. I didn't want to live my life the way he'd been living, always wondering if things would have been different if I had only mustered the courage to fight for what I wanted.

But how to do it? How could I convince Henry that what we had was worth taking a chance on? Which brought me to a whole other conundrum; I'd already accused him of being willing to settle for me, so if I went back, how would I ever know that he wasn't doing exactly that? I didn't mind being the one to humble myself, but I knew I would always wonder if he would have been just as content on his own as he was with me.

This was completely maddening. I couldn't live with Henry, and I was having a hard time getting by without him as well. Maybe I should take a walk, get some air to clear my head. I wished that Hannibal had a little leash so I could take him with me. I didn't know much about cats, but I was pretty sure people didn't walk them like dogs. I didn't think he'd be too fond of the drizzling weather anyway.

"You keep the couch warm, and I'll be back in a bit," I said, scratching behind his ears. He purred, and I couldn't believe how much I'd come to love the sound, even though I'd never admit it. It was so . . . soothing.

As I stood up, a knock on the door startled me. When I saw who it was through the peephole, my heart went crazy. I opened it quickly.

"Waldorf, what are you doing here?" I asked. He stood there, dripping in the hall in a rain slicker, holding a box.

"You know me; I do what Henry needs to be done. Like you used to."

I flinched.

"He's in bad shape, you know. Why did you quit?"

What could I tell him? I couldn't say I figured out Henry never needed a secretary in the first place because Waldorf might get suspicious about his own job, and I promised Henry I would never tell him. "It's . . . complicated," I said finally.

"Don't break his heart, princess. He's suffered enough already."

In my pajama pants and sweatshirt, I looked like the least likely princess candidate ever. What could I say to make him understand? He looked so sad that I felt like I'd betrayed him and Henry. "I'm a lawyer. Did you know that?" I said.

"No, I didn't."

"Henry knew I'd only be able to work for him until I found a job, and I think I might have one. That's why I left. But that doesn't mean I don't have feelings for him."

He softened. "You're one of the good ones; I knew you were."

"You look cold. Would you like to come in and have something to warm you up?"

He looked like he was cheering up already. "Now that depends. Do you have whiskey?"

The look on my face must have been priceless. "I'm pulling your leg," he assured me.

I laughed. "I have hot chocolate."

"Thanks, but I better get back to work. I don't like to be too far away in case he needs something."

"Henry's lucky to have you, Waldorf."

He shook his head. "I'm lucky to have him. Where would you like this, princess?"

"I can take it," I protested.

"It isn't any trouble."

"On the counter would be fine." He didn't comment on my humble surroundings, and I found myself wondering where he lived. "Thank you for coming all the way out here."

"I hope you like your new job. And I hope you patch things up with my boss."

"Can I ask you a question?"

"Sure," he said.

"You've known Henry a long time, right?"

"Most of his life."

"He told me once that you and his grandfather basically raised him. What happened to his parents, if you don't mind me asking?" I asked.

"He'll tell you when he's ready."

"I understand. I didn't mean to pry."

He hesitated for just a minute. "His father died when he was just a little boy, and his mother couldn't function after that. She's a good person, but she was so dependent on him. When he was gone, she couldn't make herself get out of bed anymore, not even to take care of her own son. So Henry's grandfather took him."

I nodded, hoping he would continue.

"She tried to make up for it later, but I think Henry has a hard time trusting anyone now. His father left him with enough money that he wouldn't have to work, but he's always been good with computers. He's done well, considering the start he had in life, but I guess we all have to find a way to get past the hand we're dealt."

"You are very wise, Waldorf. Thank you for trusting me with that. It helps."

He beamed. "You're welcome."

After Waldorf left, I stood in front of the box, wondering what could be in it. I knew now that I would give Henry another chance, but I hoped whatever was inside was something that would remove the doubt that he really wanted me.

I didn't need to worry.

Inside the box was a record player—red, white, and yellow, exactly like the one I used to have when I was a little girl. There was one record in a sleeve—Billie Holiday, "All of Me." I plugged the record player in and put the record on. There was a sheet of paper with the lyrics of the song tucked into the bottom of the box, in what I assumed was Henry's handwriting—apparently he could remember how to write after all.

The few tinkling piano notes at the beginning were crackly on the little player. Hannibal thought we were under attack and flew into the bedroom, but nothing ever sounded so good to me. Even Henry's amazing setup could never compete with this. When it was over, I played it again . . . and again . . . and again, until I knew all of the words by heart. And then I knew what I had to do. I put on my shoes, feeling feverish with the need to be somewhere immediately. I wished I had the time and resources to plan something as perfect as he had, but at the same time, I didn't want to give Henry yet another opportunity to second guess himself.

I got halfway down the four flights of stairs before I realized I was still wearing my grubby sweats. I was in a hurry, but I didn't want to arrive looking like a homeless person either. I ran back upstairs and quickly put on my good jeans and a sweater—casual but not unemployed chic. Now I had the whole bus ride to figure out the rest of my life.

Chapter Twenty-Seven
"If You Were Mine"

I WAS WET FROM RUNNING from the bus stop to Henry's office, and I still had no idea what I would say, but I had that feeling you get when you know something important is about to happen. My brain was in hyperdrive, and everything around me seemed sharper—the earthy smell of the rain, the splash of my sneakers in the puddles, the cold of the water seeping into the cuffs of the too-long legs of my jeans.

I ran up the stairs to Henry's office, a little out of breath. I was shivery, but I wasn't sure if that came from the cold or the nerves. I stood outside the door to collect myself. There was no music coming from the office, but there was still a light on inside. I realized I'd been afraid I might not catch him. Even though it was only four o'clock, it was overcast and gloomy, giving it the feeling of being much later.

The door was open, so I let myself in. The lights were out in the main room, and my desk was empty, making the room seem deserted. Funny how I still thought of it as my desk. Henry's door was open a crack, and there was a little light coming from that direction. I couldn't hear any noise in there, though, and I was relieved that no one else was here. It would be a little awkward if I came to make up with Henry and he was in the middle of a business meeting.

I was stuck with my hand on the doorknob to his office. I really should have some sort of plan. I should have prepared better. But something told me this was one of those things you couldn't really prepare for. This was one of those times where I'd just have to make it up as I went. But I'm a lawyer, so I should be good at improv, right? Thinking on my feet? I couldn't think about it too much or I'd chicken out. *Open the door, Rachel. You're halfway there. Just open the door.*

I pushed the door forward enough to peek around the corner. Henry was at his desk—asleep. I'd thought there couldn't possibly be a less comfortable place for him to sleep than his couch, but I was wrong. The way his face was smushed into the desk looked even more cramped. I chided the cowardly part of me that whispered it wasn't too late to back out. Henry would never even know I was here. But I didn't really want to run away. I was tired of hiding from people who would never really know who I was underneath the layers I used to protect myself. I thought that maybe I'd finally found someone who could see through it all, someone I could talk to and let the conversation take its natural course instead of steering it away from anything personal. I was ready to give it a chance, see if I was right.

I walked as quietly as I could to the desk, but I needn't have bothered with stealth. Henry didn't even stir. I was suddenly having a déjà vu moment of dinner at his house and finding him dozing. I wondered briefly if he might be narcoleptic. Hmmm . . . Awkward Decision #1: wake him or don't wake him? I couldn't exactly just stand here and watch him sleep. What if he woke up and caught me watching him? Spying on him in his sleep at his house once was forgivable—chalk it up to curiosity. But twice would be something he could legally press charges for. Which brought me to Awkward Decision #2: how to wake him.

I tapped him lightly on the shoulder. No response. I nudged him a little more firmly and said, "Henry?" in my quiet voice. That seemed to do the trick. He opened his eyes and looked around.

"Rachel? What time is it?" He rubbed his eyes with the back of his hand. "Maybe we should start with what day is it?"

I smiled. "At least you remember who I am. It's Thursday."

He looked at my dark, damp hair. "I'm guessing it's raining outside."

"Nothing gets by you, does it?"

He blinked. "I must have dozed off. Uh, why am I still at the office?"

"It's barely after four. It only looks like it's nine."

He sat up and stretched a little. "And why are you at the office?"

Barely Awake Henry didn't seem as pleased to see me as I thought he would. He was the one who made the overture, so surely it couldn't have been a complete disappointment to find me here.

"Waldorf delivered your gift, and I wanted to . . . thank you?" Although this was meant to be a statement, my sudden insecurity turned it into a question. This was not at all how I saw this scene playing out.

Henry's eyes opened all the way, and I knew he'd pieced it together. "Of course. I'm sorry; you'll have to forgive me for my vagueness. I haven't been sleeping very well lately."

Why haven't you been sleeping? I wondered? *Secretary, possibly turned love interest, turned non-secretary/non-love interest troubles? Almost orphan troubles? Or was it just your garden variety millionaire work troubles?* He still looked a bit wary, and I was beginning to think I'd misinterpreted the whole thing. "Well, I won't keep you, but I wanted to let you know how nice it was for you to think of me. It was very sweet."

"I do, you know," he said, and from the way his gray eyes locked on to mine, I could see that he was totally awake now.

"You do what?"

"Think of you. All the time. Did you listen to the song?"

I gulped. "Several times. Hannibal didn't like it, but it sounded pretty good to me."

"I'm glad," he said.

My initial bravery had all but fled. It was now or never. "Look, Henry," I started.

"I know. You can't work here anymore because it wasn't a real job, and you'd rather starve than not earn an honest wage. But I don't want you to starve."

"Actually, I have a second interview tomorrow."

His face lit up. "That's awesome!" He stood up and gave me a big hug.

"Maybe there was something in all that confidence stuff you said," I said into his chest.

"Hey, people would pay for advice like that from someone as wise as myself."

"Well, if I get that job, the check will be in the mail."

"*When* you get that job," he corrected.

"Yes, when I get that job. Let's be positive—why not?"

"I truly am happy for you. I knew you'd never be my office girl forever," he said.

"Don't congratulate me yet—I still have to sell them in this last interview."

"You will."

We were still hugging, and that was the moment I knew I needed to tell him I wanted to be more than his secretary. Or ex-secretary, as the case may be. Confessing that seemed doable at the moment, perhaps because my face was buried in his shirt.

"Henry?" I mumbled.

"Yes?"

"I need to tell you something, and I need you not to run away until after I've finished."

He peeled himself away from me enough to look at me, and the security I'd felt vanished with the sudden space between us.

"Okay," he said.

Ugh. This was going to be much harder if I had to look into his uncertain eyes while I said it. "I like you," I said.

"I like you too."

"No, I mean I *really* like you. I think I like you more than I've ever liked anyone before."

"Well, that's a relief."

I choked out a laugh. "It is?"

"I thought you were going to tell me you had a terminal illness or something. You got so serious for a minute."

"You don't seem very surprised," I said.

"I've been liking you more than anyone else for much longer than you've been liking me."

I was speechless. All this time I thought Henry was still pining over Shannon. Could he really be ready to move on? If he was going to be brave, I could too. I felt a rush of something that was a combination of nerves and adrenaline as I stood on the precipice of victory or ruin. Well, here goes nothing.

"I'm going to tell you a secret," I said. "That night when we met, at Jill and Jake's wedding? I played it off pretty cool, but I had kind of a crush on you."

Henry looked surprised. "You did?"

"I'm sure you didn't notice. Over the years I've gotten good at covering up my feelings, and besides, it was obvious you only had eyes for Shannon."

Henry looked a bit sad; maybe my earlier observation about him finally being over Shannon was just wishful thinking. I wondered what it would take for him to finally be able to hear her name and feel nothing. I walked over to one of the windows and looked out at the rain that was pelting the sidewalk.

"I spent my whole life telling myself it was easier to be alone," he said. "But Jake was my best friend. I saw how happy he was, and I wanted that. So I decided to take a chance. I would go after the first single girl I saw that night that I was attracted to." He rolled his eyes. "Great timing, huh?"

"I just wish you had seen me first." I touched the window pane, and it was cold on my fingers. "But maybe that wouldn't have made a difference . . ."

"Don't say that. You're beautiful. I can't believe you're not in a relationship."

I didn't know how to respond to the "beautiful" comment, so I filed it away to consider later. "Shannon used to joke that if she and Nathan ever got together, I should go after you. She always said you were the perfect guy, just not the perfect guy for her."

Henry didn't say anything, and I knew that this was where it could all go incredibly right or spectacularly wrong. If he stayed silent, I could let it go and figure he wasn't interested. Or I could plunge ahead and make absolutely sure he knew what I meant.

There wasn't an option. Standing here now, I realized how much I'd truly missed him the last few days. I didn't know for sure that we could make it work; no one can ever know that. I walked back to where he was standing and put my hand tentatively on his arm. Looking into those eyes I'd avoided earlier, I knew I wanted to try.

"Here's the thing—I know we haven't known each other that long, but I think you may be *my* perfect guy." The words whooshed out of me; there was no turning back now. It felt like there was a tornado raging in my stomach. Everything inside me was being shaken up and rearranged.

"Really?" he said. His voice was so quiet that if I hadn't been standing right next to him, I wouldn't have known he'd spoken at all.

"Really."

He smiled. "I think I like you better as my girlfriend than my secretary, and that's saying something. You were my best secretary by far."

My heart thumped wildly in my chest. "Girlfriend, huh? Is that what I am?"

His eyes had a sparkle I'd only seen a few times. "I don't know. Does that sound like something you might be interested in?"

"Well, that depends. I think before we go any further with this relationship, you might need some therapy."

He looked confused. "You want me to see a therapist?"

I stood on my tiptoes and put my hands on his shoulders, pulling him down to where I could better reach him. "Not that kind of therapy—kissing therapy."

The smile on his face was back. "I think that might be very helpful for my condition." There was no question in his eyes when he leaned in to kiss me, and running away seemed to be the last thing on his mind. His lips pressed against mine as though they'd always wanted to, with no sign that he was holding on to the past. His fingers brushed against my neck before tangling in my long, dark hair. To my amusement, I was the one thinking about Shannon this time. She was right; Henry was a really good kisser.

When he finally stopped to breathe, I giggled. He was wearing more of my lip gloss than I was.

"What?" he said.

I rested my hand on the side of his face, using my thumb to wipe away the lip gloss. "Red is a good color on you."

"I'm sure it looks better on you." He reached for my hand and kissed my palm. My face felt as though it were ten times redder than the lip gloss. "So what do you think, Dr. Pearce? Am I cured?"

"Well, I think you're making great strides, but I'm not entirely satisfied with your progress."

His face fell.

"We're going to need to schedule lots of practice sessions to make sure you don't relapse. Is that something you're willing to commit to?"

He wrapped his arms around me and kissed the top of my head. "You tell me when and where. I'll do whatever I have to do to get well."

"You know what they say—the first step is admitting you have a problem."

He kissed me again, and it was even better than the first time. His hesitation seemed to have all but vanished, but I would make him do the time anyway. Practice makes perfect, right?

Chapter Twenty-Eight
"I Can't Give You Anything But Love, Baby"

I DIDN'T GET THE JOB. But with Henry's coaching I got better and better at selling myself, and a month later I finally heard those magic words—"Congratulations, you're hired." It was a smaller firm, but it was a great place to start, and I was thrilled to finally have something to put in that expensive bag of mine besides breath mints. Granted, it wasn't exactly the *Law and Order* gig I'd been picturing; right now, I was just working on wills and trusts. I'd only been there two months, but I felt like I was finally on the path where I belonged.

In exchange for Henry's expert business advice, I continued to provide him with plenty of therapy. In truth, he probably had more experience in that field, but he very wisely let me think I was in charge. Most nights after work, we'd hang out at his house. I was working on crocheting a blanket for Shannon and Nathan's baby, which they had recently discovered was a girl. Maybe I really would have a namesake.

The endless worrying about what Nathan would say about me dating Henry was ultimately unnecessary. When I finally came clean about my new secret boyfriend, Nathan said he thought it was great that I found someone who made me happy. Either Shannon had given him a heads-up or he was secure enough in their relationship that he was over hating Henry. Maybe he was just a good actor. Since the four of us were supposed to have dinner together in a few weeks, I'd find out soon enough. Last I checked, Shannon still hadn't told Nathan about our pending double date. Some things never change.

Henry and I sat around and talked and listened to music or watched movies. Sometimes I cooked, sometimes we got takeout. One night Henry made me show him how to cook the prime rib. I thought it was kind of sweet that he wanted to help me until he said it was so that one day when I got tired of him and moved on, he'd know how to do it himself. He said it jokingly, but I wondered if he still expected me to leave him one day. Things seemed to be going pretty well in general, but I kept wishing I could come up with some grand gesture to let him know I wasn't going anywhere.

Until one day, I had an idea. It wasn't exactly a grand gesture—it started out as a little thing, but I hoped it would convey the message. I needed some help. It took some time and a little convincing, but I was finally ready to put my plan into place. The fruits of my labors were in a smallish cardboard box that I carried up the stairs to Henry's office. There was only one problem—I was starting to chicken out.

What had seemed like a good idea now struck me as embarrassing at the least and incredibly forward at the worst. The Rachel of a year ago never would have even considered doing something like this, but between struggling to get a job and this thing with Henry, I had learned something. You can't always leave things to fate and hope the universe will hand you what you wish for. Sometimes you have to pretend you're confident even when you're scared to death. Sometimes you have to make your own fate. Which was why I was walking through the door to Henry's office, holding my little box, and trying to act like I wasn't crazy nervous.

There was a bag of cherries sitting on my desk, and this reassured me a little. Even though I didn't work there anymore,

Henry continued to buy me fruit when he knew I was coming by the office. It always made me smile that he kept up this quirky/cute habit even though I could afford my own produce now. *Surely a man wouldn't keep buying fruit for someone he didn't want to keep in his life, right?* This random, nonsensical comment from the voice in my head struck me as so ridiculous that I had to hold back a nervous giggle. Next to the cherries was a little dish of colored paper clips, and that did make me laugh. Gotta love a guy with a sense of humor.

I could hear Henry's voice in the other room. I was relieved he was on the phone because it would give me a few minutes to gather my thoughts. I poked my head around the corner and waved, and he smiled and waved back. He held up one finger to indicate that he was almost done, and I nodded. I went back into the outer office and sat down at my desk. I was more nervous holding the box, so I pushed it to the far corner of my desk, but I still felt like it was looking at me. I turned my chair toward the window and picked at the cherries instead, making a small pile of pits on a Kleenex.

I had been nervous before I saw Henry, but I think my anxiety had multiplied since he smiled at me. I couldn't hear the words, but I could tell from the tone in his voice that his conversation wasn't winding down yet. I hoped he wouldn't be too long because I was sure to talk myself out of what little initiative I had left. At the same time, I found myself hoping it would be the longest phone call in the history of the world. I felt silly now, but maybe by the time he was done, I would come full circle back to where I thought this was a good plan.

Oh, seriously, stop with the drama. It's not like it's the end of the world if he thinks this is presumptuous and odd.

Except it kind of was. Henry and I had made significant progress, but I still thought of him as a skittish animal; I was afraid that if I made any sudden, unexpected moves I might scare him away. When Shannon suggested that Henry and I might end up together after the first time I saw him again at the café, I thought she was nuts, but the more time I spent with him, the more convinced I was that we were perfect for each other. I was getting so attached to him now. I couldn't believe I'd finally found someone I could talk to, someone I didn't have to hide from.

"Hello, my little lawyer. How are you?"

I startled. So much for thinking I was so clever at discerning Henry's conversation status. He'd finished up with his call, and I'd completely missed the whole thing. Now he was here, and I was thrust into carrying out my plan. I swept the pit-filled Kleenex into the garbage and stood up, smiling. Henry kissed me briefly and hugged me. I still wasn't used to his height. I wasn't short, but anyone under six feet was dwarfed next to Henry.

I was taking too long to answer. "I'm good. How was your day?"

"Oh, you know—same old. You look a little tired. Rough day at the office?"

Great. He thinks I look worn out. Already this wasn't going the way I'd hoped. "I didn't sleep very well," I said, which was true. Last night I was too excited thinking about this moment. I lay in bed and rehearsed this over and over until there was no way I could sleep, and now . . . well, I never imagined he'd be telling me I looked tired.

He frowned. "Did your manic cat keep you awake?"

I'd finally introduced Henry to Hannibal, and they were both jealous, which was flattering but frustrating at the same time. I hated to show him my place, but he'd kept asking, and I'd finally caved. He was amazed. I think it never occurred to him that anyone could live in a space that small.

"Hannibal kept me company," I corrected. "He's a good cat."

"I'm sure he is."

He wasn't convinced of Hannibal's charms yet, but it had taken a while for them to grow on me too. He'd come around. I tried to steer the conversation back in the right direction. "Did you eat lunch?"

He looked guilty. "I got busy, and I kind of forgot."

I gave him a dirty look. "Just because you don't have a secretary to cater to your every whim anymore doesn't mean you can neglect yourself. Call and have something delivered if you can't bother to go out."

"I'm fine. But now that you mention it, I am starving. Should we go have some dinner?"

I panicked. If we left now, I could always give him his surprise after dinner. But the more time that went by, the more chance there was I'd lose my nerve. "Okay, but before we go," I charged ahead, "I have something for you."

For the first time, Henry noticed the box sitting on top of my desk. "Really? Is it edible?"

I couldn't help laughing. He was like a little kid. Now that he'd realized he was hungry, he couldn't focus on anything else. "Maybe."

"Mmmm, what is it? It looks like a bakery box." He went for the lid to open it, and I slapped his hand away.

"Be patient. I have to tell you something first."

"I'm sorry. I'm just so *hungry*."

"Honestly, I'm going to have to start packing you a lunch."

"With Doritos?" he asked.

"What?"

"My grandpa used to pack my lunch for school, and there was always a little bag of chips. Doritos are my favorite."

"Which flavor?" I'd lost complete control of the conversation, and despite my initial irritation at being derailed, I was curious. Any time Henry talked about being a kid, I was fascinated. Aside from what Waldorf had told me, I still knew relatively little about his childhood, so whenever he volunteered information, I soaked it up. I knew he would tell me about it when he was ready, and I wanted to make sure he knew I was interested, no matter how trivial the information seemed.

"Cool Ranch. Or Nacho Cheese. Or the Spicy Chili ones. They all sound pretty good right now. Ask me again when I'm not so hungry," he said, grinning.

"Okay, noted. Unfortunately there are no Doritos in this box."

"Is it cake?"

"If you'd calm down and listen to me, I'll tell you what it is!" I had the perfect picture in my head of how this would go, and in no version of it was Henry so ravenously hungry he was unable to concentrate. To his credit, he waited for me to tell him, as patiently as he could under the circumstances. His eyes were fixed on the box as if he was hoping to suddenly develop x-ray vision so he could see the contents.

I sighed. "It's cookies."

"Can I have one? I know you probably think I'll spoil my dinner, but I'm really hungry. It would be like a little appetizer."

"These aren't just any cookies."

His eyes lit up. "RubySnap? But where's the bag?" He looked so confused it was almost comical.

"No bag. I told you, these are special."

"A whole box of RubySnap!" He looked positively gleeful. "Are they Vivianna?"

"No, they're Rachel." I hadn't intended to reveal this little bit of information until I played with him a little more, but obviously he wasn't going to be able to think about anything else until I fed him.

"Rachel? But there are no Rachel cookies."

"Well, there are now." I opened the box, revealing the contents; three rows of gorgeous cookies studded with raspberries and chunks of dark chocolate. My heart was jumping like a caffeinated squirrel. For a minute, he just stared, and all I could do was guess at what was going on in his head. Was he flattered, or did he think this was silly? When he finally raised his eyes to meet mine, he looked awed.

"How did you do this?" he said.

"Well, as it turns out, the owner is a bit of a romantic at heart. When I told her I needed a favor for one of her best customers, she was only too happy to help."

"You *created* a Rachel cookie?"

"You created a job for me; I created a cookie for you."

"This is amazing!"

"I have to admit, my intentions weren't completely honorable. I was a little jealous of the attention you've been giving Vivianna."

He laughed. "I can't believe you did this for me."

I sighed. I couldn't help it. I was so relieved he didn't think my surprise was completely lame. "I wanted you to know that I'm not going anywhere. I keep trying to show you, but I wasn't sure I was getting through to you. I thought cookies might make a more tangible impression."

"I've never had anyone give me such a thoughtful gift. Thank you," he said, his voice completely sincere.

"I certainly hope cookies aren't the most thoughtful gift you've ever gotten."

"You know what I mean." When he leaned down to kiss me, I put my hand on his chest, and I swear I could feel his heart beating through his shirt.

"Is everything okay?" I asked him when the kiss ended. Why would Henry be nervous? I'm the one who should be nervous.

"Well, I had something more extravagant planned, but this seems like better timing. Besides, it pales in comparison compared to your surprise." Henry reached into his pocket and took out something small before he got down on one knee.

I wasn't sure how much more of this my already overworked heart could take. I'd hoped that he'd see the Rachel cookie as a cute gesture, but never in my wildest dreams had I imagined it going this well.

"Rachel Pearce, you are the only cookie for me. Would you do me the honor of being my cookie for the rest of our lives?" He cracked open the ring box, and I gasped.

"That's way too big. I'll have to carry something heavy in the other hand all the time, or I'll fall over!" If this represented three months of Henry's salary, I'm guessing he had trouble finding ways to spend it all. Suddenly, exotic produce in the middle of winter seemed completely reasonable.

He threw his head back and laughed. "This is what I love about you. No other girl would ever say a ring was too big, but if you don't like it, we can trade it in for whatever you want."

"No, no, no! It's perfect. We might have to hire a bodyguard when I go out so no one decides to kidnap me though."

"That could be arranged."

I rolled my eyes. "I was joking."

His grin was wider than I'd ever seen it. "So is that a yes?"

"Yes! I will be your cookie!" He laughed and slid the ring on my finger. I'm not sure when I started crying, but my face was already wet when he jumped up and started kissing me again. Part of me was convinced that I'd finally managed to fall asleep last night and I was still dreaming, but the ring on my finger felt real enough. I didn't think it was possible, but Henry was getting better and better at this kissing thing. I finally had to disengage to catch my breath.

Henry brushed the hair away from my face. "Well, are you ready to go to dinner now?"

"I thought you wanted to attack the box of cookies," I teased.

His eyes twinkled. "Oh, I can wait until later now. I'm sure the cookies are spectacular, but I have the real thing."

About the Author

AUBREY MACE LIVES IN UTAH, but every winter she considers moving somewhere warmer. She enjoys her job in an infusion center but wishes she had more time to spend with the people in her head—the ones who lure her in with the promise of a good story and never fail to surprise her. When she's not consorting with them, she likes to hang out with her family and friends—the ones who walk the delicate line between supporting her writing addiction and keeping her grounded in reality.

You can meet Aubrey's other characters in *Before the Clock Strikes Thirty;* the Whitney Award–winning *Spare Change; My Fairy Grandmother*; and Whitney Award–nominated *Santa Maybe*. You can also visit her at her website, www.aubreymace. com.